INTO THE FOREST

TALES OF THE BABA YAGA

EDITED BY
LINDY RYAN

ISBN Print: 978-1-64548-123-2
ISBN Ebook: 978-1-64548-124-9

Cover Design and Interior Formatting
by Qamber Designs and Media
Edited by Lindy Ryan

Published by Black Spot Books
An imprint of Vesuvian Media Group

To the mothers, grandmothers, aunts, nieces, sisters, daughters, wicked witches, and fairy godmothers who have left their mark.

To the ocean, to the forest, to the wild.

To women in horror.

PRAISE FOR INTO THE FOREST

"A lovely, thorned, haunted gathering of tales of what it means to occupy a woman's body. Baba Yaga serves a reminder of the wildness sleeping within all of us. This collection brings her roaring to life."
—Kristi DeMeester, author of SUCH A PRETTY SMILE

"INTO THE FOREST explores the folklore of Baba Yaga through new tales, filled with transformation and retribution, from a masterful group of authors. We travel back and forth in time, from Europe to the American South as violence and madness drive the used, abused, and betrayed into dense stretches of trees. There we find a path to strength and power, to unearthing or becoming the otherworldly Maiden, Mother, Crone."
—Linda D. Addison, award-winning author, HWA Lifetime Achievement Award recipient and SFPA Grand Master

"I have loved Baba Yaga since I was a girl. Her wild disregard for the "rules of man" inspired me. She isn't bound by hearth and home, rather it is bound to her. Baba creates her world, remakes it in her image, and the world—the wild world—loves her for it. All else trembles. Here are 23 stories that pay proper tribute to Baba Yaga's wild nature in all its facets. From Yi Izzy Yu's horrifically charming "The Story of a House" to the sensual tale of revolution and magic in "Water Like Broken Glass" by Carina Bissett, each story explores what it means to be untamed. These aren't just tales of a child eating witch, though there is plenty of that. These are stories about what it means to be a woman fluent in darkness. Each of these authors speaks Baba Yaga's language. It's the language of starlight, shadow, bone, and blood. They have borrowed the witch's spirit, blended it with their own and created a grimoire from which all of us can draw upon."
—Angela Yuriko Smith, multiple Bram Stoker Award®-winning and Elgin Award-nominated author

TABLE OF CONTENTS

PREFACE
by Lindy Ryan

When the idea first came to put together a women-in-horror anthology, it took some time to decide on the theme. There have been several incredible female-focused anthologies of late. We wanted to add to that growing library with a collection that captured the very essence of those who identify as female horror writers: wild and fierce and feminine.

Baba Yaga is all of those and more. Thus, she became our muse and our subject.

With mortar and pestle in hand, we set out to create an anthology. Instead, we found a sisterhood. Hundreds of submissions flooded our call—stories from women worldwide, from every walk of life, and each breathtaking and inspiring in its own right. As we commenced the arduous but exciting task of selecting the right pieces for this collection, we were reminded of something wonderful. There is a wealth of talent among women-in-horror today and *women* in horror today. Wild women. Women with imagination, with power, and with voices demanding to be heard.

Women who, regardless of any differentiator that might be applied to separate us, retain the spirit of Baba Yaga.

Slavic in origin, many have grown up hearing folktales about Baba Yaga, though she will undoubtedly be new to some. Whether you're meeting Baba Yaga for the first time, or this is one of many trips to her familiar chicken-legged hut, we invite you to journey with us to meet the witch who waits deep in the forest and read her tales. Many will find her warm, while others will pronounce her wicked. These stories are, like Baba Yaga herself, limitless and unpredictable.

They are wild. They are fierce. And they are feminine.

Thank you to every woman who shared her story. Thank you to every contributor whose name appears in this book. Thank you to every reader who picks up this collection and finds their sisterhood.

We are Baba Yaga, and it is with great delight that we take you *into the forest...*

A special and not insignificant thank you is due to Toni Miller, our favorite Baba Yaga, without whom this anthology would not have become the powerful collection that it is.

FOREWORD
by Christina Henry

Baba Yaga is a character who almost needs no introduction. The broad strokes of her are there, embedded in our collective memory—the long-nosed crone with her walking house and iron teeth and penchant for cannibalism. We know her comic forms of locomotion—her house has chicken feet; her flight is powered by a mortar pushed along by a sweeping broom. This whimsy should make her more accessible and less opaque, yet it somehow increases her menace, makes Baba Yaga's cruelty sting more.

In the traditional stories, Baba Yaga is always ugly, always old. She has no need of the male gaze, nor the beauty standards that come with it. This is no Snow White's stepmother, admiring her beauty in the mirror. Her ugliness is, too, not necessarily a descriptor for the personality within. In folktales, being physically unattractive is often a shorthand for villainy—the beautiful are virtuous, and the ugly are not. While Baba Yaga is rarely virtuous in the traditional sense, she is often fair and sometimes even kind, though these qualities are not easy to predict.

She lives on the borders of places, in the margins far from a safe and civilized society. Her house will appear at the edge of a wood, or sometimes deep in a forest but on the thin line between kingdoms. Sometimes it is on a seashore, where the safety of land becomes the uncertainty of the ocean. She is a wild thing, tied to the earth. She can be a friendly hand to a passerby or a monstrous one—a snake that can choose to strike or turn its fanged head away in mercy or indifference.

Even her name, *Baba Yaga,* is a reflection of the uncertainty of her identity, of her core character. *Baba* is, depending on the Eastern Slavic language and the time period it is spoken, either "grandmother" or "old woman" or "fortune teller" or "midwife" or perhaps "foolish woman" (though only a true fool would think Baba Yaga foolish).

Yaga is a term of even more mysterious provenance. According to Andreas Johns, author of *Baba Yaga: The Ambiguous Mother and Witch of the Russian Folktale*, the word *Yaga might be sourced from the Serbo-Croatian jeza ("horror," "shudder," or "chill") or perhaps from the Polish jędza* ("witch," "evil woman," or "fury"). It might be, according to Sibelan Forrester's essay *Baba Yaga: The Wild Witch of the East*, "that *yaga* originally meant 'horrible,' 'horrifying'… if Baba Yaga originally played a role in the secret corpus of myths or initiation rituals, a taboo might have discouraged people from saying her name in other contexts." The scholarly speculation on the source and meaning of Baba Yaga's name is vast and deep, probing the roots of languages that have been traditionally tied to her stories, searching for one clear and defined answer. But, ambiguity remains. Her name might mean nothing, and it might mean everything. Baba Yaga's name remains as shrouded in mystery as her true nature.

The vast body of folktales around Baba Yaga reflects these many natures. Baba Yaga isn't always, strictly speaking, the same woman from story to story. She is not always even one woman. Sometimes she is three sisters, each more crafty and cruel than the last. Sometimes she is a single benevolent wise woman, assisting fair maidens and lost princes. Sometimes she is a trickster, offering weary travelers comfort while waiting for her victims to fall asleep before murdering them. Sometimes she is both mother and daughter, crone and maiden in the same tale. She often longs for the sustenance of "Russian blood," which she could sniff out even if she were blind. She frequently asks the rather loaded question, "Are you doing a deed, or are you fleeing a deed?"

In one story, a nameless lovely maiden is pressed into Baba Yaga's servitude by her cruel stepmother. Baba Yaga assigns the maiden several tasks and leaves the chicken-stilt house. Several friendly mice offer the maiden help, and because she is a good and kind girl, she listens to them and completes her tasks. Baba Yaga showers the girl with riches, for Baba Yaga rewards those who do their duty, and eventually, the girl makes her way home to her sour-faced stepmother. However, upon seeing such wealth, the stepmother greedily sends her own daughter to Baba Yaga, expecting the same end. Of course, since blood daughters of stepmothers are often as foolish and cruel as their parents (see *Cinderella*, which coincidentally may or may not also feature helpful mice), this particular maiden screams and beats the mice that try to assist her. The mice, now dead, cannot help her complete the difficult tasks assigned. She does not perform as Baba Yaga expects.

When Baba Yaga returns, she discovers the girl has not done her duty. There is no opportunity for pleading and crying on the part of the maiden, no arguments before the court. Baba Yaga immediately breaks this unfortunate into pieces and puts the girl's bones in a box. This is not a woman to be trifled with.

She is not always cruel, though—perhaps we might call her capricious. In the tale of Finist, the bright falcon, and the maiden who loves him, Baba Yaga appears three times in the form of three progressively older sisters. Rather than hinder the maid on her quest to find her beloved, the sisters inexplicably assist her, providing precious gifts to aid her and ask for nothing in return.

In her trinity form, Baba Yaga functions not as the terrifying antagonist of the tale (that is left to the maiden's rival for Finist's affections) but rather as the kindly wise woman of the wood bestowing favors upon the good-hearted. The less optimistic among us wonder, though, if Baba Yaga would not demand some price had the maiden failed in her quest and wandered in the witch's path again. Baba Yaga will give presents when it suits her. But it also suits her to punish the foolish and the failed, to carve girls into pieces small enough to fit into a box.

DINNER PLANS WITH BABA YAGA

A POEM BY STEPHANIE M. WYTOVICH

I tattoo a chicken's foot onto my thigh, your eye
a looking glass resting atop my bones. I walk on
broken acorns, braid my hair with the thread from
a lost boy's jacket. You scream from the pepper
plant growing on my porch, and I nod and nod,
agree with the spells pouring out of the earth.

> *I'll be sure to mind the roots,*
> *collect the honey from the hives*

You tell me to make a stew, to chop up the
onions, pull the radishes from the ground. I bite
my tongue, let my tears fall into the bowl, the salt
a sealant, a locked door boiling beneath the peas.
I stir clockwise to summon you, imagine the rancid
perfume of your ghost.

> *Yes, I have spiced the two-lips,*
> *marinated the girl meat overnight*

There's a routine to this, a ritual, the way
the kettle is forever on, screaming like a dying
red fox. I drink a broth made from feathers stewed
with baby teeth and sage, chop up potatoes
still covered in dirt, half-eaten by wireworms,
the taste of flea beetles still strong on my tongue.

> *I put the rhubarb on the table,*
> *milk the snake over the sink*

At nightfall, the scent of jasmine mixes
with the pine needles on the porch, cuts
through the musk of leftover promises
still lingering in the woods. If you listen closely,
there's a song in your soup, an alphabet
in your blood, each mouthful a child lost,
a child consumed.

> *I throw their clothes in the fire,*
> *Eat their names under the light of the moon.*

LAST TOUR INTO THE HUNGERING MOONLIGHT

BY GWENDOLYN KISTE

Greetings, and welcome to our perfect little neighborhood! We're so very happy to have you here. You'll be a lovely addition to our community.

Follow us now, and please come see our beautiful homes. Matching shutters, matching cars, matching families at neatly-set dinner tables. Everything's absolutely flawless, don't you think?

(Pay no attention to the clogged gutters or the cracks in the foundation or the mortgage bills piling up in the kitchen corner. This tour should have a little fantasy, shouldn't it?)

One home after another, we want to show them all to you. Our vaulted ceilings, our vaulted lives. This is our little pocket of paradise, you might say. After all, we have everything we could ever want. Our gleaming white walls as plain and straightforward as each new day in our lives. There's nothing out of the ordinary here, nothing calling to us from just beyond the property line.

Where are you, my girls? And who's the new face among you?

Please keep up now. We've got one last place to show you. At the end of the cul-de-sac, past all the pretty little houses and the pretty little families locked up within, there's a final sight you should see. It's easy to miss if you don't know what you're looking for. And why would you know? You're new here, the same way we were all new once.

Look there among the dense patch of pine trees, and you'll spot it. A dirt path, the kind that could be no more than an access

1

road. And as it turns out, it does access something. Or someone.

We never say her name, but that's because we don't have to. We could recognize her in an instant, even though we've never seen her up close. She's always with us, a whisper on the wind, a shadow passing over our eyes when we're looking away. Something so near it makes the hairs on the backs of our necks stand on end.

(They say her house in the deep, lonely woods is propped up on chicken legs and filled with a thousand bones. Late at night, we sometimes lie awake and wonder if those bones make her home stronger than ours. We also wonder if maybe we should find some bones of our own.)

Tucked there in the gloomy forest, she's our unlikely den mother, the creature of the green, the enchantress you'll never tame. And why would you want to tame her anyhow? She's better wild.

(Everything's better when it's left to run wild.)

It's getting dark now, so we should get a move on. But this isn't the last time you'll come here, is it? You might settle in for a while, unpacking all your porcelain and linens, and pretend you don't care about this secret place. But it will needle you, just like it needles us.

When you go jogging in the evening or take the stroller out at noon, you might want to creep a little closer to the path. Just for a moment, just to get a better look. That's when you'll see how terribly overgrown it is, all clotted with brambles and darkness. It doesn't look very welcoming. It doesn't look like home.

(Yet it feels like home, doesn't it? Somewhere you thought you'd dreamed up, somewhere you'd always longed for.)

So now that you're part of our neighborhood, the important thing to remember is to never take that path. If you're smart, you won't even stand at the mouth of it, the heady scent of pine and promise filling your lungs. You especially won't stare down its winding turns into the eager darkness looming there.

In fact, it's best to pretend the path doesn't exist at all. Please won't you forget we mentioned it to you? That would be safer for you. And for us.

Where are you, my girls? What are you waiting for?

We tell ourselves we're satisfied here. Our hands aching and raw, we scrub the filthy dishes and spritz Windex on all the windows, and pick out a new Whirlpool refrigerator as all the dreams we've surrendered whirlpool down the drain.

Still, not every evening is quite so bad. Sometimes, there's a strange shift within us. That's when we find ourselves restless at midnight, standing in murky hallways, a mortar and pestle gripped tightly in our hands. We didn't even know we owned a mortar and pestle, yet here we are, like the witches of yore, conjuring magic when we don't mean to.

We wander to our front windows and stare up at the dark clouds. Our breath twists in our chests as a shadow passes over the moon, and we know she's so near to us. She can emerge from the forest anytime she wants. Only she rarely does. That's because she wants us to come to her. She'll answer any question we ask, fulfill any wish we desire. Of course, it might come at a price. But then again, what doesn't have a price?

What are you willing to surrender, my darlings? What parts of yourselves are you eager to slough off like thin skin?

Despite ourselves, she sees us for what we are. Obscure power tingling in our fingertips, rage boiling in our bellies. All the things we could have been. All the things denied to us. This fear we share, these tired bodies the world battles over. *Our* bodies, even though we're told they don't belong to us at all. They belong to men with gavels, men in suits, men without souls. Without decency, either. The kind of men who would mock us like we're silly schoolgirls, men who would hold us down on a bed and guffaw while we thrash and scream and cry.

Men that aren't so different from the ones sitting across from us at the breakfast table each morning. Faces that we used to know. Faces that are no more than strangers to us now.

Come to me, my darlings. Come to me and be free.

But we've got to make the best of things. We've got to keep pretending not to hear her. On warm summer days, we sit together in sun rooms and sip fresh iced tea and smile at each other for hours, the corners of our mouths twitching from the weight of our make-believe mirth. We compliment each other's decorating schemes and act like we honestly give a fuck about things like crown molding and matching dinnerware and how to choose the best duvet.

At last, when the sun is dipping in the sky, and none of us can stomach the charade any longer, we each walk home alone, the neighborhood deteriorating around us. Our front steps cracking in two, the frosted sconces on our porch lights shattered to dust. This once-perfect neighborhood, turning to cinders at our feet.

We'll make the best of things, though, we'll make the best of it, we will, we will, we will.

Yet all day and all night, we find our gazes set on that dirt road that extends beyond the cul-de-sac and into the hungry trees.

The men do their best to distract us. They coax us back to them, tying the apron strings so tight we can't catch our breath. We tell ourselves we should stay. But the world's crumbling around us, and there's nothing we can do to stop it. Not unless we run.

Not unless we take the path that's calling to us.

We could wait until midnight. Listen for the screech owl serenading the moon as we slip out the back door and disappear into the dark toward the verboten path.

Or we could do it in broad daylight. In front of the passersby and the postal workers diligently delivering little brown boxes from Amazon. Everything so nice and normal until we do the one thing we know isn't allowed—make a choice of our own.

Or we could be polite about it. Fix a nice dinner first. Maybe a pot roast or a honey-baked ham. Sit down together as a family for once. Do the dishes afterward, since nobody else will help us. Fold the laundry. Make sure the children have done their homework. Check all their math problems. Check all their spelling, too. It's potato without the 'e' at the end, darling. Please remember.

But even as we do our best impression of ourselves, the men sense it in us, they sense our resolve, and they're suddenly hovering nearer.

"You'll stay right here," they whisper, their eyes darker than every sin they project on us. "You're ours."

But this time, we can't help but laugh because they're wrong. After all, these bodies do belong to us, and we'll do with them what we please.

For so long, we were told we needed to be perfect. But all we ever really needed was to be wild.

Still smiling, we turn away and march out our front doors toward the end of the cul-de-sac. The path is open to us now. The brambles have cleared, and there's a faint light ahead in the woods, ready to guide us.

Somewhere back in the lonely houses, strangers are calling our names. They screech and weep and beg and bargain, but that's no matter now. That's all in the past, and we have no need for it. Our hands entwined, we drift down the dirt path, the brambles and thorns closing in behind us like thick blood filling a wound.

Welcome, my girls. I've been waiting a long time.

Together, we'll rush into her arms, the moon slicing through the sky, and we'll dance on a floor of a thousand bones. And with our wild hearts gleaming and new, the forest will sing dirges around us, and our dreams will burn so bright and furious they'll sear everything and everyone we've ever known to ash.

THE STORY OF A HOUSE

BY YI IZZY YU

In the beginning, House had many brothers and sisters—cheeping and chirping, hopping and pecking.

It had a normal head, too.

Two eyes instead of windows. A beak. A gizzard in its throat. Then one night, the fox came and blooded the coop with the guts of House's brothers and sisters, leaving the survivors trembling because no one warned them about the world's true nature, that it was not all seed and warm feathers.

Even then, House had been an exception to its siblings. Moments after the fox fled back into the forest, House stumbled out of a mass of chicks huddled against the persimmon tree trunk to which they fled when their mother screamed at them to scatter.

House darted up to its mother's body first, felled like a mountain. Warm and fat just blinks ago, now half of her was eaten away, and the other half glistened dumbly—no more alive than an unkindled egg. House sniffed once at its heartbreak and then raced to the forest's edge, making a loud, otherworldly cry of grief that no chick had ever made before.

The forest was full of glowing eyes, of moist beetle smells, of snapping twigs and fireflies blinking between the branches. House stared into the arboreal darkness, breathing hard, broadcasting hate and a challenge to the coward, narrow-skulled fox to return. The act was unhinged. But House, in a fit of birdbrained madness, mistook the size of its rage for the size of its small twiggy body and was convinced it might fight a fox and win. That it might fight a whole forest.

Fortunately for House, no creature answered its unbalanced call. The snakes took its behavior as an ill omen and thought House too diseased to eat. The tigers found it too inconsequential. The foxes were full. Other things simply didn't notice a small chick grieving in the dark.

Nevertheless, House remained in its roost all night, bloody and fuzzed, staring hard into the forest with eyes black while behind it rose weeping from the chicken yard.

When the farmer got up early the next morning, sensing something was amiss, he hurried to the coop where he was greeted by bright red slaughter and zzz'ing flies full of guts not their own.

In response to the annihilation, the farmer nodded to himself. He then ambled around, stooping to collect bodies and parts of bodies as if bowing repeatedly. Some of these he kept to eat, and some he threw into his refuse pit, which also held a goat dead of old age. Once this sorting was done, he rode off on a melancholy white horse with a jagged scar under one eye.

When the farmer returned, Baba rode with him.

House did not like Baba one bit. Not at first. Dressed in deer and bearskins to which colorful scarves were attached, along with metal amulets hammered into mirrors that flashed back warped reflections, she looked discomfortingly strange. So too was her smell off-putting. Fungal, sea-like, sulfurous, and rotting all at once. Still, no one asked House for its opinion. And after Baba paid the farmer coin, she was allowed to eyeball then pluck eight chicks from the site of the previous night's slaughter.

She seemed to favor those who wore the most resilient expressions. House was among these.

"Down you go," Baba said when they arrived at an old pine-plank cottage. The habitable part of the cottage was dwarfed by a low roof that hung down so far and mossy that Baba's home resembled a very small person wearing a very tall green hat.

Inside the cottage, Baba dumped the chicks out of the farmer's sack and onto a hard-packed dirt floor where a circle was drawn with bone dust.

Immediately, the chicks began to run about, cheeping and crying.

"What's this? What's going on? Where are we?"

All except for House, who stood its ground and cast sharp glances around the cottage.

Baba thumb-rubbed her tattooed knuckles and grinned as the chicks tried to penetrate the invisible barrier of the circle. Each time, it bounced them back.

"Not you though, eh?" Baba said to House. Instead of rushing the circle, House crouched catlike and glared at Baba, stubby wings partly lifted as if it might use those like claws—despite their downiness—to scratch out her eyes.

"Smart," Baba said. "You seem to have a will on you, too. Like a pair of jaws. That'll help you with your next lives."

After saying this, Baba stuffed plant matter in her mouth, chewed and swallowed, then licked her lips with a slug-like tongue and picked up a large oval drum, the skin on just one side.

Boom. She struck the drum, and all the chicks looked around for thunder.

Boom. Her hands tom-tommed faster and faster as she lurched around the circle, half-walking, half-dancing, necklaces and scarves swaying, hypnotizing all the chicks—even House—until her eyes rolled back, and she jerked up straight.

Baba then stepped over to a rough-hewn stone pedestal. It sat knee-high, just outside the bone-dust circle—a worked remnant of a stone that had fallen from a crack in the sky eons before. It lay crying like a child until found by an ancestor of Baba's.

Three things lay on the pedestal: a piece of chalk, a pair of oversized iron scissors, and a bouquet of leopard's bane.

Baba took the chalk, her eyes still rolled back, still staring far away.

Srtttch. Scrtttch. She drew a white line across the top of the pedestal.

"Two worlds," Baba said. She scribbled tiny human and animal figures on each side of the line, buildings too, and arrows between them. House did not understand her words but did understand that Baba was drawing two very different places and that in moving from one to the other, a thing became another thing, and this was somehow a secret that held all of reality like an ocean.

"Ready, little ones?" Baba said to the chicks as she opened her eyes.

The chicks craned their necks at Baba's voice—intrigued by the humor, sadness, and cruelty all mixed together.

Lifting the scissors with one hand, Baba raised the bouquet at the same time. Eyes fixed on the chicks, she put the bouquet between the scissors' blades.

The handle closed.

Twppt, yellow blooms fell from the leopard's bane.

Twppt, in response so too did the chicks' heads fall from their shoulders and onto the floor.

House and its brothers and sisters went running around, this way and that, knocking into each other and against the walls, spurting blood, until only House was left standing, breathing hard, air bubbling up at the severed bone pipe of its throat.

"Ah-hah," Baba shouted, picking up House with a pinch. House tried to peck her to no avail, now both beakless and headless.

"You'll do," Baba said, and she blew into House's neck as if into the neck of a balloon.

House felt pain then—crippling, bone-cracking pain. Its skin ripped and shredded, billowed larger, larger still, unfurling and hardening into wall and floorboards, except spaces left for the windows, which became its new eyes. Its down became carpets, while its bones crept and divided, splintered and stacked, into all the furnishings that one might find in a house. Except for the leg bones which elongated and thickened like tree trunks—raising a cackling Baba, who hopped onto House's throat now doorway, up into the violated sky. As for the consciousness of House, it lay sparkling everywhere.

"We've got some work to do," Baba said. "Think you're up to it, little chick?" She kicked House's floor with the toe of a rounded leather shoe.

Headless, of course, House couldn't answer with a cheep. But it did answer by taking off running, letting the wind rush through its windows and open door as a kind of response cry, eager now that it was as large as its rage to snatch up foxes from their lairs—whether they were in the ground or in the souls of children—and tear them in two like the day was torn when House's mother died.

House kept running and snatching up foxes until centuries later when Baba was killed during a revolution. Ironically—given her fame—she was not killed for any specific crime but executed anonymously, alongside cart-loads of teachers, shamans, anarchists, freethinkers, and other such undesirables.

Baba's last words to House were, "Run. Hide." And it did because her magical words could not be argued with—across the border to China and all the way to the city of Hohhot, where it tucked its legs under and assumed a building shape. There, House remains to this day, half-asleep but with an open door.

OF MOONLIGHT AND MOSS

BY SARA TANTLINGER

W e do not speak her name. My father has forbidden it, and as ruler of the kingdom, what choice have I ever had except to obey his wishes?

Deep in the bog lives a mysterious woman, a guardian of an eternal flame. She hasn't been seen in person for years. I wonder, if she appeared to us now, would the townspeople look at her the way my father looks at me? In his eyes, I am reflected as nothing more than a bloodied smear. My blemished sentience exists only because of a mother no longer alive to defend me. She died shortly after my birth, and eighteen years later, the pain of it all never leaves my father. When he gazes upon my older sister, the radiance that is Vasilisa, I know with finality I will never be accepted here.

"Fetch the blue fire," he tells me. "If you wish to prove you are worth anything, take it from the bog. Bring its light here."

An ancient magic. Each dancing flame promises power to the one who carries its torch. Father's assets are in ruin, and desperation carves new lines into his face. Nearly all of the ornate furniture and Mother's jewels have been sold. Servants left long ago with a few exceptions, but it makes no difference to me. Most of them took on my father's countenance of treating me cruelly. Little good did it do, for a king has not possessed such negative status for eons.

I know these things, but do I care? I have tried. After all, I don't aim to be as merciless as my father, but I can't deny the way cruelty lingers beneath the surface. Somewhere in my marrow, resentment brews.

When he asks me to retrieve the fire, I know this is to be my death sentence.

So let ruin become him.

But my sister ...

Vasilisa's recent marriage offers small comfort—her dear prince will not be enough to save Father from debt. He brought wars to our land in the name of promised glory, but instead, he found devastation so great only a miracle could bring redemption.

Or magic from a blue flame.

To trespass on the witch's territory will surely lead to an ill fate, yet, I pack a small satchel and prepare to leave.

Not for my father but for Vasilisa. She is too good to decay here, damned by Father's mistakes. If I save his fortune, I save my sister.

"Daria," she whispers, her voice a songbird come to chase away my room's silence. The single ray of morning sun peeking through my window catches the golden curls of Vasilisa's hair. Where she is every bit the dainty princess depicted in classic portraits of past families throughout the castle, I am the opposite. In fact, the last word I'd use to describe myself would be "dainty."

"Don't ignore me." She sits carefully on the bed's edge, her pale gown spread around her like waves from the sea we visited as children.

Everything about her reeks with enchantment, but it's impossible not to love her. Yet, if I did not care for her so, if she was a stranger I passed on the cobbled streets in town, I think I might resent her—the beautiful princess with a doting prince, a man who still can't remember my name. I am, and only ever have been, an invisible spectator hovering outside of Vasilisa's light.

It's never been her fault. I cannot blame her for my own insecurities, though I wish at times she'd try to understand me better.

"No words you have will stop me from leaving."

"There must be another way. Father is mad for even asking you."

"It wasn't a request."

She huffs out a cloud of air. "Why doesn't he send a worker?"

At that, I laugh. "In his eyes, the few workers who remain are more valuable than I am."

Puzzlement creases her pretty features, for Vasilisa could never know what it is to be unwanted.

Not much remains in my room. A decent bed, cobwebs, a few belongings I stashed away before Father could sell them. I turn over a loose stone near the bottom right corner wall. My hiding spot where I stored some of Mother's jewels. Just a few rings and a cameo brooch carved from a shell. I take the brooch for myself, fasten it inside the satchel.

"Take the rings," I tell my sister. "If you need to escape this place, they might be enough to help."

Tears mist her eyes as she delicately strokes the jewelry. "Mother loved this one," she says of a gold band studded in rubies. "Oh, Daria, how did you manage to hide these? Father is like a bloodhound for anything he can sell."

She steps away from the hiding spot, and I press the stone back in place. "Promise me you won't show these to him. They're for you, not him."

Vasilisa nods, still sniffling, and I hope I can rely on her.

"You make it sound as if you don't intend to return, but you must bring the flame."

Desperation does not suit her, but I can't pretend Vasilisa's life is perfect either. She will starve because of Father's recklessness, or suffer a worse fate as his lonely eyes focus only on her, this replica of our mother.

I hug my sister one last time, an embrace that becomes a promise.

"Remember what you are," my father hisses as I pass him by in the corridor. Vasilisa follows, and Father puts his heavy hands on her shoulders.

I say nothing, only stop to stare at him one last time. Part of me wonders if saving Vasilisa is worth the cost of saving this wretched man, too.

"You are the unwanted germ that slithered from your mother and killed her. Do not return here without the blue fire."

At the stable waits one of our remaining workers. A kind man, one of the only people here who treats me like a real human. The sight of his flushed cheeks from the chilled air do much to soothe the anger kindling within me.

My gloved hands grip my satchel as I arrange the layered fabrics of my skirts.

"Hello, Ivan," I say as the man hands me the reins to Gala, my pretty Orlov Trotter. A prized animal. Too precious for even Father to sell.

Ivan nods, and the troubled look on his face does not go unnoticed.

"You know of my adventure?"

He laughs, a deep throaty sound that sends shivers across the back of my neck, not unpleasantly.

"Adventure is a nice word for what your father has demanded, dear princess."

Princess. How wrong the title feels.

"Call me anything else."

He furrows straw-colored eyebrows. His own steed, a white beast, whinnies nearby as Ivan secures my belongings to Gala's saddle.

"Once you reach the bog, tie Gala to a tree before the soft grounds begin. Otherwise, you'll both sink. If you fail to return, I'll make sure she's retrieved safely."

"My return is doubtful, so thank you." I stroke Gala's strong flank, hating the idea of parting with her.

Ivan steps closer, hesitates. His warm breath ghosts across my cheeks. If I had been surer of myself, maybe I'd have run away from this castle long ago. Maybe I would've asked Ivan to come with me.

"What do you hope to gain from this, Daria?"

While I don't care for the question, I do like the way he says my name.

I focus on Gala, think of her running across wildflower meadows at the control of no one.

"Freedom."

"You think the Baba Yaga will grant you that?"

My head whips toward Ivan so fast I'm surprised my neck doesn't break. Those words Father has forbidden, and yet Ivan shows no dread. I've never been sure if Father prohibits the name because he fears the witch or if he wants no one else to know the rumors of the powerful flame.

The last person to speak the witch's name had the misfortune of Father overhearing. The poor man was made an example out of in the town square. All were forced to watch the downright medieval punishment ... the Pear of Anguish. A torture device not seen for years, but oh, Father knew an executioner for the job. The pear-shaped metal mechanism was placed inside the man's mouth, muffling any hope he'd speak of the witch or anything again. With the turn of a key, the device expanded, gagging him. Father said to keep going. The executioner did so until the victim's skull shattered.

The shredding of the man's face into fleshy ribbons haunted my dreams. When I tried to speak of it to my sister, Vasilisa shrugged it off and repeated Father's words. The man got what he deserved. It was the only time something cruel slunk from Vasilisa's mouth, but she so believed in Father's mighty judgment.

"You're either brave or foolish for speaking the witch's

name," I say. Ivan grins in response with something fearless in those strong teeth.

"The Baba Yaga is an idea, not a name."

"Really? Father always made it sound like that was her name."

"Well, so brilliant, is he?"

I hide a smile of my own as Ivan helps me onto Gala's back. My sight lingers on his white horse, and I wonder how he keeps the tall creature so pristine despite the dirt and hay on his own hands.

"Will you miss me? I mean, after all, my sister is still here to gaze at."

"She isn't my type," he mutters. "Of course, I'll miss you. You are odd and interesting and beautiful."

No one has ever called me beautiful before. And I'm ashamed I'm so drawn to the word, hungry for approval.

He clears his throat. "I mean it."

"Thank you."

A sigh drifts from his lips. "I know you are close to tasting freedom, or death, or perhaps both. If you survive the bog, you may not survive the witch. If you do, beware of how sweet lies may taste. Beware of the fate you accept."

"How do you know these things?"

A sly look overtakes his face and leaves endearing dimples in his cheeks. "Some things must remain a mystery."

"Helpful." I roll my eyes.

"Be careful," he says as Gala trots away from the stable. "And don't eat the pears."

"No pears. No lies. Got it." I wave farewell, will my heart to calm its frantic beating, and try to make sense of Ivan's warnings.

The journey takes over a day, and I am lucky no robber murdered me in the few hours of sleep I stole during the night. We reach the bog's edge, marked by a faded wooden sign and an abundance of twisted overgrowth. Morning sun breaks through, casting the sky in tones of pomegranate.

I secure Gala on sturdy ground to a thick tree near a stream ending before the marshy land. She has water, a supply of apples and carrots, and a blanket on her back to keep warm until she's retrieved. I kiss my dear horse on the nose and ignore the wrenching in my heart to leave her.

Rotting wood greets me, a short bridge that leads halfway into the wetland. Pitcher plants shoot up with thick, fluid-filled bodies, lining the path after the walkway ends. A moss-covered trail of dirt sits on a mound higher than the surrounding water. I aim to keep light steps on the route, but sinking is a constant danger. Different hues of moss catch the sunlight peering through the canopy of tall trees. Light green patches in the distance, deep emerald clumps near the path, and every shade in-between.

Insects swarm, leave bites to swell on my exposed neck. A flash of pure white distracts me as I swat away the buzzing things, and I nearly fall into a burbling pit of brackish water.

Perhaps the bog causes hallucinations. I shake away the thoughts and move onward, past Venus flytraps, their red tongues covered in crushed bugs. The tail of some scaled creature slaps the dark water, and I jump backward. Razored scratches catch my cheek, slicing deep enough for blood to bloom. I've stumbled into a thorned tree in my fright. Wiping the blood away, seeing its crimson stain my hands and coat, it's almost enough to make me turn around.

Frosted movement flashes again from my peripheral vision, and no, dear wandering mind, stop these ideas because it's not a horse. It's not Ivan. They could not run here without disappearing into watery graves.

Liquid leaks through my boots, weighs down the hem of my layered skirts. Smeared blood from my cheek burns my eye, but still, I walk on, tripping over roots and rocks.

Two hours later, I am lost. Everything looks the same in this mossy dome, and I barely catch myself from tumbling face-first into oxygen-deprived waters. And then from behind me, the whinny of a horse.

An impossibly white steed stands about ten feet from where I've tripped. On top, a rider also cloaked entirely in white. With a pale glove, the figure points east. The horse, so like Ivan's, but how could any horse be here? I haul myself up, call out to the person, but the horse gallops into invisibility. Gone.

I walk east.

Another half-hour. More bites, more blood. But finally, there. A glowing blue flame sits behind caged bars. I laugh aloud because how could I ever think surviving the bog would be enough to simply take the fire?

From a wide torch, sapphire flames dance. The cage surrounding the torch sparks as if possessed by lightning. I toss a stick toward the metal. The shock pulls back the bark, blackens the stick into a smoking heap—and I can infer my flesh would also peel and crackle from burnt bones if I try to touch the cage.

Before defeat takes me, the white rider appears again and points behind the cage. A hut waits, concealed in thick vegetation. Dark stone walls with black feathers thatched on the roof glimmer around brown moss. Below, the house stands on two large, coal-colored bird legs. The front door nests between overhangs in the shape of an inky beak. Beneath the door, a staircase lolls down like a diseased tongue.

Too curious to leave, I amble up the stairs. A wide keyhole on the door invites me to peek through, which proves to be a mistake. The keyhole is filled with human teeth. Some of the molars are so tiny ...

Before I can back away, a voice fills my head like static.

In the jar sits pieces of the moon. Take a sliver and consume it. Prove yourself worthy to obtain what you seek, what you came here for.

Pieces of the moon? Ridiculous.

Yet, there is a jar on a moldy tree stump resting on the terrace's moss floor. Whispers in my head entice me forward. An invitation to unscrew the lid, examine the glass filled with paper-thin disks.

Prove yourself worthy.

When Father asked me to prove myself, it was an attempt to either get rid of me or miraculously have me return with power to gift him. This woman's voice, though, melting into my mind, is gentler. A reminder that I am worthy, but I must prove it to myself.

There has never been anything to lose.

I remove a wafer, examine its cragged surface and gray coating. I place the circle on my tongue, let the smoky, foreign flavor curl inside my mouth. I feel as if I've licked the stars.

Silence at first, a great calm. And then ocean waves lapping over me. I see it in my mind, a bright day at the beach with Vasilisa. Just us, far away from Father's stern rule. A happy memory, but the sea pulls me down. Too soon. It blocks out the sun with salted darkness.

The day dissolves into a frozen lake. Vasilisa stands beside her prince as he makes a joke, insults my appearance. Asks if I am truly her sister.

Vasilisa laughs, asks him not to be so mean.

She laughed. She laughed at the joke. At me.

She knows she is the sun. She convinces herself she loves me, but I have been wrong about her lack of cruelty, for I see it now, the malice of Father polluting her heart. My own sister, would you cast me to the shadows?

If I cannot share her daylight, I will take the moon.

You consume the pieces and survive because we have always been creatures of moonlight, Daria.

"How do you know my name?"

One more vision.

This one is short—to the point, perhaps. But there is Vasilisa, in her buttery gown, showing Father the jewelry I stashed away.

"She wouldn't do that. You lie!"

The door with the keyhole of teeth swings open. Behind me, the white rider waits at the bottom of the staircase with a spear in hand. He points forward, and I walk into the house's beak.

"I am sorry to say you have seen truths, not lies. You are, however, just in time for the autumn funeral feast, and this is good news."

I follow the saccharine voice, aiming to keep my hurt tempered, but the anger of Vasilisa's betrayal boils inside. If she truly did those things, then she does not love me as I thought I loved her.

Subdued light obscures much in the cottage, but I spy oak shelves lined with jars. Something gooey and dead in those containers reflects back. The whole place smells of rotten fruit.

A woman walks away from the dim and hovers near a grand table. She is dressed in scraps of silver fabric as if she'd put on a thin gown only to have claws shred through it. I can't look away from how perfectly it wraps around her. She stretches, body rippling with muscles and curves, and though I am not short, she towers over me. White hair falls in waves down her back, and irises glow the same silver color as her clothing. She looks both young and ancient, something undefinable in her strong jaw, long nose, full lips—an androgynous kind of face like an actor in disguise. All so different than the painted princesses decorating Father's castle walls. Words abandon me as my tongue sits heavily in my mouth.

"Do you think me a prophetess?" she coos. "A cannibal? The Venus flytrap in human form come to eat you? Perhaps I am all of these things."

Her proximity sends quivers through my body in the pleasant way Ivan did. Confused, I follow her to the table where she gestures for me to sit. Empty obsidian plates line the surface, shining in the hazy light.

A basket of rotten pears rests in the middle, brown mush crawling with flies.

"You have passed two trials and only the third remains."

"Trials?"

"You survived the bog. Ate slivers of moon, and they decided to let you live after showing visions you weren't meant to see."

The hurt of those scenes cuts me again, and the woman watches my face with intense curiosity.

"If you pass the final trial, the fire is yours to command."

"I'm meant to bring it back to the castle, to save my father and sister from ruin."

She lights a candle near the putrid pears, and I notice her necklace made of bone has a single toe tied to it.

"Would they do the same for you?"

The words strike me like a slap to the face. Have I been so blinded by Vasilisa? The idea of her marching into the bog to save me is laughable. She would never, and this I know.

"Do you have a name?" I find my voice again.

"I am called several things in legends. But I am an ancient idea more than anything. I have many sisters, and together we have many faces, which, of course, leads to many names."

"You don't really look ancient."

She laughs, and it's like lightning mixed with honey. An electric sweetness drawing me in. Her exposed flesh sends an ache in my chest to shed my own layers of skirts and this thick coat. I glance away, afraid of the temptation. Is this the power my father so feared of the bog-dwelling witch?

"Appearances are the easiest to shift. Besides, my appetite keeps me young." She winks, and I blush.

"What is this place?"

"My home, with its raven feet and feathers, prepared to fly away, but recently we have been too starved to travel. Not many visitors to the bog, you see. It leaves us famished. Do you hunger like we do?"

"We?"

The witch leans closer until our breaths puff in the air and mingle. Specks of lavender shimmer from her lips.

"Do you want to know what you could have if you don't take the flame back to your haunted castle?"

I nod, my eyes focusing on the strange light glittering from her mouth.

Slowly, she tilts her head down. A strong hand holds my chin in place as she pulls me toward the purple gleam. Her lips overtake mine. Promises of power blossom in my mind's eyes as her radiance pulsates. She shows me freedom. There's Gala, running through green fields. And there's me as her apprentice. Free and loved. Wanted. But there's always a price to pay, isn't there?

Her tongue tastes of pears, fresh ones at least, not rotten like the centerpieces. I move away from the witch's kiss, silently apologizing to Ivan because I did not stay away from the pears, after all. Not quite.

"You're different from how the townspeople speak of you and how they draw you in secret books," I say, breathless.

She raises an eyebrow. "I have seen their crude renderings, grotesque at best. Do you think me ugly?"

Heat flushes my cheeks. "Clearly not," I mutter, my lips still aching. "You are ... ethereal. Plus, my father fears you."

A chuckle shakes her shoulders, and I want to explore her more, almost with a desperate need to understand how she breathes, how her magic works. What is she made of besides lightning and lavender?

"People like your father, I don't fit in their world. I am not the whimpering woman they covet. I don't meet their standards, and I don't care, which scares them."

"I want to understand."

"You've been chasing beauty, little Irbis. The chase of fools."

"Irbis? Snow leopard?"

She nods. "Big cat who lives in the high mountains. Your father, a poacher. Your sister, too domestic. You are the wild thing running free, or trying to. Together, we are feral, shedding our coats beneath moonlight."

I feel as if she's looked into my heart, pulled out the shadows, and translated them into something glorious.

"What's the third trial?"

"It depends. Will you use the fire to save your kin or yourself?"

It is not lost on me that the visions could be what Ivan warned me of. Lies created to change my choices. Maybe it doesn't matter. My whole life has been spent seeking something I could not name until now.

Freedom. Strength.

"If Vasilisa dies," I muse. "It becomes my fault for not saving her."

"Guilt makes you weak, little leopard. Who will save you when you're done saving everyone else?"

I hesitate, absorbing her words.

She retrieves a rotten pear from the table's center, squeezes it until the pulp oozes down her fingers. I think of the man's shattered skull from that day in the town square.

"We could return this place to life. To feasts you've never imagined, if you give me the souls of those in the castle." She flings the soggy mess of rot away.

An appetite for souls. I should have known.

"Together, we can dine, Daria. Think of it as your sister's spirit living on through you but not controlling you."

"My sister doesn't control me."

The witch crosses her arms, and my eyes drift to the veins visible on her wrists, then on her chest as she breathes in and out, how the blue of them shines like constellations.

"Their wishes for a secure future control you. I don't have to show you a vision to see that. Your sister's love, my Irbis, is a lie. She is using you to spin love into riches."

Such deception doesn't sound like Vasilisa, but then again, I doubt all I thought I knew.

"Give me something to call you, please."

The woman stretches long legs out in front of her like a great tiger. "I will tell you my favorite name, the one I called myself in a past life if you complete your last trial. Decide what you want. Consequences find you either way."

I don't feel lied to by this Baba Yaga, but I'm not sure if I felt lied to by my sister, either. Maybe that's part of Vasilisa's charm; after all, she didn't try to prevent me from leaving. She didn't volunteer to walk by my side. My older sister, but has she ever defended me against Father's vicious words? It all makes a sick kind of sense in my head.

Vasilisa may have hoped I returned, but she wanted the blue fire, too. The restored wealth. Not a sister.

"I know you're afraid," the woman whispers in my ear from the front terrace where I have walked to stare down at the cage guarding the flame.

"I am."

Sweet, earthy breath tickles my ear. "I can teach you to overcome fear. I can show you many things if you stay. I have been so lonely, and who would dare walk beside me in the moonlight through bogs and desert and snow. A wild leopard, perhaps, hungry for life."

A hot finger traces down the back of my neck, and then those hands unlace my coat's ties. I shed the first layer, let the bog's haze cool my fevered skin.

26

"You can have another if you wish. We always journey together." Her fingers squeeze gently around my waist until a mess of ribbons uncurl, sliding skirts past my hips as I step out of my shoes. I stand atop the moss in my loose cotton shift and nothing else. A state of undress I've never allowed anyone to see, but the witch's caress excites me, and she points to the white rider when I ask her who she means by "we."

The figure removes its white helmet, and there, Ivan's sweet face. His expression unreadable. Strange Ivan upon his white horse, a beast so pristine it possesses the power to hover about the bog. My stableboy, all this time, keeping the company of a witch.

"I share my power with the white rider, protector of this place."

"Ivan," I let his name escape from my breath like a promise. He rides to the bottom of the stairs, and I meet him there. Ivan slides off a glove, reaches for my hand from where he stays perched on the snowy horse. I touch his fingers, feel his solid heat, and it calms something in me as the witch who hides her name strokes my hair. I am connected to them both, to this place.

Though I wonder ...

"How many others do you lure here like this?"

Ivan chuckles. "I told you to beware what fate you accept. I wasn't sure if this path would be right for you, but if it is, then I'm glad to see you again. Will you stay with us?"

"We collect the lonely, it's true," the woman says. "But it doesn't mean we don't love them, Daria. Here, you are wanted."

The words stir heat in my barely-clad body. They have chosen me, and I can choose them, too. Belonging, it's something I achingly need, and perhaps I am mad for it, but would freedom ever come to me without a bit of madness?

Moss tickles the soles of my feet, dampening my toes as I walk to the flame. The lightning striking the cage stops, and it opens.

"What do I do?"

"Speak to the fire. Tell it what you wish."

I steady my shaking hand and wrap fingers around the torch handle. Sapphire flames smolder in front of my face, different tones of blue speckled with silver.

I never wished to be cruel, but maybe this is mercy. The castle will never regain its fortune, and it stopped being a home long ago. I whisper freedom into the fire, for myself, for my sister and father, but in different ways. The kingdom granted much pain, but I will see it end. Let something peaceful be rebuilt by better people than my family, than myself.

Here comes your precious blue fire, Father. Now choke on it.

Guilt pinpricks me for Vasilisa, but the witch promises I can have my sister's soul all to myself at the autumn funeral feast. The rest of the spirits, whomever remains in the castle alongside Father, their souls appear on the obsidian plates in the cottage, and together, we will dine. Together, we will restore strength and life here.

My trials, complete. Ivan and the Baba Yaga surround me. Their heat encompasses everything as we fall on a bed of moss. There is lightning and lavender, skin everywhere. She whispers her name to me, her favorite name—a secret I cradle in my mind. I store it next to these lavish emotions of autonomy, of what it is to be wanted.

In the distance, blue fire and smoke rage, consuming the castle of my childhood. It crumbles to ash as wild creatures emerge from the bog and run free beneath silver moonlight.

WORMWOOD

BY LINDZ MCLEOD

Mirrors tell the wrong stories. They may reflect what is present, but the naked eye deceives worse than a clothed hand ever could.

Baba Yaga's mirror is a portal into any swollen droplet of moisture; several are better, offering more clarity, gathered together like a modest woman's skirts. As she rides through the darkening sky in her mortar, the afternoon's brilliance dips below the horizon, leaving only a final, bloody finger of light. Below, the snow-tipped trees sway in a gentle lullaby. Inside the curve of the mortar bowl, noise is ensnared and amplified, bouncing back between her skeletal knees. Her ears are pricked—not for the sound of life but for the resonance of grief.

To the south, a slumbering child wrapped in a stained, threadbare sheet. Baba Yaga can peer out from the beads of sweat on his brow, can see his mother press a hand to her mouth and catch a rabbit-sob before it can escape the steel trap of her fingers. Under the sheet, the boy's skin glistens like the moon's pockmarked surface. Pustules weep, and skin cracks, revealing scarlet chasms underneath. The door is locked; there are several deep gouges on the external wood. The boy's father did not take kindly to being locked out, but in doing so, the mother has spared her husband almost certain death. At least, for now.

To the west, a young woman is sitting by a frosted window, her breath puffing clouds on the glass. A half-sewn shirt sprawls forgotten in her hands—not a lover's shirt, but a brother's. Beyond the cottage, a new grave for a young man, who holds two bullets in his chest where a heart once beat. The girl weeps for the brother she hardly knew and the opportunity to marry his handsome comrade—now vanished, along with her scant dowry. Baba Yaga sees all from the tears that track down her soft, plump cheeks.

To the north, she hears a man already deep in his cups, despite the unmilked cow lowing outside. Baba Yaga stares up at him from the bottom of the mug, where clear, acerbic liquid pools. She flits to the floor of the back bedroom, to where several beads of blood glitter. These traces were not the only things the man missed during his hurried cleanup; blood dots the snow outside like an unfinished game of dominoes, leading to the buried body of a young woman. The crime is written on the man's throat, in words that didn't come up with the bile he vomited earlier, although he's doing his best to drown it.

Mirrors tell the wrong stories. When Baba Yaga looks at herself, she sees an ugly woman with a nose so long it can almost touch the ceiling of her low-roofed house. A skinny hag with flesh like a blanket draped over couched bones. Mirrors may reflect what is present, but a lamb never stops to comprehend the beauty of the wolf—the grace of a lope, the elegance of a bite. Old does not mean useless. Ugly does not mean unkind. Grotesque does not mean unworthy. In any case, she has always been old; the magic infused into her soul comes from the forest itself. Her appearance conflates with her level of experience. Innocence is overvalued, in her opinion. Basing one's worth on what one hasn't done seems foolish.

She returns home, thinking of all the herbs she will need for her next journey. Something sweet for the child, to encourage him to eat a little, something that reminds him of a much-loved grandmother. Something savory for the girl, to remind her that there will be other men, other matches.

When the mortar bowl touches down on the rimy ground, Baba Yaga hops out with an ease that would surprise an observer.

Her chicken-legged house is roosting mere inches off the ground, clawed feet dug in comfortably. The fence surrounding the house is made from human bones, scavenged from corpses long dead and never missed. The lock on the gate is reachable through a complete human jawbone—the teeth sharpened into points—rendering the house accessible only by those desperate enough to leave something behind. To that end, a pale hand lies amongst a clump of sparse, withered weeds, fingers curled toward the sky. A scarlet trail of bright beads lead to the porch, where a woman in a brown dress curls into herself like a slug scenting salt.

Baba Yaga approaches with caution. Anyone who has made it this far has very little left to lose.

"Child?" she whispers.

The woman looks up. Pain draws her features into sharp lines; all agony is angles, after all. Through gritted teeth, she manages to grunt one word. *Sestra*. Sister.

Baba Yaga requires no further explanation. This woman's kin is—was—the woman buried outside the cottage down the road. The blood spatters on the bedroom floor sang the same song as this supplicant's blood, something low-pitched, harsh, thunderous. Not unlike the cawing of a crow.

"Inside." The door of the house swings open on command. She helps the woman in and hefts her into a chair. Rubs a poultice on the wound until the woman nearly passes out from the pain. Wraps the stub in clean bandages. Makes hot tea infused with healing herbs and sets a chipped mug down in front of the woman.

"Drink."

The woman drinks. She hasn't said anything else, but Baba Yaga knows what she wants. Justice or vengeance boils down to the same thing, anyway.

The hand will grow back in a week. The woman will have to stay here until it does, so Baba Yaga can be certain she doesn't show the magic to anyone. Once out, she won't tell anyone. No one would believe her anyway since her hand would appear entirely unharmed. Still, Baba Yaga will make her understand that she'd be doing a disservice to others in similar situations. The purity of her desperation—an honest need—was what saved her. If she'd known her hand would grow back, the act would have been dishonest. Temporary. To enter Baba Yaga's house, one must always leave something behind. To enter life means leaving the safety of non-existence behind, while the adventure of death cannot be had without first shedding the cloak of the living.

She helps the woman onto a small, hard cot at the side of the room and draws a blanket over her. The fire crackles. The room is suffused with homely, amber light. Apart from the shelves groaning with strange plants, dried herbs, and pickled animal parts, this could be mistaken for any cottage for a hundred miles. Baba Yaga selects a few jars, packs what she needs, and heads back outside. No time to listen for grief on this journey; all her attention must be on cultivating the perfect punishment.

Mirrors tell the wrong stories. The man believes he was driven to the act. His unhappy wife, finding herself pregnant, obtained certain herbs to rid herself of the baby. The man, suspecting her of adultery, figured that in either case, she was guilty of a terrible crime and should therefore be punished. The punishment simply went too far—he enjoyed himself too much, allowed his base impulses to take over. A moment of weakness, lasting an hour. The tiny mirror on the mantelpiece reflects a strong jawline, dark-lashed green eyes, a twice-broken nose. It shows himself as he believes himself to be; handsome, noble, honorable. He imagines that he is the true victim, and his wounded pride almost alleviates the crushing guilt. The vodka is helping repress the remainder.

On approach, Baba Yaga uses her pestle to slow down the mortar, swinging the bowl into a wide arc. She carves a circle in the air, twenty feet above the cottage, and adds sprigs to a jar while she chants a spell. Rosemary, to force memories of his wife. Iris, for a message not yet sent. Rue, for clear, inescapable vision. *Brosok*, she whispers. Cast the spell. And then, the same meaning but a different shade. *Ottenok*. Let the hues of the memories take shape.

The spell descends on the cottage, a great pale mist seeping through the cracks, invisible to all but Baba Yaga. The man is sprawled over his small table, both surface and shirt wet with spilled alcohol. The spell mutes the sharp scent in favor of the ones chosen by Baba Yaga. The man wakes, flounders, falls to the floor. She waits, watching from the puddle on the table, with a handful of wormwood poised over the jar.

He grabs the table and hauls himself up. One of his boots has come off, but he is too drunk to notice. Still, something is cutting through the haze—a deep, feral sense, instilled in the guts of all animals—a warning of impending danger. Something is wrong. He staggers to the bedroom and stares at the empty bed, then the clean floor. Runs a hand through his hair. His wife had always smelled of flour, of pig-fat soap, of smoke from blackened logs. Like home. Regret swells; he chokes, retches, but anger surges up, overtakes the emotion.

He stumbles back into the front room, toward a small shelf beside the fire. He grabs a jar of wild garlic and upends the entire thing into the still-smoldering fire. Flames lick up the side of the stems. Baba Yaga, in her position above the cottage, smiles. The spell dampens the scent, producing its own invasive smells and flavors. The man tastes fresh bread, then staleness. Hard cheese, then soft green mold. Salted beef melts on his tongue, followed by rank rotten meat. He gags again. He upends every herb his wife ever picked into the fire. Scrabbles around for a bottle of something—anything—to take the scent away. He licks the table like a dog, lapping at the small puddle of spilled alcohol, and Baba Yaga, unable to bear the disgusting sight of his white-coated tongue, drops the wormwood into the jar.

Wormwood has a bitter taste, but it is also the true scent of grief. The man recoils instantly, wipes his tongue on his shirt. He cannot bear to swallow, cannot bring himself to vomit, therefore, he stumbles in a circle, weaving, before heading for the front door. Fleeing into the forest, he presses his face into dry puddles of pine needles—pine, the scent of humility—but his nostrils are full of his wife. Her skin, flushed and rosy after a village dance. Her dark hair, like gathering clouds ahead of a storm. His mouth is full of her kisses, her taste. Even with his cheek and chest pressed against the frosted grass, he can feel the weight of her head on his breast. Even missing one boot, toes curling against the frozen earth, he can feel the heat of her blood splashing against his bare feet. In the silence of the forest, he can hear her last whimpering cries, bouncing from trunk to trunk. The birds that perch on branches above him caw only her name until the sound maddens him.

A passing neighbor hears the man's screams. Rushing in with an ax, they find him alone and gibbering. The man confesses his sin and begs to be put out of his misery. The neighbor, frightened by the look in the man's eye, is unwilling to pass such immediate judgment. The local authority is summoned. They put the man on trial and hang him in the forest, far from his home. It is neither a quick death nor a pretty one. They leave the body up for the birds, as befits a murderer. If they knew Baba Yaga lived so close, perhaps they would have buried him after all. She has a taste for human flesh, the stories claim, and it would not do to encourage her. His wife is dug up and given a proper burial in the local graveyard for much the same reasons.

Baba Yaga does her best. She gives people what they need, not what they want. They love her and loathe her in equal measures, but all fear her power. Strange. There isn't much to it, apart from common sense. Crimes require punishment. To take something requires that you give something back in equal measure. A hand for a spell. A life for a life. She cannot judge—she leaves that to the people, according to their own laws.

They call her a witch. They call her a goddess. They call her a cannibal. But mirrors tell the wrong stories.

And so do people.

MAMA YAGA

BY CHRISTINA SNG

Sometime during the first season of my life, I developed a taste for human flesh.

It is an acquired taste, much like blue cheese and black truffles, a vile abomination to the tongue until it eventually, over time and exposure, becomes accepted and appreciated.

It was during one of the famines when droves of parents abandoned their children in the woods and left them to the wolves, simply so they could feed themselves that one more meal.

There was no more meat in the villages, and vegetables were scarce. Many starved rather than exchange children to eat, but my sisters and I had no such qualms, despite having no children to trade.

With so many little creatures wandering in the woods, we decided to try eating one of them, they who so frequently trampled on our vegetable patch and trespassed near our home. The leprechaun tasted terrible. But human children were a different story.

We began to take them in, but like people affectionately bonded to their pets, we couldn't bear to eat them. Not at first.

My favorite pet thus far was endearing and sweet.

Stick-thin with large goldfish eyes resembling clear sky-blue marbles, she looked like a fairy child.

She gladly helped us clean the cottage and forage for berries in exchange for food and shelter.

We even used her name, Gretel. Such a strange-sounding name, even during those progressive times.

She called me Mama Yaga and treated me with deference

and respect while only nodding to my sisters, who never acknowledged her anyway.

Gretel worked hard and quietly. We barely noticed her as she slipped in and out of shadows. I often wondered what happened to her parents, but I did not care enough to ask.

Most likely, it was the same awful story I heard over and over again. After all, loving parents did not abandon their children in the woods. Especially not during a famine.

Gretel seemed grateful to be taken in and given a place in our home. But I don't think she ever forgave us for eating her pompous, rotund brother Hansel who had arrived with her.

To my defense, I simply could not bear his constant wailing about his hunger.

Every day, he sat around, whining about how bored he was, while Gretel quietly helped out around the cottage.

I never liked children, even though I was one a very long time ago, as were my sisters once, but we never behaved this way. I think our mother would have skinned us alive if we did.

So one day, while Gretel was out foraging for berries and my sisters were tending to the vegetables, I lured that pompous creature to the kitchen and shoved him into the oven. I left him there to bake in his own fluids till his skin was golden and crisp.

Gretel returned that evening with a basketful of blueberries. How her nose perked up and her mouth salivated at the aroma of fatty meat roasting in the oven.

"Have we caught a boar, Mama Yaga?" she asked while handing me the basket. I merely smiled and embraced her. "Thank you for the berries, dear Gretel!"

Gretel screamed when she opened the oven and found her brother's crisp dead face staring back at her.

She raced out of the cottage and did not return for several days.

I felt a tinge of remorse pierce my heart, seeing the stream of tears trail behind her, but I shook it off. It was dinnertime, and we were hungry.

My sisters and I tucked into a feast. Hunger does strange things to your mind while fatty, grilled meat soothes it.

We ate till we were full, and the rest, we salted and dried as jerky, to be savored another day.

Starvation must have brought her back, for Gretel appeared at our door a week later, even thinner if it were possible, and collapsed onto the ground.

After we nourished her with vegetable soup and blueberry pie, she murmured in her delirium that she was lost in the woods and kept walking around in circles.

Silly me, I forgot to lift the spell cloaking our cottage from the rest of the world. It stretched till the woods' edge before the flat plains leading to the village.

Often, I cast that spell when I got tired of encountering strangers by our cottage.

But during these perilous times when everyone was starving, it was necessary to keep those with weapons from coming to attack us weak old women until we were replenished. And now we were.

We kept Gretel. I suspected she had some kind of revenge in mind. She refused any kind of meat, worried it might be her brother, and subsisted only on vegetables and fruit. While she fattened up a tinge, she was still thin as a willow branch.

I grew fond of her, like I did my own daughter from another age, Marinka, until that fateful night Gretel killed both my sisters in their sleep and nearly carved off my head with a kitchen knife. But with her brother's flesh in my belly, I was faster. Much faster.

I caught her hand and twisted the knife back at her, watching her enormous eyes bulge so much that I felt certain they would pop out of their sockets.

At that point, I realized I only had one option remaining.

I stabbed her in the shoulder to stun her, then dragged her

by her hair to the kitchen and shoved her into the oven. How she cried when I turned on the heat.

I told her I was sorry, but I'd lived long enough to know that it was critical to exterminate my enemies before they came back to finish me.

As she cooked, I carried my sisters' bodies to the vegetable patch and buried them deep so the wolves wouldn't get to them. When I was done, I turned off the oven and buried dear Gretel out there with them. We don't eat family, no matter how hungry we are.

Afterward, I never took in any more children. It was too painful. I did keep a cat or two, and at one time, a wolf. They hunted for their own food and regularly brought me back treats.

Despite everything, I never lost my taste for human flesh. Remembering an anecdote from Gretel about the candies she loved, I taught myself to tap trees for sweet sap and extracted dye from flowers and berries.

In time, I became a master candy maker, selling them at the village and decorating my cottage with them. Only spells stayed the tyranny of army ants that loved my creations too. But the candies lured food to my cottage, and so, the spells stayed up.

In my second age, I wrote a book to commemorate young Gretel. In it, I made her the brave heroine, triumphant over her enemy, the wicked witch with the candy house.

It became a bestseller, and till today, many curious children still wander the woods, looking for my cottage. I always welcome them in with a smile and a basketful of candy.

FLOOD ZONE

BY DONNA LYNCH

T he forests were dying.

Well, not so much dying as disappearing, so Gran decided it was time for us to move on.

Having shed the snake body I'd been born into, I was ten times larger than the burrow where I grew up, so any home I could fit into, in any place she chose, was as good as the next.

After Gran turned me, I would leave the forest whenever I could to find *people things*, so when she said she wanted to move, I pilfered travel magazines to give us ideas. She was a little bit blind, so I did most of the looking, and when I saw the pictures of all the houses up on stilts along the coast, I knew it was the perfect place. We wouldn't have to hide in the thickets, a million miles into the wilderness when all the houses had legs.

And *less hidden* meant *more people*, and *more people* meant *more food*.

So, you are fine with my appetite if it means you get to live seaside, she said.

I didn't like that she ate children, but I didn't want her to starve. And in truth, I very much longed to live by the sea. In pictures, it looked so lovely. I imagined living on the shore was like being in a home with only three walls. The fourth opened out into the world where everything could be free. It wasn't so in the forest, with too many things to ensnare you, so many obstacles. So, yes. Living by the sea would come with a heavy cost, measured by my desire and my guilt. Gran let the decision fall upon my shoulders—one of the countless human lessons she was forever forcing me to learn.

It was never this hard when I was a snake.

I was perfectly fine eating small animals since I could still unhinge my jaw, but Gran was deeply insulted when I suggested she do the same. I told her I'd rather her eat adults, especially the cruel ones with their ugly hearts, but she said they didn't appease her. They tasted sour and were made of poison. She needed the bones supple, the flesh tender, and the hearts pure. These were the children of men and women who would go right ahead and trade them for their own material desires. What kind of life would a child have with parents like that? A mother who would give us their little ones in exchange for riches. A father who'd pay for vanity and unending virility with the flesh of his own daughter. It would be nothing but tragedy and heartbreak for these children, to be so unwanted, to be of so little value beyond that of currency—the sacrifice was a kindness she provided and a benefit to all parties.

A merciful act, she called it.

I understood, but if I had my druthers, I'd suffer the bad taste and sour belly so the children could go free.

That's because you don't know the world, Zmija. Where do you think orphans go? They are not all so lucky to have a grandmother to protect them. You're too young and new to the ways of humankind and much too stupid to make those decisions.

She was forever saying that sort of thing to me and I didn't like it, but she was usually right. Things were so much simpler in my former life. We were born, we fed, we made more of our own, and we died. Owls and foxes could injure us, but nothing ever broke our hearts. In our world, being stabbed in the back meant a human with a garden spade cutting us in two, not betrayal. So beautifully simple. Our whole existence painless by comparison.

Winter came, and I made the decision. Gran bade the house to go, and off we went to the shore. With her magic, she could make people think they hadn't seen what they saw, but only for a short time, so we had to move quickly. I don't know how long we traveled. It was cold, and since old ways are wont to linger, I slept, buried deep in blankets for most of it.

I could smell the sea before I saw it, and soon after, I felt the house's feet sinking and fighting against the terrain as it changed from soil to sand. As it settled, Gran stood on the white beach in the biting wind, her silver hair flailing with it, her thick and yellow-clawed toes burrowing deep into the sand. She smiled with her sharp and jagged teeth, like stalagmites, surveying the line of opulent houses up on all fours that ran as far as we could see to the north and the south.

You did good picking this place, Zmija. We fit just like a button to a loop.

But other than the stilted houses, we didn't fit at all. Our house—like its owner—was a weathered, old crone from the darkest of the woods, and now, here on the beach, a piece of dirty coal amidst shimmering diamonds. *Nothing a little magic can't correct*, she said, so I stopped my worrying and smiled along with her because she was happy.

By the morning, if you weren't looking closely, our house seemed to blend perfectly well with the others.

If you weren't looking closely.

A light haze of magic like a perpetual fog would keep people from noticing straight away that our house sat precariously atop two crooked legs rather than on multiple stilts. It obscured the rotting mosses and ancient, knotted roots that had clung to and woven themselves into the wood over centuries. It concealed the pungent odor of wet earth and decay, and the fainter smell of a viscous stew of unfathomable ingredients. Of course, Gran used as many parts as she could—which was just about all of them— so the scent of death was rarely present. There were no wolves here to clean up after her, but the ocean was the largest maw in the world. It could devour anything that remained.

The other houses along the shoreline were mostly empty and would remain so for several months. I wanted to look inside them to see what treasures people filled their spaces with, but nearly all were shuttered against the winter storms. I imagined them filled with piles of jewels and lush fabrics from faraway lands, and the heads of rare, exotic animals. It would be many months before I could know.

But the small houses to the west of the dunes were inhabited year-round. They sat upon the sandy earth, beneath pines, in the flood zone—as it was called in town—and were much easier to see into. These belonged to the people who didn't have a second home filled with jewels to board up in the winter. The people who lived here were desperate for more, in a purgatory somewhere between those who made do with next to nothing and those who had everything they could ever desire. Their lives were filled with big televisions and bigger trucks and any other thing to make them feel closer to the latter than the former, at any cost—even that of joy and kindness. Gran said the story was the same no matter the time nor landscape—people in palaces didn't need her magic, and the people in hovels treasured their families and faith above all else. There was nothing she could offer to make them trade.

But when you are in the middle, you can see how close you truly are to either place, and if the jealousy doesn't eat away your heart, the fear surely will.

The small morsels of greater excess they clamored for only made them hungrier, and so it was in their insatiable purgatory she would sate herself.

I went to their meeting places, their pubs, and their shops and listened to their chatter, which was mostly about their troubles and the troubles of others. There was so much bitterness, and the only thing that seemed to make them happy was spreading it around.

Gran gave me some magic to help things along, but I did very well on my own making up stories to entice them, to get them thinking about all the things they didn't have yet but, *maybe* …

Since becoming human, I got very good at stories.

Gran only needed *one or two at each new moon* to keep her belly full, and I only needed to guide the parents to her. She would take care of all the rest.

It wasn't long until the first of them came knocking, and by the beginning of the new year, there was knocking every day. It seemed everyone was hungry for more.

Zmija, this place is filled with poisonous souls, Gran said to me, as she called the fog every few days to cover us like a heavy curtain. People came again and again, eagerly, *desperately* willing to exchange their little ones for their desires. On the days we hid, we would watch from behind the veil as men and women would ascend the dunes, eyes scouring the beach, hands at their foreheads like sailors searching for land, pointing to where they were certain our house had stood.

We never want, we never ask for, nor do we ever take more than we need, she'd say, her quiet, brittle voice full of disgust as she watched them from the window come and go. *May their gluttony and greed split them in two from the gullet on down.*

Once again, I suggested that if it didn't, perhaps *we* should.

And before I could say it yet another time, she reluctantly agreed.

But as fate would have it and as stories will go, our new arrangement was far from perfect. The town, suspiciously, said nothing of the three missing children she'd devoured but took immediate note of a man and a woman who'd vanished into the ether within a month.

They tasted terrible, just as she said they would.

I—never having eaten a child—could only compare them to woodland fauna, whose meat was gamey but pleasant enough.

These people were neither. They tasted like sour, overly salted fat.

I was content to return to my new diet of fish and crab, but Gran could not thrive this way.

I could not ask her to poison herself, yet I could not watch as she butchered any more tiny bodies, boiling down their soft, little bones and burning their clothes in the fire. We were at an impasse, she and I, and both miserable for it.

I love you, Zmija, my chosen grandchild, my most precious creature. But perhaps it is time we let our paths diverge.

And so, we did.

She dried my tears and gave me some magic, pulled from beneath her ribs that I could use as I pleased. Then she gave me some more, pulled from her throat, with which I could speak things into existence and truth. It was not more than I needed or wanted. It was exactly enough.

Then, hungry and resigned, on the cold beach in a sea of dense fog, she kissed me goodbye and bade the house to go. The sand and the thickness of the air around us dampened the thunderous cracking sound as it lifted its taloned feet and stretched, preparing for its next journey. I didn't ask where she would go. It didn't matter, as our time was done, so I merely watched until they disappeared, leaving only footsteps that I would never follow and that would be gone with the tide by morning.

There are many versions of the story of what happened next, but I will only tell you mine.

It was not the season for hurricanes or floods. They preferred the warmth, it seemed. Now, it was cold, and the town was not prepared for much more than winter winds off the sea, but it was time to wash away the poison, and there was no need to wait until fall.

I used up quite a bit of my magic the night I gathered the children—thirty-one in all—and ran their cats and dogs and every other innocent, captive creature to higher ground under cover of night. I led them to the abandoned armory—a weather-beaten yet sturdy structure nestled between the dunes where they'd be safe until it was over. They were confused but not frightened. Of this, I made certain. They huddled together for warmth at my feet, and deep inside the shelter, I told them wild stories of my time as a serpent. I told them of my time with my grandmother—the witch who changed me—and of our adventures. I told them of lands they'd never seen and times they had never known and kept them as enthralled as I could while the growing storm made its way to land. We all felt the change in the air as it passed over us, and though the dogs whimpered and whined, I kept the children laughing, I kept them in terrific suspense, and hinted at what was to come. It would be painless, but I kept that to myself. They'd never need to know that there was any pain to be shielded *from*, and they'd be unaware anything had ever happened.

In the dark, across the dunes, the men and women who'd been so eager to sacrifice the only things that mattered for everything that didn't, had no warning. I made certain of that, too. The winds took down the trees and wires. They shattered windows and slammed trash cans and lawn chairs against their precious trucks.

Then, in the dark, the waters came, and all their time ran out.

It took quite a while for the debris to be cleared away. Quagmires of wood and metal appliances and bloated bodies had damned up streets, even the hurricane evacuation routes. Flooded trucks turned in slow circles, caught in spontaneous whirlpools that formed every time a clot of detritus would loosen from a storm drain. Sheets of siding and uprooted fences drifted through the neighborhood like primitive rafts bound for the sea. The dunes were smaller now, and the beach freshly eroded, but the remains of the town would not traverse the sandy tract of land. They would collect and rot at the edges of an unnatural lake, formed from catastrophe until disaster relief arrived with their earthmovers and testing kits. There was not much else they'd need—no food, no potable water, no medical supplies. Only coroners and containers.

The news traveled far and wide, as it does in these times. A town, taken from the map in mere minutes, was unusual enough, but when the word came that there were no children found among the dead, the story became something far more powerful than a tragedy. It became legend—more than thirty children lost in a storm that left a watery battlefield of the floating dead. Nearly every fully grown person, bloated and buoyant, slowly coming to pieces in the black water like soaked paper accounted for. But not one child.

With the corpses retrieved, for twelve moons, the stagnant lake remained, filling the air with an unbearable stench. It would forever be the home to a submerged ghost town, but in my mind, I could see deeper than the wreckage and far beyond the devastation to its true form and purpose, the very way that Gran had seen the girl within the snake and the very way that I still sometimes see the snake within the girl.

I still had enough of Gran's magic to bring it through.

And so, with the herons, and egrets, the kingfishers, and pelicans, and hawks—thirty-one in all—the drowning ruins of purgatory became a place of refuge, where nothing of man would be rebuilt, and nothing would be poisoned. The cats and dogs posed no threat to the ecosystem, as they remembered life before the flood.

I stayed and built a house of my own where hers had briefly stood amidst the elevated beach homes that survived the storm. I saw no point in bringing about their destruction. They stood tall among the landscape like the Hydra. Cut them down, and they would rise again at the cost of the forests my Gran yearned for. I filled my space with things that reminded me of her— shells and bones, smooth glass, and ferns. It was a place she would be comfortable if she ever returned, even though I knew in my gut she wouldn't.

I set the house upon four legs instead of two if only to blend in. Though it had no discernable feet, I used almost all the magic that remained to ask one thing of it—when the rising, unyielding sea ate away the shoreline, just as it would someday swallow my lavish neighbors, that it should lift its sturdy legs and take a few steps back.

And with the very last bit of Gran's magic, I made sure only the birds would ever notice.

THE PEDDLER'S PROMISE

BY CATHERINE MCCARTHY

While she slept, the forest spruce grew beards of hoarfrost, the lichen and moss donned silver-gilt coats, and Baba Yaga woke to a winter-white world. Cupboards bare and heart stolid, she blew on her fingers with brittle breath and wrapped a shawl about her shoulders before setting off for the village.

Despite the frost-hardened ground, her footsteps kept her counsel as she approached the first izba and rapped on the door. A welcome blast of warm air greeted her from within, and a young girl, with a quizzical look in her eye and a dusting of flour on her cheek, stood before her.

"Something smells delicious," Baba Yaga said, sniffing the air with her pointy nose. "If I'm not mistaken, you're making piroshki." Her stomach gave a well-timed rumble. "Oh, dityatko," she said, circling a hand over her swollen belly, "this old peddler will die of starvation if she doesn't eat soon. Do you think your mother might take a look at my wares?" A basket rested in the crook of her arm, and with the charm of a seductress, she peeled back the cover to reveal a cornucopia of colorful boxes in every shape and size imaginable.

The child's eyes lit up. "Mother," she cried. "Come and see."

Hands thrust deep in the pocket of her apron, the child's mother regarded the peddler with suspicion.

"Might I tempt you with a little treat?" Baba Yaga said. "A puzzle box for the dityatko, perhaps, or an embroidered scarf for your hair?" Before the woman could refuse, Baba Yaga slipped out a spherical box and held it up to the child.

The girl reached out with both hands, enraptured by the miniature scene painted upon it—a field of chamomile, in which a bare-breasted Bereginya lay fast asleep beneath a birch, the broken bough of which protected her modesty.

"It's beautiful, Mama," the child said, stroking the curve of the wood with one finger.

"Klara, we can't afford such frivolities, you know this." The woman yanked her daughter's hand away and glared at the peddler.

"Ah," Baba Yaga said, "but these boxes are special. Not only are they beautiful, but concealed within each of them is the very thing your heart desires. That, I promise."

Klara's mouth fell open at her words. "Please, Mama," she said. "Never again will I ask for anything."

Baba Yaga sensed the woman's heart soften and smelled victory. "Do you have a son?" she asked, though she already knew the answer.

"I do," replied the woman.

"Then perhaps this might be to his liking?" This time she held out a box in the shape of a cube, a rag of colts, pulling a troika through the snow, painted thereon. A tiny plume of breath rose from the horses' nostrils as the woman leaned in close, and the faintest clip-clop of hooves sounded.

"And what do you ask in return?" the woman said, swiping the air to clear the vapor.

Baba Yaga licked her lips. "All I ask is for a share of what you have cooking in the oven. Piroshki, I believe? The aroma of minced beef and onion has whet my appetite."

The woman studied Baba Yaga's lean frame, her bloated belly, her pinched cheekbones, and sighed, then she disappeared momentarily before returning with a steaming bundle wrapped in a pristine cloth.

Saliva frothed at the corner of the peddler's mouth, and the light in her eyes brightened. "Thank you," she said, turning to leave. "At least I shall not starve to death this day."

"Wait!" The girl's voice called the old woman back. "How do I open the box?"

Baba Yaga grinned, and her teeth glinted in the sunlight. "Ah, dityatko. That is something you will have to determine for yourself. Good luck!" And with that, she scuttled off to the woods, taking with her the scent of pepper and pastry.

When Klara's brother, Igor, returned home from working the fields, he was surprised to find that a gift awaited him, and when his sister explained it contained his heart's desire, he chuckled with mirth.

"Now, how might that be?" he said, pointing to the picture of a fine white colt hitched to the troika. "A horse is too large to fit inside something so small." For as long as he could remember, Igor had wished for a horse of his own but had never thought it possible. Nevertheless, he spent some considerable time attempting to open the box. Indeed, both children twisted and turned, pulled and pushed, squeezed and prodded their boxes, but without success.

A hearty supper of piroshki and pickled cabbage softened the blow, but still, both children went off to bed with full stomachs and empty hearts.

Three days and three nights passed, by which time they had almost abandoned hope, when suddenly the lid of Igor's box sprung open with a sound like a horse chomping at the bit. Eyes wide and hearts aflutter, the children peered inside. A bed of straw concealed the prize within—a lump of old bone, shaped like a horse's toe.

"So much for the peddler's promise," Igor snarled, then he opened the door of the izba and tossed the bone on the frost-hardened ground where it landed with a dull thud.

Late that night, Igor woke to the sound of neighing. He crept downstairs and opened the door. There stood a fine colt, its coat as white as the snow on which it stood. It pawed the ground and whinnied, the whites of its eyes desperate for Igor to follow. And follow he did. Barefoot and dressed in nothing but a nightshirt, Igor tracked the horse through the forest, all the way to Baba Yaga's hut.

In the morning, Klara woke to find him gone. The box lid yawned wide beside his bed, and a fresh fall of snow covered his tracks.

Igor was not the only one to go missing, for word soon spread throughout the village that several other boys had disappeared during the night. And there was one thing they all had in common—each and every one of them had received a box from the old peddler in exchange for a tasty treat, a bundle of kindling, or even the odd ruble.

The villagers gathered in the square.

"All my grandson ever wanted was to become a soldier and serve his country," Babushka Ivanova said. "His box contained a handful of gunpowder, and, mistaking it for soot, he threw it onto the fire. Frightened my daughter out of her wits when it exploded." She shook her head and smiled sadly. "Fool of a boy, but I'd give my right arm to have him return home to us."

"And there you have it," said another. "The foolish boys must have hatched a plan and run off to join the rebels."

"Not my son," said another. "He's too feeble to fight."

The crowd mumbled and murmured, but none could come up with an answer.

Then a softly spoken woman stepped forward. "Have any

of you wondered why not one of our daughters has been able to open her box?"

"It must be a trick," someone said. "Our daughters are every bit as clever as our sons. Perhaps the boxes the peddler gifts the girls are impossible to open."

"Huh," a wise old woman said. "Our daughters learn from an early age that what one's heart desires can never be found inside a box, no matter how prettily packaged it comes. Better to accept life's disappointments and get on with it. Whereas our sons—well, let's just say they learn their lessons the hard way."

"Are we to stand here gossiping, or shall we muster our strength and send out a search party?" It was Pavel Volkov who spoke. Gray pallor and unshaven, he appeared every bit as downhearted as he felt, for it had not been three months since his beloved wife had passed, leaving him to raise his son, Samuil, alone.

The crowd shuffled their feet and huddled in small groups, eager to get back to work.

"My Samuil would not have left me, not after his mother—" Pavel's voice broke, and he pinched his nose hard to stem the flood.

"But there is work to be done," a childless woman cried. "How will we pay the rent if our men down tools and wander the woods instead?"

This led to much debate, with the crowd seeming split on its views.

The village elder raised a hand and called his people to order. "We shall put it to a vote," he said. "Sofia is right, there is much work to be done, but Pavel is also right, and if he believes our children have come to harm, then it is our duty to do something about it."

After considerable debate, it was decided that a search party would be sent to look for them if the boys did not return home by the following morning.

One by one, the crowd dwindled, all except Pavel Volkov.

Samuil was all he had left in the world, and he did not intend to let another day and night pass without searching for him. He had witnessed what the other villagers had not, such as how his son's eyes had twinkled when the peddler passed him the box. A heart-shaped box, upon which mother moon shone down on the Volga, seeming to guide its flow with her luminescence. Unlike the other village boys, it had taken his son less than a minute to open the box and uncover the gift inside, such was his longing for it. And he had watched his son on the brink of manhood fight back the tears as he held the lock of his mother's flaxen hair in his hand.

"How could the peddler have known?" Samuil had said, to which Pavel had shaken his head in bewilderment.

He had not, however, heard his son rise from his bed and follow his dead mother's footprints into the forest.

So Pavel returned home instead of to the field and collected his scythe with no intention of cutting grain.

Childhood tales of Baba Yaga consumed his thoughts, and logic refused to dispel them. Could the peddler be the witch in disguise, and if so, what did she want with Samuil and the other boys?

In the heart of the forest, the light was dim, a weak, winter offering of elongated shadows. If Pavel's instinct were correct, he would need to follow the path right to the other side, for Baba Yaga lived at its farthest edge, away from prying eyes.

A bitter wind did its best to dissuade him, but Pavel's determination remained strong. A covey of grouse took sudden flight, the sound of their wings startling him, and the mew of a solitary lynx set his teeth on edge. Well aware of Baba Yaga's camaraderie with the animal kingdom, he wondered if their intention was to warn her of his approach.

Soon Pavel spied a distant hut, elevated on long legs that bent at the knee and transposed the weight of the hut from one foot to the other every few seconds, just like a chicken. He stopped in his tracks, listening for signs of life. Two blackened windows watched him sightlessly while the chimney breathed no smoke. If luck was on his side, the witch was not at home, and if it wasn't? Then his anger and his scythe would come in useful.

Pavel took tentative steps toward the hut, a frozen mist shrouding his view. A fence of bones guarded the perimeter— femur and fibula, humerus and ulna, some of which were capped with skulls. His blood ran cold. So it was true then? The witch of the woods really did harness human parts for her own employ.

An icy pathway threatened to bring him to his knees as he navigated the route, but he dug his heels in firm. As he approached, the hut turned its back to him, just as he suspected it might. Remembering the words spoken by his old babushka, he summoned to mind the incantation. His breath was a cloud of despair as Pavel spoke. "Hut, hut, turn your back to the forest and your front to me."

With a whoosh of air, the hut swiveled. A rickety door, secured by a metatarsal bolt, neatly slotted inside a hollowed vertebra, sent a shudder along his spine. The thought that this carnage, any of these human remains, might belong to his beloved son made blood pound in his ears, and his chest tighten. He threw the bolt and crossed the threshold.

What a sight to behold! A butchered limb lay strewn on the table, strips of sinew trussed a fattier cut, complete with navel, from which sage and onion oozed, green and pungent. And to the right of the joint sat a mortar, in which bone marrow, salt, and parsley had been pummeled to a paste by the pestle.

Pavel retched. "Not my Samuil! Dear God, don't let it be my Samuil!" Yet deep down, nestled between sternum and scapula, his heart said otherwise. The horror of what he was witnessing was too much to bear. The whole hut reeked of death, stank of sweat and sorrow, and Pavel's prevailing thought was to thank God that his beloved wife would not witness this carnage.

When Pavel returned to the village with his head bowed low and his heart in tatters, no one needed to ask what had happened. The look on his face spoke for him.

The villagers gathered all the weapons they could find—knives and pickaxes, mattocks and crowbars, and followed Pavel into the forest. A trail of harrowed souls, intent on bringing home their loved ones' remains. Bury the boys together, that was what they would do. There was no other choice. And the witch? How they would make her suffer!

They wandered the forest, each lost in thought.

Klara recalled how Igor's face would brighten whenever he was around horses. She held the memory close, refusing to picture anything else.

Babushka Ivanova's cane was a Burdan rifle in her hand, one her grandson would never get to hold, but with which she would end the witch's life in a heartbeat, given half a chance.

And the son whose mother deemed him feeble? In her eyes, he became a valiant knight, thwarted by the enemy whilst trying to save others.

The mood turned more solemn as the villagers drew close to the forest edge. Every man, woman, and child trembled with the thought of what they were about to witness.

As leader of the troop, it was Pavel who saw it first. In disbelief, he fell to his knees, dug dirt-encrusted nails deep in his scalp, and roared.

Nothing but a patch of bare earth, roughly square-shaped. No chicken-legged hut, no snow, even the fence of bones had disappeared into thin air.

While Pavel wailed, young Klara searched the ground, hoping to find some remnant to prove her brother's existence.

And find it she did. There, on a clump of bright green spleenwort, lay a toy soldier, whittled in wood by an amateur hand, though painted with precision. The soldier rode a white colt, and in his left hand he carried a rifle. His face was spattered in soot, his expression one of agony, and the horse's tail? A plume of flaxen hair hung limp and lifeless on the palm of Klara's hand.

THE SPACE BETWEEN
THE TREES

BY JO KAPLAN

I have never understood my mother, or perhaps I have never tried. In my life, she is writ large, as any daughter's mother must be. Her presence hangs over everything. Sometimes I hear her voice in my head, where my own thoughts ought to live, and it rings with such clarity I could almost believe she's managed some telepathic trickery—but that is not a magic she possesses.

Love and fear arrive in equal measure when she shouts, "Girl!" The sound sweeps over me as an avalanche does a mountain. I am not so much a girl anymore. Even in my younger days, it was always, "Don't let that fire go out" or "Slice the meat at an angle, you heathen!" I must have cringed when I was little. But I've never had any occasion to argue, for she has always taken care of me.

We are alone out here.

At night, the forest is black as death.

But my mother is a hard woman. She isn't afraid of whatever could be lurking out there.

We hunt and fish. I tend to the hearth while she communicates with the earth. The space between the trees is impenetrable; you always hear something before you see it. Often I find myself listening to the subtle shifts in the forest's utterances while whittling my wooden dolls, timing my strokes with the rustling branches and birdcalls. It calms me to blend into my surroundings. I become invisible.

When the dark falls, it falls swiftly and without mercy.

Then being closed up in our little hut feels cozy rather than claustrophobic. We read by the hearth's blaze, we dine, we paint protection sigils in blood on the doorway. Behind the drawn shutters, I know our lamps watch over us. We lie down on our beds, listen to the nocturnal woods, and let the joy of this pulsing darkness fill our hearts. It has always been a feeling without a name—something primal, rooted in the basest sense of being alive.

This all changed when he arrived.

Of course, I heard him before I saw him. There was something unnatural in the rhythm of scratching leaves—and the forest was never unnatural unless an intruder disrupted its harmony. Somewhere, a thrush tittered. There was a flapping of wings. The erratic snapping of branches. He had drawn close by the time I saw him—a man with dark hair sweat-plastered to his forehead and sad, desperate eyes. When they struck me, they widened.

"Don't come any closer." I stood, half-finished doll in one hand and whittling knife in the other, which I had instinctively pointed outward.

The man's hands rose slowly. "Please, help me. I'm lost. I've—I lost the trail." He trembled as a chill wind blew from the darkening east.

I lowered my knife but hesitated otherwise. One of my mother's rules is never to invite anyone inside without her permission. But she was out performing her rituals and likely would be until after the sun departed. Meanwhile, this man had a bloodlessness about him that worried me.

"Come," I said. "You look like you need a warm fire."

He approached me slowly, the way I might approach a deer I aim to kill. For my part, I froze as if to become invisible. His hand rose delicately to my ear and promptly lowered again. He was smiling in a bemused sort of way. "You have leaves in your hair."

"Of course," I said, returning his smile. "As do you."

The hearth returned blood to his hands while I prepared supper. He crouched close to the lambent flame, clutching the woven blanket I had draped around his shoulders. As I chopped, each slice of the knife was a clock tick counting down to my mother's return.

"What are you making?" he asked.

"A hearty stew. For strength and longevity."

"I could use some of that right now." His shoulders hunched together as a shield against the cold, and his face bore the ghostlike melancholy of a man beaten down to his ragged edges.

I asked the stranger his name and where he was from.

"Yakov. From the village."

My knife slipped, and I regained my grip. My mother has always told me not to trust a villager. They tried to kill her once. This man, however, seemed without energy or desire to do anyone harm.

"And what are you doing this deep in the woods, Yakov-from-the-village?"

He gave a hollow laugh. "Trying to gain my father's approval."

I stopped chopping to raise my eyebrows at him.

He elaborated. "My brother has always been the favored son. He hunts and plays sports. I like to read and paint, which are apparently not manly enough endeavors. But my brother ... he lost his child. God, this sounds terrible as I say it out loud." Yakov rubbed his hands over his face. "With him grieving, I thought it might be my turn to ..." He barked a laugh. The hearth cracked a spark in the air. "My God, I am a terrible person, aren't I? Taking advantage of my brother's grief to turn my father's favor to me. I went hunting because I thought it would impress him if I shot a bear."

"The world is cruel," I told him as I pushed aside the sliced carrots and peeled the onion. "We must all snatch whatever opportunities we have, however unpleasant they may seem."

"I don't think I was meant to succeed," he said. "I lost the path and ended up wandering for hours. Even managed to lose my gun. I thought, wouldn't it be ironic if I were eaten by a bear? My father would probably laugh, knowing I couldn't survive a single night in the woods. If I hadn't run into you before dark—" He sucked back his words and shook his head.

My knife danced over the vegetables. "It's lucky you found me."

"I never expected to find anyone so far out in this remote wilderness. Do you live here alone?" My sniff brought his gaze to me as he stood. "I'm sorry, I didn't mean to upset you."

"Upset me?" I wiped my nose on my blouse and blinked away tears. "Oh, no! It's just the…" I gestured to the chopped onion. "I am not alone. My mother will be home soon."

"Oh," he said, and I thought he sounded almost disappointed.

My heart trembled as I wondered how my mother would react to finding a strange man in her home. She might smile and laugh, or she might shove me into the corner while she dealt with him. She is a mercurial woman, given to abrupt and often extreme shifts in temper. I have found it best to heed her without trying to please her, for she can never be pleased.

"*Are* you all right?"

I looked up to discover him watching me, his eyebrows drawn in concern. Too long, I had been standing there with the knife in my hand, staring at my worktable, motionless. Feeling the worm of dread wriggle within me.

"Yes," I said. "It's just …" I set down the knife beside a runnel of onion juice that mingled with blood leaking from tender chunks of raw meat. "We don't see other people very often. Almost never. She doesn't like people, my mother."

"I imagine one really must hate people to spurn society and live in such an isolated place."

"We didn't always live so far from the village," I said. "But the forest has always been my home."

"God, it must be lonely!" he cried out. "I love having people around me; can't stand it when I'm left alone with myself for too long. Other people are a great distraction from oneself." He stopped babbling and peered at me. "Why doesn't your mother like people?"

There was something clean and soft about him, like a baby, and I became conscious of the dirt caked into my every groove of skin, the leaves tangled in my matted hair, my black and ragged fingernails. Though he had some of the forest on him—grass stains and mud up his legs—his was a fresh coat. What I wore was an accumulation of crusted-in grime. I had the wild urge to lean over and lick his soft face. I wondered what he tasted like.

"I suppose it's because people don't like her," I said. "She is a hard woman to like."

"Well, her daughter isn't."

We looked at each other, and I felt a warm buzzing within. Another wild impulse stole over me, this time urging me to grab him and keep him here with us forever. He could take on the chore of chopping wood, which I find tiring, and help me with my more repugnant tasks.

My thoughts were interrupted by a deep and rhythmic pulse like the beating of a great heart, which resolved into approaching footfalls so heavy they rattled the knife on the table.

My mother was home.

The door swung open, admitting a swirl of leaves and cold. In the darkness beyond lay hints of light—the lanterns my mother would have lit on her way in, well-enough ensconced in trees as to be unnoticeable in daylight. A moment later, my mother's form loomed into that open doorway. The fire was livid on her scarred and narrow face.

"Who," she said. "Is." She stepped inside. "In." Yakov shrank in his blanket. "My." She gave a great sniff from her dripping nose. "HOUSE?" She took two more heavy steps that shook the floor. Her voice roared and shrieked at once, and its sound was enough to slam the door shut behind her. "*Who is in my house?*"

Though Yakov cowered, I stood firm in the face of her thundering. "He was lost and needed help."

Her hunched and weathered bulk hovered, her yellow eyes bore into Yakov. "Lost and needed help?" she said blankly before a smile broke over her face. "Oh, you poor thing!" Then she turned to me. "Cook us supper."

The stew did not take long, though I ought to have let it simmer to help the flavors blend, and that's the thing, isn't it? One must choose which is more important—convenience or quality. It was not my tastiest stew, but I felt hastened by my mother's eyes on my back and the silence between her and the stranger.

He made no pretense at civility once the food was in front of him. When reduced, we are all beasts at heart. He must have been starving.

Wind shivered the trees outside and berated our creaking wooden walls. In the snapping light from the hearth, my mother's face refused to settle into one shape but wavered with ghastly shadows.

"Yakov is from the village," I told her.

"Your daughter saved my life," he added through a mouthful of stew. "I don't know how I can repay her. Your hospitality is much appreciated. I was so lost—I don't think I could find my way home again. Especially not in the dark."

My mother's sharp laugh made him flinch. When she

slurped from her spoon, broth snaked down the grooves of her wrinkled chin. "I suppose you want to keep him?" she said to me. "You want to fall in love and be swept away?"

My chin lowered so that I could not see Yakov's expression or give away the truth of her words.

The fire sparked and threw dark shapes that cavorted against the walls. Though my mother did not stand, her presence formed a shadow of impossible proportions that rose above her like an ephemeral double.

"You want to be a slave to a man?" Her voice became something more than itself—wild and cruel. "Clean his home, cook his meals, make yourself always pleasant for him, suck his cock when he desires?" The fire steadied, and her shadow shrank back into her. "And when he is done with you, all that will be left is your empty husk."

I stole a glance at Yakov, whose expression mingled surprise and trepidation.

"You cannot trust a villager," she said. Her voice cut with the sharp edge of glass. "They come with their torches and pitchforks."

She took a bite of her stew, and its magic smoothed some of the lines on her haggard face.

Now that Yakov was done eating, he had begun to peer shrewdly around the hut, taking notice of things he had previously paid no mind—the small bones that hung like charms from the ceiling, the flaking brown blood painted on the doorframe, the jars of herbs lined up on the mantle. He landed on one of my wooden dolls which sat on a small cushion. I saw him observe its carefully-carven details and thought he must be admiring my skill. But his voice came out flat. "Those are yours? The dolls?"

"Yes," I said proudly. "I whittle them myself."

Yakov stood abruptly, pushing the table so hard my mother's stew slopped over the edge of her bowl.

"What have you done with them?" he shouted, a deranged fury grown sharp as flint in his eyes.

"With what?"

"The children!" His chest heaved. "In the village, the babies—all those that have gone missing over the years. There is always a wooden doll left in its place like some perverted exchange. A doll just like that one. They say it's the curse."

My mother chuckled deep in her throat. Strands of silver hair dipped into her stew.

"My curse," she said, lifting her head.

He stared back. "You're the witch."

Her mouth curled into a rictus with teeth like broken woodchips. "My daughter took them. She left the dolls."

"Oh, God," Yakov said, stumbling away from the table. "You killed them! All those children. Those poor ... my brother's child." His look grew pained. "Why?"

My mother slurped and gnawed on a tough bit of meat. "For the stew, of course." Then she let her mouth hang open as she laughed.

Gagging, Yakov stuck two fingers down his throat. I knew he couldn't stomach knowing what it was he had eaten.

Still laughing, my mother reached across the table, and her arm grew longer and thinner until it had stretched to the far wall where Yakov bent over trying to expel what he had unknowingly consumed. Her claw seized him by the neck.

"Don't hurt him, Mother."

In that moment, faced with the terror bright in his eyes when he looked at me, something within me lurched out of place. I suddenly had a new context in which to view my mother and me, and I found myself horrified at what I saw. I saw our spells and rituals using the blood of murdered children whose bodies we consumed, whose bones our mortar and pestle has ground to fine powder to summon the spirit world, some of which I carry with me always. I saw the grieving parents of all the babes I have snatched from the village in the night. I saw these terrible things in Yakov's eyes.

My mother threw him against the wall; his head cracked once hard, he slid down to the floor, and he lay there insensible.

Hatred lurked in the depths of my mother's eyes. I cowered beneath her, but she took my chin and lifted it, and made us share a gaze.

"Your father was from the village," she said in a voice gone thin as moonlight. "He was lost, too, but he found me. For a short time, we found each other. He told me he loved me. Since I was with child, he promised to marry me. He returned to the village to tell his family the good news, but when he returned, he did so in the night, surrounded by a mob that tried to burn my hut with their torches. They came to kill you. They came to tear you from me. They could not abide such an abomination."

A stabbing pain entered my heart. "My own father tried to kill me."

"They are snakes," she hissed. "Lying snakes. The villagers tried to kill you, but they did not succeed. I would not let them have you. You are *my* daughter. My power burns within you."

Never had I felt such fierce love burrowing into me as I did then, so much that the hut held its breath, and the air crackled with possibility.

My mother placed her hands on my shoulders, bringing us closer together. "Now we can taste their fear. Now *they* can understand what it is when someone comes to kill your child." Her grin crept up again. "Except I succeed."

"Maybe Yakov is different," I said as I turned my head, hoping to see him coming round. Instead, I found a bare patch of floor, stained red. "Yakov!" I spun. The door was flung open, and I caught sight of him as he ran out into the dark. I followed into the rustling forest obscured by the veil of night. When he stopped abruptly, so did I, and when he turned around, he was brandishing a knife, which he must have snatched from the kitchen. "Yakov, please!"

"You fucking monster!" he shrieked, his voice high and unhinged. In a moment, his gaze moved behind me, where he finally saw our lamps, firelight beaming out through their sockets and grinning jaws. Remembering the pouch of bone dust in my pocket, I pulled out a handful and blew it into the air, where it shimmered into a cloud that surrounded him and turned the knife to ice.

He let it go and turned from me.

Then Yakov-from-the-village ran off and vanished into the darkness between trees. I picked up the knife and carried it back inside the hut, shutting the door behind me. My mother was waiting. She stood by the window, staring out into the dark.

"That was a stupid waste of bone dust," she spat.

I joined her in gazing out at the forest which had hidden itself from our eyes. It was so dark out there, and the stranger so lost already, it seems likely his doomed escape would lead him only farther into the endlessness of the forest, where he would perish. Even so, I imagined, from out that darkness, a sea of glowing eyes weaving among the trees, drawing closer until they resolved into torches, and the shadows wielding them would shout their anger as all the villagers Yakov had gathered came to kill us and destroy our home.

"Suppose he comes back?" I said.

My mother laughed. "They won't find us."

The world lurched beneath my feet, and the darkness out the window rushed away as the stars drew nearer. We rose into the air as the hut stretched the creaking length of its legs until we stood among the treetops, their black leaves fanning just outside the window. One of my dolls tipped and clattered to the floor; the bowls on the table rattled and shook; my mother and I held onto one another for balance. Then, with the slow lumbering gait of an ancient creature, our hut took one heavy step and another through the trees, a trail of burning skulls floating after us as we headed in a new direction for our home.

SUGAR AND SPICE AND THE OLD WITCH'S PRICE

BY LISA QUIGLEY

The irresistible aromas arrive suddenly. It's late afternoon. I have just stepped outside to retrieve the latest packages—more diapers and wipes, a seemingly endless need—and the smells are just there, as if they are an ordinary occurrence.

Of course, they aren't, but they *are* distinct—baked goods, with a rustic artisan flair. The kind lovingly kneaded before being baked in an ancient stone oven. I have smelled them once before, and I know exactly where these yeasty sweet aromas originate.

I look toward the foothills of the mountain reserve, just at the edge of our small, quiet neighborhood. The golden sunlight hits the crystal suncatcher that hangs just outside my front door. The light refracts through the glass. Tiny dancing rainbows scatter across my front porch. My breath catches, and I am filled with unnamed longing.

"Mom!" My daughter's shriek comes from inside the house. "MOMMY!"

I cast one last aching glance at the foothills, longing curdling into resentment. I breathe deeply of that intoxicating scent, just as my daughter screams for me again. Just a few more hours until bedtime.

The hut in the woods will have to wait.

My skin feels like it's on fire. It isn't, of course, but I always feel like this at the end of the day.

I am in the kitchen, a giant pot of spaghetti noodles boiling on the stove, a skillet of red meat sauce simmering on another burner. No one would ever call the smells coming from my kitchen "artisan." These smells are generic, scents originating from boxes and jars from a grocery store shelf.

My four-year-old daughter is in the side room, yelling for me to come put on a different show for her. The baby is wrapped around my ankles, tears streaming down her face, longing to be held.

The "witching hour."

That's what the mommy blogs call these last hours of the day. Just before dinnertime, when bedtime is so close and yet still somehow feels eons away.

Mommy blogs. If someone would have told me when I was younger—when I still believed anything was possible—that I would spend my free time scrolling my device, eyes glazing over, reading "mommy blogs" to try to make some sort of sense of my life, I'd have sneered at them. That was when I still thought the world was magic, that when I grew up, I'd have a fairy cottage in the wooded preserve at the edge of town.

My headphones are shoved into my ears, a sweating glass of half-drunk white wine on the counter, and all I want is a half-hour of quiet children, so I can cook and listen to my favorite podcast—one where my two favorite actresses talk about their experience on my favorite show—in peace.

But the children keep screaming, and I swallow a mouthful of rapidly warming wine. For a brief second, I close my eyes and imagine dumping the boiling water from the stove onto them both.

I open my eyes, glance at the stovetop. I down the rest of the wine in one gulp.

My husband will be home from the office soon, tie loosened, and I will ask him to help, but he will tell me he's so tired and needs just ten minutes to himself. He will strip out of his button-down shirt and slacks (leaving his clothes in little piles on the floor), pad wordlessly into the bathroom, and close the door. I will hear the faucet screech on, the thunder of water from the showerhead. I will push a strand of sweaty hair behind my ear and finish getting dinner on the table.

I am not a psychic.

It's just that is this the usual pattern of our lives. Why would today be any different?

The baby's crying becomes so insistent that I swell with guilt and bend down to pick her up. I wipe the tears from her cheeks with my thumb and shush into her ear.

"I know, baby," I whisper. "Dinner is almost ready. I know. I'm going as fast as I can."

"MOM!" my daughter shouts again. "My show turned off. Help me!"

The meat sauce bubbles furiously. I need to stir it. I need to soothe my crying baby. I need to help my oldest daughter. Need, need, need. Their needs are endless. The water from my husband's shower shrieks through the pipes in the walls.

My baby wails in my arms, and I sag with the weight of her. I glance at the clock again, desperate, hoping for a miracle, but bedtime is still an eternal hour and a half away—and we haven't even made it through dinner.

I take a deep breath and try to remember a time in my life I had dreamed of becoming a mother. Back when I still had dreams.

I sigh and go into the next room, sauce for sure sticking to the skillet by now. With my clinging baby sobbing, I help my oldest daughter locate her TV show.

Somehow, we made it through dinner, though it was chaos as usual. The scene unfolded pretty much as I had predicted, but what else did I expect?

Now, finally, finally, both our girls are in bed, sound asleep. And finally, finally, I have time to myself. But we are both collapsed on our couches in front of the television, and my husband is already asleep. It won't be long till I am also asleep. This is the alone time I crave, and I will waste it sleeping.

I am just beginning to doze when my eyes pop open and I am suddenly alert because the aromas are stronger than ever.

I sit upright, glance at my husband, who is snoring loudly. I stand. He doesn't wake. For no clear reason, I am compelled to move quietly.

The front door opens with only the slightest creak, and the aromas of baked goods are heavy and sweet in the night air. I glance down the rows of houses on the darkened street to see if anyone else can smell it. But there is no one, and, of course, I didn't really expect there to be. This invitation is just for me.

I prop the screen door open, go back to the couch, and sit. I breathe deeply, slowly, savoring the sweet sensation of a watering mouth. There are so few pleasures left in my life. I glance around the room and notice it's not just a smell anymore—the aroma has entered my home, and it's thick now, like a fog, or oven smoke.

I remember, then, what the old woman in the woods once told me.

"My cookies are messengers," she had said. "And they will help you see things as they really are."

I was too afraid to taste them that time so long ago. I ran off before I had a chance. But I am not afraid of the old woman anymore.

I cast a sidelong glance at my husband.

The aroma fog has filled the living room so much I can barely see through it. I strain my eyes to see my sleeping husband—and recoil.

My breath comes in shallow gasps, and my hands shake, but I do not look away. After all, the smoke is not telling me anything I didn't already know. I get up, moving to stand directly over him, and look again. I have to be certain—and there is no denying it.

My husband is a monster.

He is sleeping soundly, his chest rising and falling. His skin is rough and leathery, and horns protrude from his head. His mouth hangs open in sleep, and his teeth are large and yellowed and fanged, like a wolf's. Silvery strands of putrid saliva stretch from his open mouth.

My breathing slows. It is a strange relief, somehow, to finally see what I've known all along. The overpowering yeasty scent fills my lungs, and my husband shimmers between his acceptable human form and his monstrous one, but I will no longer be so easy to deceive.

I stand again and go into the kitchen. I retrieve the bottle of pinot grigio from the fridge and dump a heavy pour into the glass that still sits on the counter.

I grasp the glass with one hand and go into the backyard.

It is fully dark. I am sitting in an Adirondack chair, enveloped by the night. The crickets are loud this time of year. I always prefer the night because it's more honest than the day. Everything alive is screaming.

The wine glass is sweating against my hand. I gulp a swallow of wine and feel the embrace of the strange fog. It shows me to truth out here, too.

My house is decrepit, a ruin. The siding is rotted, and the frame pokes through—not wooden, but yellowed bone. Vines curl up from the depths of the earth, choking the foundation. I drink more wine.

This isn't home. It's a house of horrors. Everything inside is cursed with decay.

Slowly, I turn my head. My neighbor's houses are rotted, decaying things, too. I stand, walk around the side of the house toward the front, keep walking till I'm standing in the middle of the street.

The whole neighborhood is a horror show—a smiling façade of fake joy, of endless monotony. Inside, everyone is rotting.

I turn, observing it all until I am facing the two mountains in the distance, the entrance to the forest preserve at the edge of town—and gasp.

Prismatic light ripples off the tops of the trees, a kaleidoscope of color, so bright and so beautiful it's almost painful to look at. My chest tightens. I don't just *feel* longing; I *am* it.

The forest is *alive*. It is the one true thing in this dreadful town.

The rainbow lights shimmer and sway above the preserve, intoxicating in their brilliance. Forgetting myself, I take a few steps forward toward the dancing lights. Then I stop.

The aromas engulf me. I turn to face my house, which I know now is a broken promise, a lie. This house was never going to save me.

I look at the upstairs window, where I know my girls are sleeping in a decaying room.

My eyes still on the window, I gulp the rest of the wine and head back inside.

When I go inside the house, I leave all the doors open. The sweet cinnamon fog fills the whole house now, and I am standing in front of the girls' closed bedroom door where the aroma has slipped in through the crack underneath. My forehead is pressed against the door's cold wood. I don't want to go in, but I need to be sure.

Finally, I step inside their room, dark except for the blue nightlight next to my oldest daughter's bed.

I stand over her, the gentle curve of her profile illuminated by the soft blue light. Her gentle snores do not betray how loud she can be. I lean over her, kiss her cheek. The mouth-watering aroma of ancient baked goods overpowers her usual lavender soap and sweat smell.

The baby's crib is in the other corner. She stirs when I smooth her crop of fuzzy hair but settles quickly.

When they're sleeping like this, I can almost forget how hard it all is, how it isn't anything like I imagined. Almost.

I could turn around right now. Go back downstairs, sit back on the couch, bask in the light of the television, allow myself to fall asleep.

I could do it all again tomorrow.

But the aroma fills the room quickly, and I am not able to unsee.

I don't *want* it to be true. I had hoped ...

But maybe on some level, I have always known. This was never going to end well.

These monsters are not my beautiful babies.

I've been holding the pillow for a long time, watching my daughter's chest rise and fall. I wonder if I still have a choice. If I can ignore what I know. If I can live with the weight of the truth.

But I already know the answer to these questions.

I start with my oldest, then move on to the baby—just as they came into this world. It's quieter and easier than I imagined, and it's over quickly.

I had expected to feel remorse, but I am just neutral. An everyday task. Like clearing out old food from the fridge to make space for the new.

When it's over, they are more beautiful than I could have ever dreamed. I have weeded out the rot, extinguished the curse. The room is filled with sweet doughy smells, and my girls are their whole, beautiful selves. Their faces glow with prismatic light.

That's when I finally cry because I know that this is good. This is right.

My husband is even easier because I have no hesitation. I know what needs to be done, so I pick up the pillow and do it.

When I leave the house, I bring the bodies of my girls with me— one over each shoulder. They are heavy, but I know where I am going. The shimmering rainbows guide me.

I walk in the middle of the street until I reach the trailhead in the foothills. I stay on the trail for a while, then I veer off into the thick woods. It's slow going, but I don't mind. My feet are certain, leading me back to the hut I saw so long ago.

These same mouthwatering, impossible aromas had lured me when I was a young girl. I stood outside the old woman's hut, arms wrapped tentatively around my middle. Even then, her weathered face was a tangled map of wrinkles. She stood before the open door of her hut, wry beneath the thatched roof, her hand extended with a cookie. Instinctively, I knew there would be a cost if I accepted—and I wanted nothing more than to pay it. I was reaching for it when my mother called out to me from the main trail. The spell was broken. Fear overtook me, and I turned away from the hut.

I thought I could go on with my life as though it had never happened, as if I didn't know such a place existed. I thought I could ignore the cries of my heart, the secrets that grew like wild vines inside my chest.

Just when I think I can't carry my daughters' bodies any longer, the hut is there. It is just as I remember it, as though no time has passed.

She is already standing on her doorsteps, arms reached out to me, worn face ancient and kind. I pause before going in and place my daughters' bodies at her feet.

"Everything is a mess," I say. "I think it's too late."

The old woman cups my face in her hands, her skin like bark, eyes clear like the deepest pools of water.

"Never," she whispers.

She stoops down then, picks up my daughters' bodies, and carries them inside the hut. I follow her, pulling my sweater closer around my shoulders even though the night is not cold. Once inside, she motions for me to sit in an old yet sturdy rocking chair in front of the stone oven.

The old woman opens the oven's cast iron door. She moves steadily, with self-assurance and grace. She picks up my daughters, pushing them gently, one by one, into the embers, which roar to life with flames. I wince, but she quickly places a clay mug into my hands and wraps an old afghan around my shoulders.

"Drink," she whispers.

The flames swallow my daughters. Like medicine, the warm liquid slides down my throat and into my belly.

The smells emanating from the flames are sweeter than ever. Gentle smoke fills the room, fills my lungs. I breathe deeply and take another drink, allowing the smoke and the drink to cleanse me. I am at peace, and so are my girls. This world was not built to contain our wild hearts.

She stands behind me, squeezing my shoulders, gently caressing my back. She is a wild, misunderstood creature, just like me. The world will make me out to be a monster. They will say I snapped. They'll write about me in the papers, analyze me in documentaries. They'll say my insides were rotted. I was a wicked woman, a terrible mother. The stories will vibrate with sensation, shock, outrage. Mothers everywhere will hold their children a little closer, look them in the eyes, kiss their foreheads—and ignore the wild vines that grow in their own hearts. Every mother holds her monstrosity at bay.

I sit back into the old wooden chair, close my eyes and feel the old woman's hands upon my back. I bask in the warmth from her fire, the heat of her tea in the bowl of my belly. I breathe deeply of the sweet, spiced scents that billow forth from the stone hearth.

Face to face with the flames, the fire is not so fearsome as I had once imagined. Monstrosity is not a cause for shame.

One last, deep breath, and the vines overtake my heart.

I am finally home.

BIRDS OF A FEATHER

BY MONIQUE SNYMAN

S plattered mud marred Olivia Donahue's scuffed high tops as she ran alongside a shallow creek. Water splashed against her bare legs, soaked her pastel pink ankle-length socks, and turned the insides of her sneakers soggy. She stared ahead, barely able to discern shapes in the dark, unfamiliar woods, hoping to find her way back to civilization eventually.

An unintelligible shout echoed through the area.

Olivia glanced over her shoulder, eyes wide and stomach twisting into tighter knots. Her heart pounded hard, adrenaline pumping fast through her body.

A gunshot rang out somewhere behind her, loud enough to send a shockwave of terror through Olivia. Someone cheered in response. Deranged laughter, laced with spite and malice, followed. A more controlled, almost reluctant titter joined the cacophony. Then, Arthur Freeman's familiar voice called to her, his anger unmistakable in the way he enunciated every vowel in her name.

"God, help me." Olivia sent her breathless prayer into the ether as she pushed her legs to move faster, ignoring the protesting muscles in her thighs and calves. She'd given up on figuring out how long she'd been on the run. It didn't matter. Nothing mattered apart from staying alive.

Her survival instincts forced her to cross the creek and take cover in the dense woods, where sinister shadows congregated. Once she stepped through the tree line, the darkness swallowed her whole. Olivia faltered, stopped in her tracks, then gathered herself mentally as she allowed her eyes to adjust. Slowly, the faint moonlight shining through the canopy illuminated her surroundings—ancient trees with broad trunks and eerie branches reaching out every which way.

"Okay, okay, we're sorry, Olivia. We were just having some fun! Come on out," Myrtle James called. When Olivia didn't respond, she continued with a frustrated, "Stop being *so* fucking serious."

Always dressed in their school's red and white cheerleading outfit, her wheat-colored hair in an impeccable, impossibly high ponytail, Myrtle had perfected the art of playing the sweet, innocent girl-next-door to put her unsuspecting victims at ease. When betrayal no longer seemed likely, though, that's usually the moment she struck. Olivia had seen it happen to others countless times—girls, boys, adults, nobody was off-limits. It could be a vicious rumor making the rounds, a humiliating "prank" that cuts deeper than any knife, or an outright lie to destroy a life. If Myrtle had it in for you, there's no way to sidestep her wrath. Olivia *knew* this, and she still fell for it. Those nice words that were used to convince Olivia to come along to … fuck knows where … and the possible popularity that would surely accompany any positive association with Myrtle James was just too tempting.

What. An. Idiot. Olivia mentally chastised herself as she carefully navigated the unknown terrain without losing too much speed.

Of course, it wasn't *just* Myrtle who had lured Olivia out of the safety of her home. Arthur Freeman, that damned handsome devil, did a splendid job at making her feel oh so special. Bringing her flowers, leaving little handwritten notes in her locker, flashing her one of his signature smiles. Every other nobody at Eisenhower High was jealous when it became apparent Olivia had caught his eye. Even more so when he draped his letterman jacket over her shoulders and asked her to prom.

Prom was still a few months away—the equivalent of a lifetime commitment by any teen's standards.

"Olivia!" Arthur's rage became more apparent, even though his voice sounded farther away.

Olivia jumped over a tree root, landed solidly on her feet, and rushed behind a nearby tree to catch her breath. She pressed her back up against the trunk and squeezed her eyes shut as she attempted to control her labored breathing.

"I told you she would bolt," Eric Smith argued. "She's no Vicky Rothman. I told you!"

"Cut it out, man," Arthur snapped.

Vicky Rothman? Olivia felt her brow furrow. At the beginning of the year, Vicky had been a lively girl, all smiles and always keen to help. She was also Arthur's ex-girlfriend. Rumor had it, he broke it off with her, and she didn't take it too well. In fact, by the time the Rothman family moved out of town, Vicky was a shadow of her former self—gone were the smiles, her light snuffed out by a new hatred simmering beneath the surface. After he finally won her over, Olivia now knew what she'd probably had to endure as Arthur's so-called girlfriend.

"Don't tell him to cut it out," Lesley Kilmer said.

"Oh, look who decided to join the party," Myrtle said sarcastically. "The little mouse—"

"Myrtle," the tone in Eric's voice cut off the queen bee's insult.

"Okay, fine, can we just get on with it? I have a curfew," Myrtle said.

"Yeah, whatever," Eric muttered.

Olivia didn't wait to hear the rest of their conversation. She pushed off from the tree and made her way deeper into the forest, determined not to become the next Vicky Rothman, or worse. She knew what weird shit they'd been doing, after all. Myrtle and her merry band of—what? *What* had they even been up to? Sure, there had been some candles, something that resembled a pentagram drawn in the dirt, a few chicken bones scattered around. One could brush it off as morbid curiosity, play-acting, maybe dabbling with dark forces. There wasn't anything illegal about it. Yet, none of those explanations had sent her off running in the other direction. She could handle paranormal crap. The supernatural didn't scare her one bit. What mattered was that Arthur had a gun; there was probably a bullet with her name on it. She couldn't take the chance to become part of their sick ritual or whatever the hell they wanted to do with her.

Branches scratched her bare arms and legs, snagged at her clothes. Olivia tripped once over a root, falling face-first. Her body ached; her mind reeled. Still, she didn't stop. She couldn't. Olivia *knew* if they caught her, she wouldn't see daylight again. Their reputations were on the line, after all. Arthur, Myrtle, Lesley, and Eric seemed clean-cut, well-rounded teenagers. Role-models. Ivy League contenders. They wouldn't let her live to ruin their carefully constructed façades.

So, Olivia ran. Deeper and deeper into the eerily quiet forest where everything looked the same. She sidestepped a tree, crisscrossed a few yards of open space, and slipped into a shadowed area to catch her breath. Every part of her mind screamed at her to continue, to put as much distance between her and the oncoming threat. Olivia's body, however, could only go on for so long.

She needed water. Food. Why had she skipped dinner? Excitement, Olivia remembered. Going out with *the* Arthur Freeman had been enough of a reason not to indulge in her mother's lasagna. Consuming all that garlic would've put a damper on any potential kissing.

Oh, how Olivia had wanted to kiss Arthur. Not anymore, though. Never again.

Be careful what you wish for, her mind mimicked her mother's voice.

Olivia listened to her surroundings, waiting to hear a telltale sound that would send her running away from certain death again. When nothing stirred, she allowed herself to relax and lean against the tree. At least, for a moment. Just to rebuild her strength so she can find her bearings and make her way to a nearby road.

A minute passed.

Her breathing evened out, and the breeze cooled her skin. Her panic faded, replaced by something resembling calm. Olivia was still on edge, but she could think rationally again.

Then, five minutes had gone by.

Apart from her soft breathing, there wasn't a single sound to be heard in the forest. The wind cutting through the area didn't even rustle a leaf. Hidden in the dark, shrouded by the shadows of ancient trees, surrounded by an intense quiet, she somehow convinced herself she was safe for the first time since she'd left her house.

Olivia rested her head against the trunk, closed her eyes, and inhaled deeply.

A waft of familiar cologne drifted on the breeze.

Crack.

Something dry crunched underfoot somewhere nearby.

Her eyes shot open; heart rate returned to beating a furious pace. She stayed completely still, allowing only her eyes to scan the area. The darkness made it impossible to see beyond the next tree, but she sensed someone in the vicinity. Had they found her?

Olivia had to make one of two equally difficult choices— she could stay where she was and risk the chance of being found, or she could run deeper into the forest and, possibly, be spotted by her assailants. Neither option felt right.

A warm trickle of air blew onto her neck. Olivia's body responded as the small hair on the back of her neck stood upright. She shifted slightly from foot to foot, then dared to peer around the tree's trunk. Nothing.

Olivia sighed in relief as she shifted back into her original position.

Thank God, she thought.

Suddenly, a flashlight flickered on and shone directly into her eyes. Whatever relief she'd felt previously evaporated as she realized they'd found her. They'd found her, and they would probably kill her. What then? Her face would probably show up on milk cartons first, then the police would stop investigating her disappearance. Eventually, there would be a memorial service. Maybe they would find a body, perhaps not. If she was lucky, a podcast could cover her death, but chances of it making national headlines were slim.

Laughter echoed through the forest—Myrtle's cruel, amused laughter.

"Gotcha!" Arthur's voice came from directly beside Olivia as a strong, large hand rested on her shoulder and fingers dug painfully into her flesh.

Without hesitating too long, Olivia did the only thing she could think of doing. She pulled away from Arthur's grip and sidestepped Eric, who tried to block her escape. Surprisingly enough, Lesley came the closest to grabbing her, but even her attempts were for naught.

"Get her, damn it!" Myrtle screamed.

Olivia sprinted blindly into the darkness, listening to the heavy footfalls trampling the underbrush as they followed her. The sudden onset of lightheadedness—a reaction to the dread bubbling through her system—made her footwork sluggish, uncertain. She persisted through the inky night, though, accepting the salient, suffocating embrace of the wild terrain.

"There, there," the forest seemed to say as its grip tightened on her. "You belong to me, not them."

"Olivia," Arthur bellowed.

Run. Just run as fast—

Before Olivia could finish her desperate thought, the forest floor gave way and, for what felt both like a lifetime and a mere millisecond, she was suspended in midair. In those moments, thoughts of a life unlived flitted through her mind. Memories, wonderful and terrible, were over far too soon. An unspeakable rage took over. How dare they cut her life short. What gave them the right to take away all her hopes and dreams, her future? And then, before she could obsess over vengeance or regrets, gravity took hold, and Olivia came crashing back to Earth. White-hot pain shot through her hip as she landed hard on her side. Olivia rolled down the steep incline, jutting rocks and gravel cutting into her skin. Dirt and foliage clung to every part of her, while blood began seeping from the various wounds inflicted on her exhausted, prone body.

Then, one agonizing hit to the head turned her topsy-turvy world into a pitch-black void.

Death would have been easier, but Olivia wasn't ready to give up on life yet. Her anger kept her from fading into nothingness. Thoughts of retribution grew, dampening the waves of pain rolling through her body. She would not give those who'd hurt her a free pass. Never. They'd do it to someone else, someone who may not be as lucky. So, Olivia fought for all she was worth, endured the anguish as she forced her eyelids open, and looked up at the starry sky peeking through the forest canopy.

Every inhalation hurt. Every exhalation felt like it could be her last.

She tasted metal, smelled the sharp scent of blood. Something else lingered in the air, though. Olivia couldn't place the odor, but there was an almost herbal quality to it. Fresh, yet somehow cloying, coating the blood in a type of medicinal layer.

"Sleep," a withered, unfamiliar voice commanded.

Olivia averted her gaze to find a rickety old woman, hunched over from age, staring at her. The years were visible on her face as deep wrinkles cut across her forehead. Even in the darkness, she could see the liver spots marring her leathery skin. Wearing a headscarf and dressed in mismatched clothing that could only be described as that of a stereotypical babushka, the elderly woman picked up a thick rope and tugged it toward her gently. Olivia's entire body jerked as the earth moved beneath her, the gritty sound of ground shifting not loud enough to muffle her groan in pain.

"Sleep," the woman said again.

"Too ... painful ..."

"Ah, it means you're alive." The woman had an accent, faint but there. Scandinavian, perhaps? Olivia couldn't be sure. "Life is good, no?"

Yes. Being alive is good, Olivia thought.

"Exactly," the woman answered as if Olivia had spoken out loud. She pulled on the rope again, hardly putting any effort into it, and whatever Olivia lay on moved forward more smoothly. "I've been where you are now. Betrayed. Broken. Left for dead. Yes, I know your story all too well, child."

Olivia squeezed her eyes shut, and a fat tear ran down her cheek. She just wanted to be accepted, loved. High school was a minefield for even the most adaptable teen, and up until Arthur started giving her attention, she'd been invisible for the most part. Her so-called friends were more like acquaintances— they talked, sometimes ate lunch together, but there wasn't the camaraderie one would expect between friends. Arthur and Myrtle offered Olivia an alternative high school experience, one to end her lonely existence.

I'm so incredibly stupid!

The old woman clicked her tongue, then said, "With time, you will heal and grow stronger, and you will live to be a ripe old age, but first you must sleep. Vengeance comes later." The old woman turned around, pulled the rope over her shoulder, and moved through the forest at a snail's pace.

Eventually, Olivia closed her eyes again. She didn't sleep— at least, she didn't think she did—but peace washed over her. Not absolute acceptance or anything of the sort, merely a realization that she was safe. The worst was over. She hoped. Still, being *that* vulnerable, and relying on a stranger for help because she was essentially half-dead, wasn't what Olivia had bargained on.

"Little sister?" the old woman's voice intruded on her thoughts.

Olivia's eyes fluttered open, and she found herself lying in a clearing, a raised house looming over her. The elderly woman's leathery face came into view, the deep wrinkles accentuated in the harsh white light of the moon. Olivia looked around, dazed by her surroundings. More than a foot of snow now covered the forest floor, and even in the darkness, she could make out the silhouette of an unfamiliar, vast mountain range in the distance. What struck Olivia as peculiar, however, wasn't the landscape. It was the house standing over them. Standing not on poles. No. Standing on what appeared to be giant chicken feet.

I must have hit my head so hard I'm hallucinating.

That simply had to be the reason. What other possible explanation could there be? Olivia blinked a few times and shook her head. The chicken legs didn't vanish, though. Instead, those hock joints bent, and the house lowered itself. The sound of wood grinding, snapping, creaking, echoed through the otherwise quiet forest as the house settled mere feet away.

Wide-eyed, Olivia turned back to her savior, asking, "W-where am I?"

"We are home," the old woman said. "You're safe."

The rustic-looking dwelling shifted underfoot, but nothing inside the house moved along. Small vials and bottles flooding the built-in shelves in the old woman's kitchen didn't so much as rattle. Not even the curtains rustled when the wind blew through the cracks and came in beneath the door. Still, the scenery outside the windows changed, and the house sometimes jerked about with indecision as if unsure what direction to go in next.

Strange as it was to be inside a cabin that stood on chicken legs, Olivia wasn't scared. In fact, she really did feel like she belonged there. In a previous life, maybe? Something about the whole place seemed to speak to an ancient part of her being, a memory etched onto her DNA. Primal fury and female intuition had activated new things within her mind—things Olivia had only imagined as fiction.

Lying on a bedroll, covered in furs to stave off the cold, with a full view of the small kitchen, Olivia remained mostly quiet as the odd old woman bustled about. Every now and then, whenever Olivia drifted back to consciousness, she listened to stories that originated in a different time, learned forgotten secrets. Healed.

Days could have gone by, perhaps even weeks. Olivia didn't know. She didn't care much about anything except her growing need to exact a peculiar type of pain on those who'd hurt her. Her anger, though justified, didn't feel like it came from her. No. Well, not entirely. It rather felt like the undiluted rage of a thousand women, who'd all been hurt—or worse—by people they'd trusted. Olivia Donahue, high school nobody, was merely a conduit.

"You feel them, don't you?" the old woman asked one evening as a cozy fire crackled in the hearth.

Olivia pushed herself into a sitting position. "Who?"

Staring into the flames, she said in thought, "The others. Our sisters. Ones who were not as lucky as you and I."

"Yes," Olivia whispered. "I feel them."

"Good."

"What ... I mean, *why*—?"

"There must always be balance in the world," the old woman explained. "There is life and death. Good and evil. We are both; we are neither. It just so happens that the world has become an especially cruel place in recent years and now—" She turned to look at Olivia. "*We* need to set things straight."

"We. As in you and me?"

The old woman grimaced. "Not *just* us. There are others."

Olivia tried to understand the underlining meaning of the riddle-like conversation, but she could only focus on the questions popping into her head.

"Survivors?" Olivia asked.

The old woman's entire face smoothed out before her lips tilted upward. Then, she cackled loudly as if Olivia had told her an especially dirty joke. When she realized Olivia wasn't joking, she pulled herself together and shook her head.

"Yes, no. I suppose some are survivors, like us. Most, not all, were victims."

"*Okay ...*" Olivia didn't understand a damn thing coming out of the woman's mouth.

The old woman raised an eyebrow as she studied Olivia. "We are changed, child. What happened to us was inevitable for our true nature to be revealed."

Confusion turned to frustration. What was this senile woman talking about?

"Baba Yaga! We are Baba Yaga," the old woman said loudly as if reading Olivia's thoughts.

The term meant absolutely nothing to Olivia, yet she felt the power it held in the old woman's accent. It meant something powerful, not to be messed with, fierce and female. All the things Olivia had wanted to be while they were hunting her in the forest. Did she feel any of that where she sat? She glanced at her hands where the smaller cuts had already healed. Parts of her body were still tender, but the pain wasn't as significant as it should have been.

"What is a Baba Yaga?" Olivia asked, returning her gaze to the old woman's eyes.

A toothy grin formed on the haggard face before she said, "We are guardians, tempests, witches. We are—" In a blink, the old woman in frumpy clothes disappeared. In her place sat a young, svelte seductress with long blond locks in a revealing red dress. "Dreams come true to those deserving, and—" Gone was the young woman. Instead, a crooked-nosed hag with jagged metal teeth and demonic red eyes stared back at Olivia. "Nightmares come to life. We are justice embodied, free to be whom we were always meant to be. You and I, and those like us, have been reborn."

Olivia wasn't like this woman, was she? A shapeshifter. Witch? Impossible. She would've known if the fall had stripped her of what made her human—if she'd lost her sanity. Then again, she wasn't running for the hills, screaming either. The house was walking around on chicken legs, and it didn't freak her out, for God's sake!

The old woman turned her attention back to the fire, settled in her seat, and said, "I will teach you the ways of our kind, child, and you will have your justice."

Olivia Donahue
November 17, 2005 – October 31, 2022
Beloved daughter

A simple, unadorned headstone marked the empty grave. There were no flowers here, no grief. Just a marker to show a short life lived and lost, a vessel no longer accounted for. When had the search parties given up hope on finding her body? When the first snows fell or when the dogs lost her scent? Did the police, townsfolk, her parents still care about who'd brought this unnecessary loss to their doorstep, or had forgiveness already taken root? Olivia didn't know. She barely cared anymore.

Now a companion and mentor, the old woman had been right about her being reborn. She hadn't been stripped of her humanity, in fact, she saw it more clearly in herself now than ever before, and her sanity was in check. Olivia Donahue, the girl who'd been so desperate to be accepted by unworthy dabblers, had become something different altogether. Something to be feared. And though she still had links to her former life, she understood her purpose was greater than giving her parents closure.

"Are you ready?" the old woman asked.

"I am," Olivia said as she turned away from her headstone.

"Then let us not dawdle."

The two hunched-over figures shambled down the hilltop side-by-side, their heavy cloaks blocking out the worst of the icy, autumn wind. They appeared to move slow, seemed to struggle as they traversed into the forest again, but that's what they wanted the world to see. Gray-haired, wrinkled, feeble old women, harmless by anyone's standards. If anyone saw them, they would think them elderly sisters.

Sisters.

They *were* sisters. Shared experiences sometimes created even stronger bonds than the ties created through blood.

Day turned to night as they quietly walked through the forest—as familiar to Olivia now as any other wooded area on the planet. She saw every tree as a living entity, each body of water as a sentient being, and all the creatures roaming those wild spaces were friends. Baba Yaga protected them, and in turn Baba Yaga was protected by them. A simple symbiotic relationship.

"The earth has soured here. Do you feel it?"

Olivia closed her eyes momentarily and allowed the earth's vibrations to run up her legs. "I do," she said. "Why?"

"You were not the last one who'd been brought to this place. Your old friends have been busy."

"They have spilled blood?"

"More than once," the old woman said. "We shall set things right."

"An eye for an eye," Olivia concurred.

The farther they ventured into the forest, the more prominent the feeling of wrongness became. Something unnatural had occurred here. The earth had soaked up the stories, and the trees now whispered those tales of death to the Baba Yaga. The dabblers were there, yes. They were already on their next hunt, anticipating their next sacrifice. For what? Success? Fame? Money? Perhaps just for fun.

One dabbler was missing, though.

"Who?" Olivia wondered aloud, and the trees showed her a vision of Lesley Kilmer—the quieter one of the gang. Unsurprised, Olivia turned to the old woman and asked, "What happened to her?"

The old woman shrugged. "I suspect she came to her senses soon after you … disappeared."

"Ah."

Did it make her better than the rest?

They turned the final corner, passed the last tree, and entered the clearing where a large bonfire blazed through the night. The deranged laughter—a sound Olivia knew all too well—drifted through the forest. Myrtle, Arthur, and Eric were nearby and getting closer, corralling their victim. She sensed it.

A scream, bloodcurdling and desperate, followed.

Olivia watched as the old woman walked to the fire and took a seat on a log. She stretched out her legs and held the cane she'd brought along by her side.

Footsteps raced toward their location.

"Wait," the old woman said, then smacked her lips. "The forest will save the girl and redirect them here."

Olivia nodded.

A few minutes passed before the homicidal trio entered the clearing, seemingly annoyed about losing their prey. Myrtle was the first to spot them.

"Oh," Myrtle said, the surprise evident in her tone. She turned to Arthur and Eric, her eyes widening. "We have guests?" It sounded more like a question than a statement.

Arthur turned up his charm by smiling widely, acting all innocent while hiding a hunting knife behind his back. "Hello, ma'ams."

Olivia showed no sign of having seen the weapon. Instead, she smiled back and said, "Hello, young man. We saw the fire and thought to come rest for a minute, warm up a bit. I hope you don't mind."

"Of course, we don't," Arthur said. "Do we?" He shot a glare at Myrtle, then glanced at Eric, conveying a message Olivia couldn't decipher, but his friends clearly could.

"No, please rest," Myrtle said, smiling sweetly.

Eric remained silent.

"What brings you out this way?" Arthur asked, looking toward Olivia's companion.

"Bit of this, bit of that," the old woman said. "The question is, what brings you here?"

Olivia was familiar with the old woman's tone by now, knowing full well there was an accusation hidden in those words. Arthur seemed uncomfortable under the old woman's scrutiny.

"These here aren't friendly parts." Olivia rubbed her hands together over the fire. "Or didn't you hear about all those people going missing?"

"You should be careful," the old woman said. "You never

know who you may meet in the woods."

"Oh, we're not too bothered by those rumors." Arthur's smile didn't falter. Even Myrtle seemed to relax, even though she'd gravitated to Arthur's side.

The old woman nodded as she got to her feet ever so slowly, putting on a show of vulnerability for the dabblers. "We'll be on our way then."

"So soon?" Myrtle asked.

"We have a long way to go," Olivia said, waiting for her companion to join her.

"You're welcome to stay awhile longer. We have food," Arthur said.

"Shall we?" the old woman asked Olivia, sounding weak. "Perhaps for a little bit? It *is* a long way home, and we have walked many miles already."

"We won't make it home by dawn."

"Come now, it's not like anyone's waiting for us."

In Arthur's soulless eyes, something unholy sparked. Excitement. Yes, they were not his usual targets, but they were here. And those were the words Arthur had been waiting for ... Not only were they weak, alone, but there was an opportunity here he couldn't let slip through his fingers.

Olivia mumbled, "Very well, sister. Let us rest for a few more minutes." She shuffled toward her companion. The time was ripe to put things right. "What harm would it do, hmmm?"

"Indeed."

She sensed Arthur coming up behind her, could see the knife in her mind's eye as the blade gleamed in the firelight. At the same time, Myrtle was moving into place, her gaze fixed on the old woman. Eric, always the third wheel, didn't immediately take the hint that something was about to happen.

Before Arthur or Myrtle could strike, however, Olivia spun around and shed her disguise. The frail, elderly woman was replaced by a more demonic shape, one resembling the Olivia Donahue they'd once hunted. Metal teeth glimmered as she grinned at him, the boy—now a man—who'd hurt her and so many other girls before, finally caught off-guard.

Myrtle's scream came from somewhere behind her.

"Fuck this," Eric shouted.

Arthur stared at Olivia, gaping in fear.

"Hello, Arthur," Olivia said. "Miss me?"

Before he could respond, Olivia pounced. She sunk her metal teeth deep into his neck, puncturing his esophagus. The tang of his blood filled her mouth as she tore away chunks of flesh and severed his carotid artery. He gurgled as blood filled his throat, sputtered as Olivia released him, and he stumbled backward. Arthur's face turned white, unable to look away, already making peace with what was to come. A quick death.

"You deserved a lot worse than this," Olivia hissed. "Be grateful for small mercies."

"Olivia," the old woman said.

She turned to find her companion transformed and standing over a cowering Myrtle. In an instant, Olivia's cane transformed into an oversized, heavy pestle, and she made her way to where Myrtle sat. She raised the stone object high above her head and brought it down fast.

The pestle connected with Myrtle's skull several times, spraying gray matter and blood across the earth. Quick, yet messier than intended.

When Olivia was done, she smiled as a new kind of vibration ran up her legs. "Do you feel that? The earth is already healing."

"Baba Yaga, do not take pleasure in this work," the old woman said as she conjured a mortar from thin air and clambered inside. "We are not like them. Come."

"Yes, sister," Olivia said as she joined her companion.

WATER LIKE BROKEN GLASS

BY CARINA BISSETT

W hen does a woman become a witch?

It's different for all of us. Some come to it naturally. Others struggle for a while.

For me, that contest of arms started in a few inches of water with my lover's hands firmly pressed down on the back of my neck.

He won.

I don't know how much time passed before I emerged, reborn as a rusalka bound to the river that swallowed my last breath. And I lingered there until a girl came to me with a plea for help spelled on her bruised and battered lips.

Luckily for her, not all drowned girls stay dead.

The first thing I notice is her shining red hair. It streams past her shoulders like a banner. Following that flag is a soldier.

"Watermeid!" The fleeing girl summons me even though I am only the ghost of a rumor, a common condition for all women who've been beaten, broken, and left for dead.

She lunges into the river as the man closes the gap.

"Heks!" she cries out. *Witch*.

I slip out of the embrace of my favorite birch and into the water below. The girl's feet crash through the river. Her bare toes cling to the smooth stones. The man's shiny black boots slip on those same rocks, but he is determined in his pursuit.

He reaches out to catch her, but she stumbles forward, and

he is left grasping at the white ribbons trailing from the girl's long hair.

The soldier's fingers close in a fist, and her flight comes to an abrupt halt. He lands a blow with his free hand. The girl crashes to her knees, waist-deep in the rushing river. She is fumbling for the trench knife tucked into her waistband when she finally spots me, drifting along the riverbed.

The soldier mutters something guttural as he draws a pistol from his belt. The girl's lips curve in a blood-streaked smile, and she raises both hands in surrender.

I might not be a witch, but I *am* a watermeid. A drowned girl. A birch bride. And *my* arms are empty.

I tangle the soldier's ankles, drag him to the deepest channel. And then I let go. He surfaces, arms pinwheeling as he gulps for air. When he sets out toward the nearest shore, I follow, hidden in the current. His strokes grow stronger, more purposeful the closer he is to safety. He grasps a handful of grass clinging to the shore before I pull him back into my domain. His eyes widen when he finally sees me as the river wraps the length of black hair around his throat. His armband pulls free midstream. The cutwater snatches at the flash of red. It curls to reveal a white circle stamped with the harsh black lines of a crooked cross. I permit him to surface, make another attempt for freedom as I gather the sash as tribute. The iron cross pinned to his gray-green collar is the price for our third encounter. And so, bit by bit, his uniform is stripped of regalia until the soldier's strong body finally fails. His lungs fill with water and weed, and I turn away.

The girl with the red hair waits for me near my favored haunt, the birch with roots sunk deep into the river. Cradled in the remains of an old channel, a pool reflects a spring sky as blue as a robin's egg.

"I heard rumor of a watermeid near here. Lucky for me, it turned out to be true." Her laugh is one of joyous discovery. "Thank you, comrade."

Curious, I drift closer.

"A woman of action, not of words, I see." She uncrosses her legs, slides away from the safety of shore, and wades toward me with her hand outstretched. "I'm Tilde."

I consider slipping away, but her bright-eyed stare dares me to stay. And so, I reach back, brush my fingers across hers, quick as a minnow darting with the current. Satisfied, she offers a mocking salute.

"Welcome to the Resistance."

Tilde builds a hut on the river bend near the silver-barked birch. The building is so close that I can climb the slender branches and lean out to touch the roof. At night, Tilde scales the walls and settles herself in the rushes. We watch the stars together, learning to navigate the silence between us.

Early each morning, just as the sky begins to blush, the hut rustles like feathers fluffed by a roosting hen. Tilde rouses with it, brushes the thatch from her clothes, and blows me a kiss before heading back to town and the patriots plotting a revolution. I wish I could follow, but I am a birch bride, a rusalka fettered to the currents of death and despair. And so, I wait each day, swimming up and down the river, waiting for her to return.

Tilde brings me stories, opens them like presents. Her sister knits cables into code, garments woven with secrets for the forces fighting against men determined to destroy an entire race. And then, an ambitious aviatrix cousin jumps a train heading east. Now she is a Night Witch, dropping fire from the skies upon unwary armies.

"I don't have the patience for knitting, and I'm afraid of heights," Tilde adds with a shrug.

I find it impossible to believe fear is an emotion Tilde is

acquainted with. She is much too fierce for that.

"I have other talents." And she does. She might not be familiar with yarn and its endless variations of stitches and slipknots, but flirtation she's mastered. And her beauty and charm are as fatal as bombs launched from a biplane under cover of a new moon.

And so, Tilde lures the unwary to my shores. With their shiny black boots and silver stars, these hardened soldiers are always so eager. Afterward, I strip their symbols, offer them to Tilde along with smooth pebbles and fish bones collected from the hollowed-out human skulls paving my river's deepest channels. She strings those red armbands, one after the other, on a piece of abandoned fishing twine from the roof. Unmoored, the sashes ripple in the breeze, and the crooked crosses dance like hanged men unwilling to surrender their last breath.

One day, Tilde steps into the water, naked and alone. I discover myself in her arms, and what was once shattered emerges sacred and complete. I remember love in its many forms. I am reborn, renewed.

We spend our days in the water, our nights tangled in the treetops. My birch stretches toward the rooftop; the hut moves closer to the river. But bound as I am to water, I shackle Tilde as well.

"Problems are meant to be solved," Tilde says.

My beloved works to set river stones and beach glass into the loamy soil for seven days and nights until the path stretches from the shore to her doorstep. But it still isn't enough.

Tilde moves forward, always forward, and visits a baba yaga who lives in the forest. I correct her when I hear the name. There is only one Baba Yaga, and she walks with Death on the eastern steppes of Russia. Tilde laughs.

"Who would have thought a rusalka would be superstitious?"

"I have a name." I slide deeper into the water.

"Yelena." She leaves her work behind and comes to me. "There are many ways to be a witch in this world."

Tilde demonstrates, and I begin to believe.

Under the baba's guidance, Tilde adds another layer of spell craft wrought in a border of foxglove, hemlock, and belladonna. She hauls bucket upon bucket of water to purify the walkway between worlds, yet still, I cannot take more than three steps on dry land before terror and pain drive me back to the river that claims me as its own.

Searching for a solution to our dilemma, Tilde's baba starts to work with the other forest mothers. Tilde is confident they will unravel the root of the curse, but still, she grows restless. They should trust her with more of their secrets. There's other work to be done. More and more often, her gaze turns back toward town and the revolution that continues without her. I hold her close, hoping I can anchor her with my love, but one day I wake, and my arms are empty.

"They killed a girl today." Tilde's bloodshot eyes stare into the distance.

Careful to keep my feet in the water, I stretch out on the riverbank to console her.

She pushes me away and rubs her cheeks.

"Pieter saved me."

Pieter. The leader of Tilde's resistance. A valiant man working to destroy the invading forces, one soldier at a time.

"They were looking for me," she says, and I find myself caught between one breath and the next.

My lips wrap around questions—Who? How? Why?—but the words are like pebbles in my mouth, so I whisper her name, instead.

Tilde ignores me. She unwraps brown paper to reveal a glass bottle filled with dark liquid.

"Her hair was red, too. Lighter than mine, but close enough." Tilde looks at me then. "Like you, she had a name, but we are now forbidden to say it."

Men and murder. Will it ever end? I edge closer, wind myself around her. This time she allows it.

"Pieter told me to run, hide. He doesn't want to lose me, too."

Tilde talks about this revolutionary hero—often. She dismisses my jealousy. Pieter is nearly twice her age. When I question his motives, she corrects me. War is cruel, and those who are young and female are the most vulnerable of all.

This leads me to memories of rushing water and hands pressed against the back of my neck.

"Stay here." Even out of the water, my voice rumbles and rolls over the syllables. "With me."

She kisses my brow. "I cannot, my love."

When she opens the bottle, I shrink away from the horrible smell and slip back to the safety of the river. Tilde ignores my reaction and applies the contents. A while later, she follows me into the water. And, when she finally emerges, the bottle's contents rinsed downstream, her hair is as blue-black as my own.

"I will find the men who killed her," she says. "I will bring them here, and you will make them suffer."

One day, when Tilde has been away for more than a fortnight, a man comes to the river alone. He strips the gray-green uniform, folds it neatly, and leaves it on the bank next to polished black boots. His cheeks are rough and red, his eyes waterlogged.

"I know you're here." He opens his arms, palms raised to the sky. Even though the day is warm, he shivers.

I swim closer.

Peach fuzz follows the softness of his jaw. Not a man, but a boy still teetering on the edge of adulthood. Although I've drowned countless men—guilty and innocent alike—he is the first to offer himself willingly.

Unsettled, I splash in the water. He flinches but otherwise doesn't move.

"Go on," he says. "I deserve it."

"Explain." The word rolls off my tongue.

"So many have died." He pauses. "My fault."

This boy is looking for absolution—something I cannot grant him. But death does not come easy at my hands. The bodies of these men are mine, but their souls belong to me as well. They flutter in the current, tethered to the riverbed paved with their bones. Tilde wouldn't hesitate in the sentencing, but even I know a single soldier could not murder millions alone.

Every question I'd like to ask is as sharp as broken glass. If I utter the words, they will slice my tongue. Besides, I already know the answer. It is folded up in that neat and tidy package left on the riverbank—another red armband to string up, another crooked cross ready to dance in the breeze.

Tears course down those wind-chapped cheeks. He takes a deep breath. "They made me do it."

Of course, they did.

I should drag him under, rip the golden hair from his scalp, shear skin from muscle and bone. Tilde would have insisted. It's a sacred duty to kill these invaders, every single one an evil to be routed from this earth. But I remember the true face of evil, and it was as familiar as my own. Strangers and soldiers aren't the only murderers in the world. So, I leave him there, still living, penance a possibility—at least for one of us.

Later, I wonder if I should have kept the boy. We could have traded stories—grief and guilt enough for sharing—a distraction from this unfamiliar loneliness left in Tilde's place. But when I return, he is gone, tracks left in the mud on the opposite shore. The discarded uniform, weapons, and boots remain where he left them.

Tilde stays away. On the last full moon, the hut moved into the shallows. It balances on two sturdy chicken legs, revealing a hatch underneath that opens through the floor. Only a faint outline remains in the spot once occupied by the original door. Two windows have taken its place, as though the hut is watching for a flash of red hair in the distance.

Three full moons pass before Tilde returns. She climbs through the trap door. Her lips are stained red, her skin as white as the belly of a fish, and I am reminded of tales filled with teeth and blood and damnation.

"The deserter, where is he?"

I shrink away until my back is pressed against one of the straw-covered walls. The hut rustles reassuringly.

Tilde scans the room, eying the mobiles I've created from polished bones and river rocks. "You've been busy."

I want to shout and scream. *What have you done? Where have you been?* Instead, I simply nod.

"Good." Tilde closes the space between us and crouches next to me. "You've never told me who did this." Cold fingers trail across my cheek.

"It was a long time ago." My teeth chatter.

She curves her body into mine and pulls me close. "Tell me now."

And I do.

I tell her of the unborn babe, the desperation, the inevitable.

"The curse can only be broken when your death is avenged," she says.

"The babas told you that?"

"The babas are gone." Her lips twist in a grimace.

"Gone? But where?"

"I didn't need them anymore." She flicks her fingers dismissively. "They refused to give me what I wanted, so I took it." Tilde's pupils are so large they eclipse all but a thin ring of blue at the edges. *Belladonna.* "Knowledge is power, and power only grows when it is *used.*"

"Tilde?" The rest remains unspoken.

The coldness of her skin against mine tells me what I need to know. The forest mothers are all dead, drained to feed the dark power of this creature I barely recognize.

She smothers my protests with kisses. I cannot leave, so I pretend I'm still with that fierce, red-headed girl, the woman who brought me back to this side of the living with the sheer force of her love. But I can't bear to see her face, paler than even mine, or the way our hair tangles together, the color as dark as a bruise. Tilde demands that I see her for what she's become, powerful and cunning, an enchantress feared by even Death itself.

"Yelena," she says. "Look at me."

The hut clucks and crows in protest.

My eyes stay shut.

It is a chilly day on the edge between the old year and the new when Tilde leads a man of a different caliber to my shores. The river roars as it nears the bend, but all the man's attention is on the shallows. Each step he takes thuds heavier on the turf until, at last, he comes to a grinding halt.

The man frowns. "Why did you bring me here?"

"You asked a question. The river holds the answer." Tilde picks up a flat stone that's worked its way free from the abandoned path. She weighs it in her palm. "There is nothing to worry about, no chance of discovery. Those missing soldiers ended up far away from here."

It isn't true, but she doesn't know that.

The man doesn't seem to notice the trail leading to an empty hollow, nor does he notice the hut huddling at the bank's edge near the stately birch. Instead, he stares into the shallows as though his rippling reflection is a ghost.

"This is where you dump the bodies?" He clenches his teeth—a muscle twitches along his jaw like a fish rising to bait.

Despite my resolve to stay hidden, I glide closer to shore.

"Something like that." Tilde grins and skips the stone across the water.

The years weigh heavy on the man's broad shoulders. Yet beneath the stockier frame and the sorrow he wears like a shroud, I know this man. I know the freckles scattered across those gnarled knuckles, the press of those strong fingers around my throat. Yet, she called him a different name than the one I once knew. This *Pieter* is the leader of her resistance. Tilde's hero, a champion of the people.

A murderer.

I reach through the water and grab the skipping stone midair. My toes dig deep into the silt, and I rise from the river like whitewater coursing around a boulder.

The man falls to his knees.

"It's not what you think," Tilde assures him. The sun catches the bold red emerging at the roots of her hair. "She is with me." My beloved looks at me with eyes as dark as nightshade. "She's with us."

"No." The word is a groan.

"Pieter?" Her gaze flits back and forth.

The river parts around me, and I walk across the slick surface of countless human skulls used to pave a path of my own making.

Tilde's eyes widen at the sight of the army laid out beneath my pale feet. So many men, decades of death doled out in the wake of my own drowning. The soldiers Tilde brought me are only a fraction of those who'd paid for the crime of another, the monster who'd damned me to this twilight life. *Wilhelm.* Determined protector.

But he'd set that name adrift long ago; it is nothing more than a river-worn memory. Now, this man is a leader of a revolution. He carries a different name. *Pieter.* A pillar of strength.

"No." Tilde's eyes widen. She takes a step back. "It can't be."

I stop just inches from dry land. The cutwater churns and boils around my feet. The river lays claim to me just as this man once did, but neither the river nor the man can deny me now.

Tilde draws a gun from her waistband. No knife this time. The barrel is covered with neat tally marks. I am not the only one keeping score.

"Is it him?"

She already knows the answer.

"I don't deserve your forgiveness." Pieter bows his head, bares his neck. "But I am truly sorry."

"Yelena, you must avenge yourself," Tilde says, her voice as cold as a winter morning. "*Freedom*—" She bites down on the word. "Is yours for the taking."

I hesitate. How many people has this one man saved over the years? According to Tilde, they number in the thousands. But a crime cannot be erased by a single act of vengeance. Besides, I am no longer a victim.

"No." The skipping stone slips from my fingers. "Freedom cannot be taken. It must be earned."

Tilde does not yield, and for a moment, I see the girl I once loved. "The baba yagas said this day would come. Your death *must* be avenged."

I tilt Wilhelm's chin so that he is looking up at me as I once did to him. "Leave this place." Even I can see he is no longer the man I once knew. "Pieter." The sound of his claimed name slides into place. "Go and never return."

"Fine," Tilde says, her voice as sharp as broken glass. "I'll do it myself."

The sharp retort of a bullet is followed swiftly by two more. Pieter is thrown forward. The whitewater frothing at my feet rises as the river greedily laps at what is left of his ruined face.

Tilde plants her feet onshore and reaches for me. "Come with me, Yelena." Now that she's seen the multitude, row upon row of bleached bone, she no longer trusts the water. "It's time to leave this all behind."

In that, she is right. I take her hand. Her nostrils flare when my grip tightens. Does she see Death coming for her? Or does she believe that her stolen power will save her from one such as I?

The moment between us stretches, a thin and tenuous thing, until I finally release her. A memory of minnows slips back into the stream of time.

I place one bare foot on Pieter's head. My toes curl around the jagged crater that remains. My next step is onto the man's broad back, a bridge between his world and mine. And then, I am on solid ground, winter grass tickling at my ankles.

"Did it work?" Tilde drops her hands to her sides. Her eyes are blue once more, and this time they are filled with the memory of hope. "Is it over?"

I nod and trace the trail she once built leading from the river to the clearing nestled next to my favorite birch. Tilde abandoned that project as she'd done with me, but she follows, wary once more. Husks are all that remains of the poison garden, but I harvest the seeds as I go. By the time I reach the clearing, the hut has returned to the spot where it hatched. I think of the stories my Russian mother told me as a child, tales of a solitary woman who roams the wilds, seeding witchcraft into stones and sky.

For the first time since I drowned, my skin dries completely. Tilde paces, watching and waiting, but there is an urgency in her stalking. She sketches spells in the air, casts a net designed to capture her enemies. She is no longer simply a girl with a gun, no witch's apprentice. Her power grows each day. I listen, make plans of my own. The sun sets, and the moon peeks over the horizon. I am reminded of those sweet summer nights when I rediscovered the power of love, but that rusalka and her beloved no longer exist. We have both changed, and with it, the connection between us. I press my forehead against the familiar bark of the old birch tree and offer thanks for those long years of companionship, but this is no longer where I belong. It is time to follow a different path.

"You're free now." Tilde interrupts my farewell. In the twilight, all hints of that red-haired girl are gone. She is Death incarnate. A creature that thrives on war, and her hunger is as bright as the full moon, as sharp as glass. Tilde faces south as though she can hear the sounds of gunfire and grenades in the distance. "Come with me. Together, we will make them *pay*."

And I believe she will, but she must follow this path alone.

It is the north that calls to me, the birthplace of my mother's mother—the roaming steppes beholden to Baba Yaga.

The hut rustles, rouses, and takes the first step toward our new life, far away from all this death. My homeland waits for me, just as it always has.

Not every woman becomes a witch. Some of us are born into it. Others struggle for a while.

A few of us—the drowned girls, the birch brides, the unquiet spirits—do both.

HERALD THE KNIGHT

BY MERCEDES M. YARDLEY

This is the tale of how Baba Yaga fell in love. Did you know such a thing was possible? It's true. The moon has its secrets. The oceans mouth the seashore. Even forces of nature like the ultimate witch are allowed a love story.

Fairy tales are full of clever young boys and beautiful, bewitching girls. The boys are good and strong. They turn into cunning young men, able to outfox the man who wants their head in exchange for gold, or the witch who wants to eat their little sisters. The girls grow into gorgeous blond ingénues. They are kind and good. They weep over the bloodied stumps of their hands until the skin becomes clean and smooth, and the devil himself can't take them.

These young men and dewy-eyed girls always meet. Usually, the girl is kept in a palace or a tower, and the ingenious boy uses his wits to win her. She is given as a trophy, a prize, and they gaze into each other's blue, blue eyes while falling madly in love.

This type of story didn't suit Baba Yaga at all. She wasn't interested in tales of simpering love. Love makes you weak. A heart isn't meant for such silly things, but it's meant to beat, flex like the muscle it is, and strengthen as it works harder and harder to push the blood through the aorta and arteries. A heart is strong. It is thick. It is a piece of meat, and it has the right amount of resistance when you bite down on it with your teeth.

Teeth are also strong, white picket fences. When Baba Yaga looked at a strapping young man or a pretty little thing, she measured them in her mind. She weighed them, seeing how much fat ran around their thighs and whether their calves curved under her hand like the flank of a deer. She checked their eyes for jaundice and the color of their soul. A soul flows through your fingers like sand, like strands of hair, like water. You can pack a voodoo doll with chicken feathers, fingernails, and tattered pieces of soul. You can sew it into a dress. Baba Yaga did all of these things.

Baba Yaga was young and lovely with piercing gray eyes. Her father, when she had a father, told her to lower her gaze.

"You have the eyes of a man," he told her. "They're fierce, and I can see fire in them instead of my reflection. What type of man would choose to wed a brazen woman such as yourself?"

Baba Yaga didn't blink. Her eyes were like the finest burnished swords, sharp and cutting.

"I wouldn't want any man that would want me, Father," she said. "I don't want any man at all. I want to learn the secrets of the universe. I want to know how to stop somebody's blood in their veins. I want to know what words to whisper to the stars so they will fall to the ground and do my bidding. A husband? What a waste of time."

Baba Yaga was clever, which was a shame, the townsfolk said, because it was wasted on a woman. Her face was acceptable, really. Her skin was creamy and hair full and lush, but those eyes held pyres inside. When a townsperson met her gaze, they saw their children shrieking and burning inside her irises.

She used her clever fingers to pound poultices. She made tinctures for wounds and poisons that turned her fingers and teeth black. She left her home and strode around the woods at night, listening to the murmuring of the trees as they called her.

"Bryony for toxin," they told her. "Lavender to sweeten the taste. Mushrooms to close their eyes for eternity."

She took a moon bath, stepping out of her dress and leaving it behind. She felt herself recharging, feeling whole and renewed while the rest of the town slept.

There was a rustle in the bushes. It was neither the rabbits that pressed against her legs nor the wind. Baba Yaga whirled, her muscles taut, as the vines and tree roots curled around her, snaking up her legs, warning her of the danger.

A man in black armor stepped from behind a tree. He bowed handsomely.

"I do apologize for startling you, my lady," he said. His voice was amplified inside his helmet. It sounded like a void and threatened to suck Baba Yaga in.

She didn't straighten but stayed low to the ground, ready to run or attack, whichever seemed best. Her growl rumbled low, and the flowers bent away from it.

"You are unclad. Here, let me shield you."

The knight removed his cape and draped it around Baba Yaga's shoulders. She made no move to cover herself.

"It's dangerous in the woods," he said. "Even more so at night. Please let me escort you back to the town."

Baba Yaga sniffed.

"I'm much safer here than I am with those horrid people. I'd rather stay, if it pleases you, and even if it doesn't. It doesn't matter to me either way."

She shrugged off his cloak, and it pooled at her feet. She heard him catch his breath, but she was already running, her long legs flashing as she moved across the forest. The underbrush pulled away from her, clearing her path. Rocks and sharp roots burrowed beneath the soil so as not to pierce her bare feet. The black knight watched her, instinctively knowing she ran toward something, not away from him, and it was no surprise when the forest closed itself behind her.

An unmarried woman is nothing but a menace. Baba Yaga heard it every day.

"You need to find yourself a husband," her father said. "I'm tired of providing for you."

"I'll provide for myself," she told him, but he whimpered and moaned, great big crocodile tears squeezing from his eyes. If she were to leave, who would cook his meals? Who would use her mortar and pestle to grind his medicine? Who would rub his bad left leg before he went to bed every night? And wouldn't it be safer if she were to marry instead of simply moving out alone? That way, his son-in-law could take care of him, too.

Baba Yaga dreamed she was a bird. She took wing and flew over her small village. She flew over the trees and across the oceans. She curled up in a tiny nest she built herself, something lovely and bizarre. It would be just right.

The forest claimed her, marking her with a smarting slap on her thigh. She grimaced as she rubbed at the spot, and her hand came away wet with blood. From that day on, she bore the mark of the trees, and her human scent was covered with that of the forest. She smelled of fresh pine and moss, fungus, and warm animals.

One night the black knight came to her in the woods. She knelt on the cool ground with the head of a deer in her lap. She rubbed her hands down its neck while it closed its eyes.

"What are you doing here?" she asked. She spoke calmly so not to disturb the animal.

"I came to see you," the knight said.

"I have nothing to say to you."

"But I have so many things to ask."

She leaned down and whispered to the deer. Secrets. Incantations. Promises or threats, it didn't matter. She kissed it on its muzzle and then snapped its neck with a quick, deft twist of her hands.

Bones cracked. The deer bleated as air rushed from its lungs.

The lights in its eyes went out.

"Do you see how cruel I am?" she asked. She got to her feet and shook the dirt from her dress. "You want nothing to do with me."

"The animal was diseased. I could smell it. You only performed a mercy."

Baba Yaga stared him down with her strange eyes.

"What do you want with me?" she asked.

The knight put his hand over his heart.

"I only want to know you," he said. "I see you in the forest like a wild thing. You live in the land of men, but you don't truly belong there. There's something unusual about you that captures my attention."

She tossed her head.

"I am not a thing created to amuse you," she said loftily. "I am simply who I am. It makes no difference to me if you're interested in that or not."

She stood poised like an animal about to bound off into the forest. The knight held still as if moving would somehow frighten her.

"Why do you wear your armor here in the forest, under the moon?" she asked. She poked the metal with her finger. It was cold, pockmarked by use and the callous weaponry of war. "Surely you'd be more comfortable without it."

"The world is more comfortable with me in it," he replied, and she shrugged.

"Don't worry about their comfort. Be more concerned with yours."

The next time she went to her special clearing, he was waiting there. He had a hammer in his hands. Tools. Nails and a saw.

"What is this for?" she asked. Suspicion lowered her voice. It made her fingers tense and her expression stormy.

"The woodlands are swallowing you up," he said. "It's as it should be. I see you crumbling when you are in the village as if the very air wounds you. You can't breathe."

"Can you?" she asked. "I saw you at the market the other day. Everyone gives you a wide berth. They say you are cursed, that you are stupid, that your face is full of scars and wounds, and that's why you never remove your helmet."

"Do you believe I'm cursed?" he asked her.

"It doesn't matter to me either way. Your business is yours, and I don't concern myself with it. Now, what are you doing here?"

He told her of his plan, and her face warmed. A smile bathed her face like moonlight, and her eyes reflected fir trees and wild brush.

"Do you really mean it?" she asked, and the knight held an ax high in answer.

"Let me help," she said and closed her gunmetal eyes. The light in the clearing seemed to dim, then, but she held her arms to the woods and spoke. It was an old language, something long gone from most of the earth, and the trees turned their ears to it. The flowers leaned closer, and the brook changed course to give her more room. A mighty oak laid itself down in front of them.

"Thank you," Baba Yaga said, and the black knight swung his ax. The tree split into neat piles of logs.

"Thank you, thank you," she said and kissed each tree as it gave itself up for her. Pines and sycamores. Redwoods and maples. The wood separated with ease, and within an hour, the clearing was full of beauty.

Seams and joints. Foundation and beams. During the day, Baba Yaga washed and cleaned and made her ointments. She catnapped by the fire and denied the suitors who came her way. At night she met the knight in the clearing, and they built a tiny, one-roomed home from the forest's offerings. They packed the chinks between the logs with sweet moss. The beautiful different woods shone, and they built a chimney from gray river rock. Baba Yaga took a vial of ink from her apron and dipped her finger into it. She traced a symbol over the door and said something under her breath.

"You may come in," she said to the black knight, and he bowed before stepping over the threshold. "The door will recognize you. Nobody else will be so lucky."

"I thank you," he said, but she was already bustling around, hanging herbs over the windows and making sure her bed and bookshelf would fit neatly against the wall.

"It will be superb," she said and whirled to face him with a grin. He gasped, the amplified sound inside his helmet caused her smile to fall and shatter on the ground.

"What?" she asked and put her hands to her face. She knew her eyes bored into souls uncomfortably. She knew her teeth were sharp, a result of being in such close proximity of her sharp tongue, her father said, and her face wasn't as comely as some of the beauties in town. But she had forgotten, you see, to be wary, and had forgotten that she didn't care at all about this kind knight, who had joined her day after day to create her cozy little home.

She stiffened. She frowned. She opened her mouth to say something uninviting, something that would cause the house to fling him outside of its walls, but the knight spoke.

"Your smile. I've never seen you so happy. It made my heart … move."

She studied his soul with a practiced eye and saw he was being earnest. She felt the colors of his confusion and shyness. It tasted slightly salty and deliciously bitter, like strychnine.

They moved her furniture inside, bit by bit, piece by piece. When Baba Yaga hung up her last dress and put her silver comb on the table, she heaved a great sigh.

"It's everything I always hoped it would be," she said. "It's so isolated and serene. Thank you so very much, knight." And she threw her arms around him carelessly. Her hair blew in the wind created inside her snug home, swirling around the two of them like a frenzy of sharks. The knight seemed stunned but then gently put his arms around her.

"It is my pleasure," he said, and they stood that way for a very long time, with their foreheads touching.

"Will you ever show me your face?" she asked.

"I fear that I will not."

"You don't trust me?"

"I don't trust myself."

"What do you mean?" she asked, pulling back. "That sounds vaguely threatening."

"Not at all," he said and gently drew her back to him. "I know what I look like. I know how others react. If I were to show you, even if you were as stalwart as I'd expect, I'd still worry. It would smolder in the back of my mind like coals and scratch against my brain like rats. I'd eat myself alive, thinking that one day your disgust would show on your beautiful face, and I wouldn't be able to take it. I think I love you, you see."

I think I love you. The words had mass, and she took her time to taste them, to test them. They didn't hold the onerous weight she had expected. They didn't wrap around her ankles, wrists, and throat. She wasn't shackled to anything. Instead, they felt more like pearls that she could choose to loop around her neck, or bubbles that rose joyously through the water. What a funny thing.

"I'll have to think on it a bit more, but I think perhaps I love you, as well," she said, and the knight shuddered inside of his armor.

"Say it again," he commanded, and she smiled.

"I might love you," she said, and he pulled her close to his metal body. She gestured behind her, and the fireplace whooshed to life. The knight's icy armor gradually warmed until she could comfortably lay her head against it.

"Perhaps you could leave the helmet on but change into

simple leathers instead," she suggested, and his laughter was beautiful, was bells, and it filled the whole house.

"Father, it's time for me to leave."

He shouldn't have been surprised, but he flapped his lips in a useless old man way and tried to bluster. "You can't leave! Where would you go?"

"I have the most perfect home far away from here. I'll stop by every now and then to check in on you, but this is best for both of us. We can hardly stand each other, but more than that, I'm becoming more unpopular in the village. It's safer for you to keep distance from me."

Her father couldn't argue with that even if he wanted to. He made a few more sad tries, but she saw the relief in his eyes when he shut the door behind her.

She was walking toward the woods when a shadow fell across her. She turned and saw a tall form cutting the sky.

"Baba Yaga," sneered a man with long hair. "I hear you've been selling your witchery to my wife."

"Possibly," she said, turning back to the woods. "I sell herbs to many people."

"This particular woman has red hair and laughs far too loudly."

"Sorry, I can't remember her. Now, if you'd excuse me—"

He grabbed her wrist and dragged her toward him. His body was hard and muscled but felt soft and flabby compared to her knight's steely armor. *How funny that I would think of him,* she mused, and even while she did so, she realized she was in some sort of shock. Her mind was trying to pull itself away from what was happening, trying to disregard the knife this strange man had pulled out of nowhere and was now holding to her throat.

"My wife came to you with child," he said, and the blade licked her neck with a forked tongue. "She took a packet from you, mixed it with water, and then had terrible, cutting pains. She started to bleed, and the baby was gone. Do you remember her now?"

Baba Yaga did, and a satisfied smile wreathed her face.

"Oh, yes. Yes, I do recall. She was a wife in your words only, forced to marry you against her will. And forced to conceive against her will. She wanted to free herself from your fetters, and I'm so delighted to hear how well it worked."

The man hissed, and Baba Yaga stomped on his foot. She pulled away from him, the blade parting the soft flesh of her neck as she did so. She dropped her basket, held her skirts high, and ran for the forest as quickly as she could. Blood ran down her throat, soaking into her blouse, and she closed her eyes at the sight of it. Far too much, so much more than she had thought, but it couldn't be helped now.

She heard a roar of rage from behind her. She picked up her pace until she couldn't possibly run any faster, but she tried. She heard his feet pounding on the ground, coming closer, and she bit out a few curses as she passed into the tree line.

Roses bloomed behind her, thorns catching at the man's clothes. Vines twined around his arms and legs, wresting the knife from him and throwing it aside. The trees filled in, blocking his path, and Baba Yaga thanked the woods. Blood dripped on the ground, pattering like rain, and the earth absorbed it ravenously. Flowers opened their mouths to catch it. Butterflies alit upon her throat and drank greedily.

Still, she ran, listening to the tortured screams behind her as the forest wrought its own justice. She didn't stop running until she reached her little haven. She closed the door behind her, threw herself on the bed, and fell into a deep sleep.

Something brushed her cheek. She pushed it away, but it came back insistently.

Wake up, she heard. It was a voice on the wind, breathing through reeds. *You need to wake up.*

Baba Yaga opened her eyes. A bunch of daisies bowed over her, dipping into her mouth. She spit them out, and a white petal caught in her teeth.

"What is it?" she asked.

Hurry.

She sat up and touched her swollen neck. She pulled away tendrils of ivy that had wrapped around her throat, covered in dry blood. She heard yelling from the forest entrance. Screams. She heard the shrieks as foliage caught fire, withered, and died.

"They're coming," she said aloud. "The townsfolk are coming."

The forest conveyed its messages to her. The people of the town saw a man eaten alive by the trees. They came with axes and scythes and fire. They were burning the place down. The animals were bolting from the danger.

Baba Yaga looked around her home. Many of her tinctures were for healing burns and soothing pox. But this one was flammable. That was toxic. She grabbed bottles and jars.

"I'll do what I can," she promised the blackberry bush peeking in her window. "That, I swear."

She heard metallic footsteps out her door. She twitched her finger, and the door swung open before her knight could even knock.

"I see you noticed the commotion," she said. She stuffed everything into a leather bag.

"Hard to miss. Are you okay? I heard you were attacked in the village."

He took her chin in his gloved hand and turned her face to the side as he appraised the wound. Something burned in his eyes, something exciting and dangerous and unholy.

"I should kill him," he said.

"The forest already did, and now it's paying the price. Will you help me?"

"Of course." He stepped back and put his hand on his sword. "The group is about two dozen strong. They're heading this way. There's a leader, but he doesn't seem to have any real fighting ability. They're running mostly on fear and rage."

"Perfect," Baba Yaga said. She put her hand on the knight's metal cheek. "Let's go."

They raced toward the cacophony of noise. Flowers shrieked. Foxes screamed. The men clawed and fought against a forest that rapidly closed in on them.

The knight ran forward with his sword drawn. Baba Yaga held out her hand, and a sharpened tree branch wormed its way into it. She tipped the end with a foul-smelling liquid from a glass bottle.

She held the poison-tipped spear to her mouth and sang to it. Brief, quick words. She closed one eye, aimed, and let the branch fly.

"Guide it," she called, and the wind abruptly changed direction. The spear sailed through the air and sank deep into a man's shoulder. He howled, and his flesh singed and curled away from the wound. Dark venom ran under his skin, eating him from the inside out. The branch blackened as he fell to the ground.

"One," she breathed.

The knight lopped the head off a bald man and then spun around, running his sword through a second person.

"Two. Three," Baba Yaga counted.

They fought. They struggled. The woodland animals threw themselves at the human invaders, tearing at their soft spots.

Eyes and throats and the tender red parts.

"Four. Five."

But they kept coming, repeatedly, and Baba Yaga ran out of her poisons. The berry branches dripped red juice on the torn earth, and worms squirmed in agony.

"There are too many," the knight said. His armor had been pierced in several areas, and his breathing was ragged. "The entire town is turning out. You have to get out of here."

"But I need to save the forest. It's done so much for me."

The knight grabbed her wrist and forced her to look in his eyes. Torch flame danced in them.

"The forest will grow back. It always does, and you're here to help it. But you need to go now."

"Come with me."

His eyes went dark, like the drowning pools. Baba Yaga hated what she saw there, the ghosts that swam in them.

"I can't. But I can protect you. I'll catch up when I can."

He pushed her toward the house, then. She took a faltering step.

"My love," he called. He turned away and raised his sword. "Promise me that you won't look back no matter what you hear."

She didn't say a word but staggered toward home.

The woods were dying. Vegetation writhed on the ground, and birds fell from the trees. The ground vomited up slugs and beetles. Baba Yaga stopped, her fists clenched.

"I can't abandon him, or you," she said and ran her hand down a decaying vine. "I don't know what to do, but I'll do something."

She turned back, stepping over the boiling mud and weeping birches. She shielded her eyes against the flames, the heat almost too much to bear. She squinted tears out of her scorched eyes and tried to find her knight.

He was backed against a tall oak, leaning heavily on his sword. A ring of villagers surrounded him.

"Knight!" she shouted, but her voice was lost in the melee. She cast around, looking for a weapon when the knight raised his head. He dropped his sword. Baba Yaga opened her mouth to scream when the knight grabbed his helmet with both hands and yanked it from his head.

His eyes, they were flames. His skull, it was fire. Baba Yaga covered her mouth with her hand. Her love showed his face of bone, a grinning skull depleted of flesh, and he was resplendent with fire. It burned hotter than anything she had ever seen.

The townspeople screamed and burst into flame. They beat the sparks out of their clothing and wiped sulfur from their eyes. They charred and turned into ash. The knight surveyed the land around him and put his helmet back on. His eyes met Baba Yaga's, and he froze.

"My love," she called, but her voice was lost in the wind. He turned, shoulders bowed, and walked away.

She waited. She waited. She stayed in that darling little house made of shining, polished wood and handcrafted with love. She took the skulls of the violent villagers, cursed them with eternal flame, and used them for lamps outside of her gate. She grew older. Her hair turned white. Her back bent and fingers gnarled, but her eyes were still sharp and her mind infinitely clever. But her knight did not return.

"I want to tell him that it doesn't matter," she told the birds of the forest. "He needs to know that he is the only man I've ever wanted."

She confided these words to the brook and the rain. Everyone knows water loves to gossip and share its stories. If she repeated it to the morning dew and the ponds, surely it would make it to him. Surely, he would understand. Baba Yaga would always be his, just as he was always hers. When two wild things are meant to be, they simply are. That's the way of it.

She grew stronger in her magic, and more learned in her

practice. She cast a spell on herself so she was wizened and old but never died. After searching the forest from top to bottom from the ending of winter to the beginning of it again, over and over for many years, she knew it was time.

She took a chicken from her carefully tended flock. She laid in on her lap, stroked its feathers, and then quickly broke its neck. She remembered the black knight watching her quietly when she did the same thing to the deer so many decades before.

"Thank you, my friend," she said. "You've done well."

The chicken's meat went into the pot. Its entrails were used for divining. She took its strong legs with its tough spurs and hung them on the outside of the door by the magic symbol she had painted there so long ago.

Spells. Incantations. Manifestations. Blood, urine, and tears. The legs quivered, twitched, and grew. They grew longer than a corn stalk and as tall and sturdy as the trees themselves. The house gathered the legs underneath it, and it stood.

"Find him," she ordered, and the house lurched off into the woods.

It climbed mountains. It crossed seas, for wooden houses can float, and chicken legs can kick. It passed through the world many times until there was only one place left.

The house lumbered until it found a man in black armor. He leaned against his dark horse and watched the strange house lower itself down to the ground.

Baba Yaga appeared in the door.

"My love," she said. "You should have come."

That was it. No more rebuke, no more tears. Simply "You should have come," and the knight knew from the shining determination in her burnished gray eyes that she meant it.

"You saw me without my mask," he said. "Aren't you afraid?"

"Are you stupid?" she replied.

An immortal man and an immortal woman, living a life

of magic and caution. Although you can't kill the witch, she can be burned and her body scattered before it puts itself back together. She must be careful. Her house shrewdly keeps watch using its burning windows for eyes. It moves about, hither and yon, keeping Baba Yaga out of reach of attackers. And the daily patrols take special care. Every morning a rider on a white horse greets the dawn. At noon a red rider gallops by on a red horse, heralding the sun. At the end of the day, the black rider appears on his dark horse, guarding his beloved and heralding the night.

ALL BITTERNESS BURNED AWAY

BY JILL BAGUCHINSKY

M y cottage stalks on little cat feet, spiriting me through the forest, never disturbing the pine-needle carpet. We slip past denizens of the wood, skirting by bears and deer and taut, nervous rabbits without drawing a whisper of attention. We creep like a pair of impossible ghosts, as silent as a shadow, as feral as blood.

We are lethal, but only to those whose actions deserve our keen attention.

The woodcutter chooses the first truly cold morning of winter to lead his two children into the forest. The wind bites at ruddy cheeks until the dawning sun rises enough to slink through the treetops and dapple the wanderers with pinpoints of meager warmth. On and on, they walk past tree after tree that all look the same until they reach the edge of a clearing. Here the woodcutter puts his children to work gathering fat gray mushrooms. He must go now and chop firewood, he says, but he will return soon, and then they'll all go home, where their stepmother will cook them a fine mushroom stew for dinner. Eyes wide, the children watch him trudge away into the forest's heart.

I watch, too. I see the woodcutter pause, hesitate, glance back, and I almost think he'll change his mind. Then he goes on, the bitterness in his heart so strong and rotten that I can smell it, an acrid musk that permeates the forest like smoke.

The hours pass. The sun arcs across the sky. The air warms, then cools. The children shiver, bellies hollow with a hunger that mushrooms will never satisfy.

This is the story I tell myself—the woodcutter will not

return for them. He will go home alone, just as his new wife undoubtedly demanded, and they will drink and carry on and laugh about no longer having extra mouths to feed. Evening will fall, and the dapple-sun will sink into nothing, and the children will freeze with their pockets full of mushrooms.

That is the way of things sometimes, but it is not the way of things today. Today I am watching.

I stoke the fire in my hearth and toss all manner of delight into the flames—cinnamon and ginger and clove—until the smoke from the chimney smells like a spice cake. The shivering children venture closer, wondering how they didn't notice the odd little cottage on cat feet sooner, because really, how does one miss such a sight?

I invite them in. They know better than to accept—they've heard tales of chicken-legged huts and gingerbread houses—but the smell of spice cake and the warmth of my hearth drown out the stories of those who live in the forest. Those are merely fables, the children reason.

Of course, most fables are anchored in fact.

I usher the children inside, explaining that I will soon be baking cookies—the most wonderful, delicious gingerbread cookies they've ever tasted, but only if they will help me with the final ingredient. Of course, they'll help, especially after I promise them a share of the cookies in return. They are eager, willing. They understand what I ask of them.

They know they were left to die.

On its little cat feet, my cottage carries us through the forest and into a clearing, where the woodcutter's house sits with firelight winking in the windows and a tendril of smoke wafting from the chimney. Now is when I need the children's help. I pour sugar into my enormous cooking pot and set them to work, stirring it as it slowly melts into caramel. "Keep stirring, or it will scorch," I tell them, "and take care, for the caramel is impossibly hot. It will cling to any flesh it touches, burning down to the bone and more."

While the children stir, I go to meet the woodcutter and his new wife. I knock on the door of their fine little home and wait, quiet rage bubbling bile-sharp and caramel-hot in my throat. The woodcutter answers and stares over my shoulder, boggling at the cottage on cat feet, and at the busy children visible through its window.

I ask him if he forgot anything in the forest.

He stammers. Babbles. Regret burbles in his half-formed words, but I've no patience for regret, not now. I take the scruff of his coat as though he were a disobedient kitten, and I march him into my cottage. He tries to pull away.

He doesn't expect such strength from a woman.

"Keep stirring!" I tell the eager children, and I shove their father into the cooking pot. He thrashes and kicks, covered in caramel, sticky and screaming and boiling alive.

The children—*my* children—stir until there's nothing left of him.

Now for the stepmother—but the children catch my hands before I can storm back to the woodcutter's house. They gesture for me to wait and venture forth with a gentleness that confuses me.

The woman they return with is young, surely too young to be the woodcutter's wife. She's no more than a girl herself, really, with skin stretched hunger-tight over jutting bones. Her deep-set eyes grow haunted as she speaks, and she keeps her voice at a hush as if she's afraid to be louder than that. Her father promised her to the widowed woodcutter, she says, just gave her away and celebrated having one less mouth to feed. Now she cooks while not having enough to eat herself, and she cleans the fine little home while her husband criticizes the result, no matter how hard she scrubs.

I notice bruises on her exposed skin, and I hear the echo

of many more in the quiet caution of her tone. The children—
my children—cling to her skirts. They love her. She took many
of those bruises for them. She begged the woodcutter not to
abandon them—extra mouths to feed, he said—and now she
begs me not to harm them. She's heard the fables of chicken-
legged huts and gingerbread houses, too. I see her steel herself to
fight, to defend.

I told myself the wrong story, then. There is no fairy tale, and
there is no wicked stepmother. But I can still end it the right way.

After calming the girl and offering her a reassuring seat
by the fire, I bake my gingerbread. I fill each cookie with sticky
caramel that carries delightful hints of fat and smoke and char, all
bitterness burned away. My children—all three of *my* children—
gobble them by the stack, dunking them into cups of tea, and as
night falls outside my cottage, a quiet security blossoms within,
here in the glow of my hearth. We sit up laughing and chatting
until well past bedtime, none of us mourning the woodcutter for
even a moment.

Then I tell my two younger children to empty their pockets,
and they heap piles of fat gray mushrooms onto the table. My
eldest slips back to the woodcutter's house one last time and
returns with stockpiles she was never allowed enough of—dried
meats, hard cheeses, jugs of wine that the woodcutter kept for
himself. Tomorrow, I promise, I will cook the most wonderful
meat-and-mushroom stew, with plenty for all of us. For now,
though, it is time for bed.

My cottage purrs, rocking gently on its little cat feet,
lulling my children to sleep like drowsy kittens. They dream
sweet dreams of cookies and caramel. For as long as they care to,
they will stay safe and happy in my cottage, learning the way of
things—as silent as a shadow, as feral as blood.

Like me.

A TRAIL OF FEATHERS, A TRAIL OF BLOOD

BY STEPHANIE M. WYTOVICH

Blair walked barefoot and desperate through the forest with a prayer on her lips and a piece of black birch under her tongue. Thorns erupted from the scattered holes in her earlobes while braided vines climbed up her wrists and arms like coiled snakes. Everything about her appearance carried an air of wildness about it. She was a warning, a cautionary tale, her dress crawling behind her like a besom collecting dirt and stains as it ripped and tore on shattered rocks and acorns.

A coupling of bats hung before her in the trees ahead, their eyes locked against hers as she dragged herself on. That night, the woods remained quiet against the winter's sky—a dark palette of moss and charcoal—the moon as full as her swollen belly that kicked and rippled with child.

Blair stopped to catch her breath, the pressure in her pelvis a building fire that sent shots of lightning through her hips and legs.

"Easy little one," she said, the scent of spoiled milk strong against her chest.

Her heart beat like a hummingbird's, her anxiety spiking as she searched through shadow and silhouette, beneath dreamscape and dampness, but the signs weren't there. No salt, no cracked eggshells in the dirt. She looked behind trees, chanted in open meadows, dared to dance near mushroom rings, but no matter what words she whispered or what honey she spun, she couldn't find the witch.

Baba. You promised ...

Blair removed a bottle of vodka from the leather bag across her chest. She took a long pull and filled her mouth until the booze seeped out the sides. She dropped to her knees—the ground was hard, cold, and unforgiving—and presented her throat to the stars. An owl screeched in the distance. A scattering of tiny legs stampeded across her back. She spit the offering into the air, a gesture of bite and comfort, warmth and ease.

"Help me, Baba. Find me, find me now. I leave this offering in honor of you." Blair's voice a cracked mug, a scratched piece of glass.

She waited a few minutes, closed her eyes, and tried to visualize the woman's hooked nose, smell the scent of stewed turnips and parsley, but there was nothing. She felt like a lost doe, a wolf separated from her pack. Baba was the closest thing she'd had to a mother growing up, and yet now as she was about to embark on the journey herself, she no longer felt the witch's guidance or pull, could hardly hear her voice or make out the grate of her mortar against the earth.

Now, there was only absence, silence.

An orphaning.

A twig cracked under Blair's weight as a sliver of wood wedged itself beneath the skin of her foot as she tried to stand.

The child pushed against her ribcage in frustration. She was running out of room, each movement a bruise, the sharp end of a knife. Blair winced through a locked jaw.

"I'm doing my best." Tears welled in her eyes. "I'm trying."

Despite the horror stories she grew up with, all those red flags and warnings about disappearances and flesh-eating crones, the woods never felt haunted to her, let alone avoidable. She'd always been drawn to the scent of pine needles and sap, to the taste of honeysuckle and wild onion, and as a child, Blair used to sneak away into the dark and spend hours counting dew drops on spider webs and collecting dead butterflies to sew into her pillow. Her father never questioned her. In fact, she doubted he ever knew she'd been gone since he was always traveling between villages or to the bottom of a jar of moonshine, forever engaged in a race to escape poverty and his wife's untimely death.

But Blair chose to grieve a different way. She cried next to creeks and streams, swam with tadpoles, floated alongside algae in the morning's light. She'd draw circles around herself in the mud, stuff her mouth full of violets, make flower crowns out of thistle and dandelions. The forest embraced her, sheltered her, and she still remembered the first time she found a heel of bread and a bowl of beans next to the tree she carved her initials in. It waited there for her—still hot—under a lid of leaves like someone was watching out for her, eager to make her acquaintance.

For weeks, she returned to the tree when she could, and like clockwork, a warm meal and a splash of hot tea or honey water would be waiting for her. One time during the summer, shortly after her first bleed, Blair arrived and found a plate of chicken beaks leaning against the tree. A red-stained note peeked out from underneath a bed of dirt: *When you're ready.*

It wasn't hard to find Baba then, her house an untamed energy Blair felt deep in her bones. She followed a trail of fallen feathers to a crooked hut that sat atop a pair of wobbly chicken legs. From the outside, it appeared small, a one-room hovel that looked tattered from ages of use and bad weather. Broken shutters hung haphazardly from fogged windows, while the roof seemed to molt as it inhaled and exhaled these big heavy gasps like it was alive.

Blair remembered the first time she touched the house's legs. The feathery tops were soft, pillow-like, and they rubbed against her like an old friend. The bottoms, though, they were sturdy, strong, their footprint a sigil, a moving protection spell. They kneeled to her, eager to come to her level as she nuzzled her cheek against its bones, its warmth a comfort even in the hot summer's sun. There was laughter and smiling at that moment—maybe even the beginning of an unlikely friendship—but her curiosity pushed her toward the front door, a splintered, uneven shape of wood that hung off its hinges and was covered in the names of what she would learn to be countless missing children.

She didn't even have to knock.

"You're here," Baba said.

Blair nodded as a lump formed in her throat. "I am."

The woman before her stood with a slight hunch. She wore a mess of faded fabrics loose on her misshapen body, her face weathered in a mess of wrinkles and age. Gray hair hung in somewhat matted strings down to her shoulders, and if she looked closely, Blair noticed an assortment of beads, bones, and what appeared to be small nests hidden amongst the old woman's dirty, dusty locks.

"Well, don't just stand there. Dinner isn't going to cook itself, and I have to head into the forest for supplies. Do you know how to make a mushroom tart?"

Blair shook her head.

"How about a lentil stew? No? Well, you'll have much to learn before the next solstice," Baba said as she handed her a broom. "Just clean the place up then, and I'll teach you the recipes when I get back."

"But how will I know where—"

"You'll find a way to make it work. Or else you won't, and then we'll have a different kind of conversation when I get back," Baba said.

Blair spent the next few hours scrubbing floors, doing dishes, and dusting spiderwebs out of the corners of rooms. She collected the old woman's laundry and took it outside to wash in a nearby creek, and when the witch came home before nightfall, a fire roared in the living room next to a pot of freshly brewed peppermint tea.

The witch nodded and smiled. "You've been busy," she said. "I have," Blair said.

Baba dumped a pile of parsnips and mushrooms on the table and pulled a bunch of green onions from her back pocket. "Can you prep these while I rest a bit?"

"Sure."

Baba limped to the armchair and draped her shawl over a pile of books that acted as an end table. She was asleep in her chair before Blair had even picked up the knife.

A contraction ripped through Blair's abdomen like a feral beast. Her body tightened, her calves clenched, her toes curled. Thirty seconds. A minute. Two minutes passed. She bent forward in agony, her breath choppy and uneven as one hand pushed against her back, eager for any type of relief.

"Breathe, just breathe," she said between the tears pouring down her face.

A wave of calm washed over her as the pain subsided, but before she could relax, she felt the squeeze of another contraction start to build. Her jaw stiffened. She bit her tongue by accident.

Blood filled her mouth.

Around her, the forest watched. It was no stranger to birth and death, a constant voyeur of cycles and the forgotten bodies of women. The moon acted as a spotlight on her person as a darkness enfolded around her, thick and potent.

It had been exactly thirteen years, six days, and twelve hours since she was tested in that kitchen. Blair had taken to the witch like a child to its mother, and Baba took her on as an apprentice, perhaps seeing something of herself in the young girl—a violent sparkle in her left eye, a cunning smile, a bit of quick wit. Together, the two of them turned poison into healing salves and harvested garlic under the supervision of the new moon. Blair learned how to cast bones and read tea leaves, and when she went into the forest to commune with the trees, she carried a torch made from mullein, a hag taper made by a curious maiden desperate for protection against those who sent her into the forest in the first place.

In hindsight, she was foolish to think she could return, to think she could have a life outside of solitude and seclusion, something to sustain her besides lavender tea and the bond between exiled women. Nevertheless, the hard truth remained— when you turn your back on what society thinks is best for you, there are consequences.

Sometimes they're wrapped in silence and the musk of drunk men.

Other times, they're delivered in blood by jealous wives, by suspicious friends.

In Blair's case, it was a bit of both, and it wasn't long before the world she used to know, the world she convinced herself wasn't *that* bad, turned on her, afraid of who and what she had become in her absence.

A witch.

A devil.

A snake.

They were happy to see her at first, convinced that after all these years, she had been eaten by the creatures of the wood. Her father embraced her; her old friends invited her to dinner at their new homes with their new families. She generously accepted their hospitality and kindness, but she took her time acclimating, struggling as she learned how to tame the dark goddess within. She wore stockings and sensible shoes instead of running barefoot through the meadows, and when night fell, she stayed indoors despite the forever pull of her body to the small lake she used to bathe in. Baba told her returning would be a mistake, that she was changed and that a butterfly should never revert to its chrysalis, but Blair had insisted, the longing in her heart too loud to ignore.

"I don't give second chances," Baba had said. "If you leave, you won't be welcomed back. Not by me, and not by the forest."

Blair had pleaded with her, begged her to reconsider.

She would not.

But like all witches, she offered a loophole, a way back to the magic.

Sacrifice.

It all happened so fast—the betrayal, the rumors—but at the same time, time itself stood still, each second crawling through the mud like the worms she used to collect after a hard rain. Blair discovered that ever since she accepted the witch's invitation, the idea of becoming small, of making herself quiet or obedient didn't sit well with her, and bit by bit, her old habits and comforts started to leak back into her daily routines.

Her neighbors watched from a distance as she brewed tea in the early morning hours, took milk baths when the shroud of the moon covered them in a deep night. They whispered about how she cooked her meals without recipes, how she mumbled spells under her breath and counted the stirs as she mixed the ingredients together. When her father got sick, they found a dead blackbird on her porch, and when she got pregnant, the father of her child denied her. Piece by piece, the stories grew, and like fire, their fear and anxiety about the things they couldn't understand or didn't want to take responsibility for started to spread like a disease throughout the village.

It was cold the night she fled. Her wrists were raw, bruised, and no matter how many times she'd washed her hair, the scent of smoke clung to her scalp, perfumed itself into her skin. She'd sensed their rage earlier in the day—it tasted like sheet lighting and stinging nettle—but she wasn't fast enough to outrun its echoes, her body stiff as they overcame her in the garden and dragged her to the village square.

"Burn her," they shouted, their voices harsh against the fire's smoke.

The father of her child let go of her hand and stepped away, but not before he spat in her face as an act of well-earned shame. He wiped the sweat from his brow and reached into his pocket for his pipe. His nostrils flared as desperation flooded his eyes, but then he lit the match and said, "I saw Blair Leyman dancing in the woods with the devil. She was his maiden, and together they made the beast with two backs."

A collective gasp spread through the crowd.

"And I saw her drinking blood from the teats of goats," Sara Fisher said. "Her stomach be filled with the crimson milk!"

Madeline Turner, the now eighty-one-year-old woman who'd lived next door to Blair as a child, stepped forth from the crowd and approached the poor girl. She reached out her hand, but when Blair went to take it, the old woman slapped her hard across the face. "Whore!"

Tears trickled down Blair's cheeks, but before she could beg and plead, a rock struck the side of her face, and her sight went blurry before it went black.

When Blair came to, she was curled in a ball on the forest floor, hugging her stomach and shaking off the early morning whispers. Blood traced the outline of her dress while the beading of clots and hemorrhages decorated her apron and shawl.

What happened?

Images of antlers and bear claws flashed through her mind. She heard the imprint of growls in the earth, the savagery of screams on the wind. She rubbed her eyes and pushed herself to her knees as she worked to find her balance.

Blair poked her stomach here and there, but nothing moved.

"Come on," she whispered. "You're safe now. You're strong. Speak to me, little one."

She slid her hands under her belly and lightly bounced the child.

A slight vibration, a subtle kick, reached against her in response.

"Thank goddess," Blair said. She exhaled what felt like a century's worth of fear as some of the pressure in her chest began to subside. "We still have much to do, you and I."

An orchestra of crickets sang around her as she got her footing, her blood trail thin but steady as she moved. *I'm making it too easy to be tracked*, she thought. Then again, it wasn't like she was hiding. In fact, she didn't know what she was doing, but she knew she needed to find Baba and that she needed to find her fast if she wanted to save the child.

Blair picked up a large branch and ripped off the leaves and twigs until it was mostly smooth. She leaned into it and let it bear her weight as she hobbled deeper into the woods. The forest welcomed her with a crown of snowflakes as she bathed in the icy whiteness of the trees, but visions of bent limbs and tortured eyes flashed through her head, the people of her village collapsed, their fallen bodies tracing a circle around what would have been a makeshift hearth.

Blair wanted to feel something, something like sadness or regret, but she couldn't, didn't.

Whatever happened to them after that first stone was cast, it didn't concern her, and if it did, she wouldn't apologize for defending herself. After all, a woman can't be blamed for doing what's necessary to protect her child, and after years of living in the wilderness, of worshiping the Horned One, there was no telling what an animal would do when it was backed into a corner, and if Baba taught her anything, it was that when push came to shove, she was a woman made of teeth.

But that was weeks ago, long and hard days with nothing but stiff hands and sore backs.

She'd looked everywhere, searched far and wide for murmurs of witchcraft or the imprint of a chicken's foot in the mud, but as she sat there in that circle with vodka on her lips and a curse on her tongue, a pool of water rushed from between her legs.

Blair smiled.

She no longer needed to find Baba anymore.

No.

Baba would find her.

It happened fast, much faster than she expected it to.

Blair dug her nails into the dirt and screamed. Something was wrong. Her contractions were every twenty to thirty seconds now, and her heartbeat pounded like a primal drum.

"You can do this," she said to herself. "Your body was made for this."

But what she really meant was *she's tearing me apart*.

Night had embraced her with moon and stars, with the fluorescent eyes of creatures large and small. She'd taken off her clothes and used them as bedding, as padding for her back and knees. Around her, sigils of protection and comfort were scratched into the earth, her blood and sweat an offering to the woods in exchange for safety.

"Please, please," she said.

Blair panted on all fours, her moans attracting the attention of owls and deer, rabbits and foxes. She dipped her hips and folded in on herself, carefully moving her body back and forth as she rode the ebb and flow of the pain.

In the distance, something moved in the darkness. A

silhouette. A shadow.

"You came back," it said.

Blair tried to focus, but agony spread through her thighs and crept up her pelvis as her body seemed to light itself on fire.

"Oh God," Blair said. "I can't, I can't do this. I'll die. I'm going to die."

A cackle spread through the trees.

"You won't die. Not in these woods," it said.

Blair began to sob. She dared to hope, but she had to know. "Baba?"

The shadow moved closer and walked around her as it spilled salt and dried rosemary in a circle. Blair closed her eyes and concentrated. She heard the familiar cracks of the old woman's bones, smelled the faint stench of cabbage in the air.

"Baba, you came back."

"No child, you did," the witch said. "And with no time to waste by the look of it."

Another contraction ripped through her, the pressure building in her stomach a bowl of lead, a concrete ball. Blair eased her back to the earth and arched her shoulders in pain.

Baba set down a worn leather bag and crouched in front of her, her hands on Blair's knees. "You're nearly there, child. She's ready and strong. When you're ready, take a deep breath and push."

Blair screamed until her throat went dry, her lungs emptied and exhausted as they ached for air. Sweat dripped off her eyelids. Her nails dug crescent-moon indents into her palms. Spit dribbled down her chin.

A vision exploded before her. A door. Wooden, unhinged. Blair pushed it open, and the smell of freshly baked bread and apricot jam curled around her. She felt safe, comforted, but when she tried to walk inside the house, a house she knew she knew, a house that was familiar to her but that she couldn't place, something stopped her from entering.

A husky voice laughed in the background, a hyena, a crow, its voice manic, joyous, like it knew something she didn't.

"I can see her head," Baba yelled.

The house faded as she slipped in and out of the fever dream, and in its place was the witch's face, her eyes wide and feral, her hands tinged black with blood.

"Push, child! Harder now. One more time."

Pressure swelled within her, a hurricane, a riptide. Blair pushed and cried and tore, her womb an opened letter, her blood the juice of a rotted pomegranate. Blair cursed as her body became a portal, a doorway, the inferno between her legs raging and subsiding as the babe's first cry ran against the wind.

Blair collapsed against her poor man's bed, her body slack and empty against the night.

"Eadie?" she said. "My sweet girl …"

In a matter of minutes, everything about her body felt foreign, useless, her stomach deflated, her womb a barren wasteland. She became personified absence, an erasure, her name a disappearance, a fading memory. In its place grew the scent of violets, the sound of footsteps and first smiles, the taste of mother's milk.

"Oh God. Thank you, thank you. Can I see her?" Blair asked as she propped herself up on one arm and reached forward.

Silence.

"Baba? Baba, can I hold her, please?" she asked again, this time with a hint of panic on her lips.

Still no response.

Blair reached in front of her, eager for the warmth of her daughter, for the solace of the witch's hand, but instead, she was met with the creeping onset of loneliness, the only thing before her a trail of white-gray feathers similar to the one she first followed as a child.

The world pulsed around her, its heartbeat loud and constant against the headache forming behind her eye. She knew she couldn't walk, her body spent and leaking. The blood loss alone made her nauseous and dizzy, but in the distance, a loud cry pierced the sky, and a guilt-soaked wrath rose within her.

I'm coming, little one. Hold tight.

Blair threw herself forward and began to drag herself across the forest floor. Pain shot through her lower abdomen as blood continued to pool beneath her. The more she moved, the more the ground seemed to shift and quake, lengthen and split, and she worried that hands were pulling her down, pulling her between the cracks and the weeds, desperate to bury the body that had walked out on it all those years ago.

"Baba? Baba Yaga?" Blair said between pants. "I know you can hear me. Where is my child? Where is Eadie?" She stopped to try to catch her breath, but the witch remained silent.

Her house, however, did not.

A short distance away stood a small shack held up by chicken's feet and magic. Smoke bellowed from the chimney as the smell of roasted pork and jelly danced out from cracked but open windows.

Blair pushed herself to her knees and crawled to the beast's lower half. She placed her hands against the scales of its foot. Its three toes curled and dug into the grass.

"Do you remember me?" she asked.

The legs responded by relaxing as they brought the front door down to her level for easier access.

"Thank you, old friend," Blair said as she stroked the right leg's feathers.

She hauled herself up the stairs and pressed her hand against the door.

A sense of unease spread through her chest as she traced the countless names etched into the wood.

Lilith. Rose. Beatrice. Daphne. Flora. Hazel. Greta. Minnie.

Pearl. Selma.

An endless list of lost girls.

Blair reached for the doorknob but stopped dead as her fingers brushed against a fresh carving, the wood still raw, splintered.

Eadie.

In a panic, Blair unraveled. "No, no!" she cried. "You can't have her, Baba. She's mine!"

The whistle of a tea kettle slipped beneath the door.

"Baba, please," she begged. "Please. She's innocent in all of this. Take me, take me instead."

"Tsk, tsk, tsk," Baba said, her short, hunched body now standing behind her. "Surely, you're not going back on your word, child. I thought I taught you better than that."

"My word? I would never promise—"

A wickedness spread across the old woman's face as she broke out in a smile, her teeth rotten, some replaced by fish hooks and arrowheads. "You wanted to return to the woods, yes? To feel the alchemy on your skin, the magic on your tongue. That requires sacrifice."

"But the village. My neighbors—"

"That wasn't a sacrifice. That was self-defense, protection. No, sacrifice is something that hurts, something that causes an unbearable weight we're forced to carry."

Shock spread through Blair's body. "No, Baba. Please, I beg of you."

"You know more than anyone she'll be in good hands," Baba said. "That is, well, until she's not."

Blair collapsed, the blood loss too much, her guilt a poison running through her veins.

The old woman cackled as she stepped into her mortar, broom in hand.

Blair blinked tears from her eyes, her gaze locked on the

witch, her mother, her friend.

"I'd hoped you would stay for dinner, but I fear you won't have the stomach for it," Baba said.

A cry shook through the bones of the house, and Blair curled beside the door, naked and numb, horrified at what she'd done, at all that was about to happen.

Those children weren't missing. She knew exactly where they were.

Her stomach growled.

"Enjoy the forest again, child. I think you'll find it much changed since you've been here last."

Blair closed her eyes and shook as a feather fell from above and landed on her cheek.

Heartsick and ashamed, the witch was right, and Blair couldn't deny what she knew to be true.

She was hungry, ravenous.

And tonight, she'd have no choice but to eat.

BABA YAGA LEARNS TO SHAVE, GETS HER PERIOD, THEN GROWS INTO HER OWN

BY JESS HAGEMANN

"Like this," the mother said, showing her daughter how to grip the razor and run its double blades up her scaly yellow legs. The girl hardly had enough hair to warrant shaving. I wish I could have told her she didn't need to—that even if she had the legs of a bear and not a chicken, she was perfect the way she was.

"Like this," the mother said, describing to her daughter how to insert the plastic applicator of a tampon. The girl tried standing with one foot on the toilet, tried lying on her back on the floor, but she was tired and stressed and she couldn't get the angle right. I wish I could have told her that menstruation is a gift, a sign of a healthy body—that even if she didn't want children, her blood was a part of her and didn't need to be hidden or sanitized out of shame.

"Like this," the mother said, demonstrating for her daughter the best way to vacuum the carpet and polish the crystal. Although the girl had been born in the city, she dreamed of a cottage, remote and sweet, that ran around on legs like hers. I wish I could have told her that control over one's environment takes many shapes—some of them resembling OCD, and some more fluid, gracious, magical, even.

"Like this," the mother said, stirring the mulled wine now scenting the air from the stove. The girl attempted to string garlands of pine and winter berries, but they always seemed to change halfway through the hanging into ropes of human skulls. I wish I could have told her that more important than decorating for the holidays is creating a space that feels like home.

"Like this," the mother said, rocking the girl's younger brother, tightly swaddled, to sleep. The girl was afraid of dropping him, of suffocating him, of what might happen if he grew into a man and suffocated her. I wish I could have told her that society needs women to cull children, too—doctors and hedge witches who know how to make a body not carry another body anymore.

"Like this," the mother said, pointing out the "civilized" cities in Europe that she expected her daughter to visit—Paris, Florence, London. The girl had wilder tastes, not for castles but casitas, towns where people danced in the streets because they knew life was short and ended in death. I wish I could have told her the world was her oyster, its pearl ready and hers for the taking.

"Like this," the mother said, applying another shade of pale pink nail polish. When the girl took the file to her own nails, though, they came out pointy, not round and smooth and pretty. I wish I could have told her that all of us, at times, need claws. And teeth. Sometimes we need teeth.

"Like this," the mother said, tipping the driver she paid to take them shopping downtown. The girl felt confined in cars, all that rubber and plastic and steel, and thought how much nicer it would be to let the wind sing through her hair as she flew among the stars. I wish I could have told her that consumerism isn't everything—we don't need more and more non-utilitarian baubles when so much depends upon a sturdy mortar and pestle beside a coop of white chickens.

"Like this," the mother said, lacquering every strand of honey-dyed hair in a tight chignon. The girl would have grown ratty Rapunzel hair down to the ground if only to wrap herself up in it at night. I wish I could have told her happiness comes from within—not from the prince who wants to rescue her, and certainly not from the one who would lock her in a tower.

"Like this," the mother said, sticking her button nose into the air, extending one pinky as she tipped the contents of a teapot. The girl's long nose reached up to the ceiling, improbable to hide, impossible to ignore. I wish I could have told her that wolves have long snouts, too—the better for smelling and, if need be, snarling.

"Like this," the mother said, throwing her shoulders back, standing proud. The girl was bone-skinny. In later years, her shoulders curled around her drooping breasts. I wish I could have told her that the body is a tool, is a sanctuary, is not an apology.

But I could not tell the girl these things, and so she nicked the hell out of her scaly yellow legs and plastered them in clay. She isolated herself on her period and moaned as the cramps held her hostage in bed. She ran away to the woods when she was older, where she lived by her lonesome in the cottage she'd always dreamed of, which she decorated with the skulls of children and all the men she tricked so they could not suffocate her. She went to Paris, but as Death's consort. (He'd promised her all the souls she could eat.) She grew claws and teeth of iron and became ferocious, terrifying, a woman twisted in on herself who snapped and snarled. At least she flew among the stars, the wind singing through her Rapunzel hair, but her body was never a tool, always a weapon. The storms she left in her wake, the souls she condemned, these were the products of her mortared womb, auto-generated by her pestle phallus—a pestle I borrow to write her story in the dirt. The tale of Baba Yaga, perfect the way she was.

FAIR TRADE

BY JACQUELINE WEST

It was still too light for summoning ghosts, and Marina had forgotten her tarot cards, so we went into the woods instead.

Late summer. Sticky heat. Blossoming weeds clustered with drunken bees. We were a little drunk, too; Alex had stolen a bottle of brandy from somewhere, and Marina had smuggled some white wine out of her parents' cellar. The air felt like the alcohol, gold and thick and dizzying, even under the trees.

At first, we weren't going anywhere in particular. We sat on a mossy log for a while, passing the warm wine around, until Alex had the idea. "We should do the wreath thing! You know, where we each make a flower crown, put it in the stream, and it tells our futures!"

And, of course, everyone said yes.

I'm not sure where the wreath game began. I'm not sure anyone's sure. It's just something we've always done in our part of the north woods, but without taking it too seriously—just like we all say that burned bread means bad luck, we all call dusk "Roadkill Hour," and we all know about the witch who lives in the woods just off Beggar's Hill Road.

So we made wreaths. Marina's was mostly dandelions. Alex's had ferns and wild phlox. Sasha and I both used columbines and violets. I didn't realize that we'd match until we all came back together, stems half-braided and fists full of flowers. I wasn't planning to imitate her. I'd never have admitted it, anyway, that I wanted to be just like Sasha.

Even though, of course, I did.

Everyone did.

"We're twins!" Sasha laughed at me as we all placed our wreaths on our heads.

We were nothing like twins.

Sasha was at least three inches shorter than me, with tiny hands and feet, red-brown hair, and such dark eyelashes it looked like she'd been born with makeup on. She was so perfect, it would have been hard not to hate her. Except that Sasha was also kind.

Another way we weren't really twins.

"Okay, remember," Marina said as we reached the creek, "if your wreath floats away, you'll find the one you love. If your wreath gets caught on something, you *won't*. And if your wreath sinks, you're going to die soon."

"It's not totally fair," Alex said, swigging from the brandy bottle. "Since Sasha already *has* the one she wants."

She and Marina nudged Sasha, laughing.

Leo. The most beautiful boy. The only one I'd ever seen who could stand next to Sasha and not seem invisible. The one whose face I carried around in my own invisible heart.

"This isn't about *fair*," I spoke up, trying to keep my own smile on. "It's about *fate*. And what kind of flowers float best. Let's go."

We all tugged off our crowns and tossed them onto the band of rippling water. Marina's dandelions went floating off around a bend, out of sight. Alex's wreath snagged on a fallen log several yards away. "Dammit!" she yelled, laughing.

And mine sank.

I knew it was mine. I had been tracking it from the second it left my hand, and I wasn't drunk enough for my eyes to blur.

But it was close to Sasha's. It looked just like Sasha's.

And suddenly, I couldn't let this be one more thing that she won, and I lost.

"Oh my god, Sasha," I said. "Your wreath went down."

"What?" Sasha turned toward me. I watched the sympathy in her eyes change to puzzlement. "Hanna, that was yours."

"No, mine was the one in front. It had more violets. That was yours."

Sasha gazed back at me.

She knew the truth. Or I think she knew. But Sasha never fought for anything. She never had to.

Her eyes left mine, and I felt something release me, something as thin and strong as a spider's thread. She shrugged, turning toward the other two, laughing. "I guess I'm dying!"

Marina and Alex gasped and argued at first. Then Alex started helping her imagine the most fun ways to die, and Marina joked about how Leo would pull out all his gorgeous black hair in grief, and we passed the bottles in another circle, all of us a bit unsteady on our feet.

Like I said, no one took it seriously. Except me. I took it seriously enough to lie. Enough that the truth fell to my stomach and stayed there, smoldering like a live coal.

When you think you're going to die—die *soon,* and you have no idea how—you get a little distracted. You make two wrong turns on the familiar route between your house and the high school. You miss simple questions on anatomy tests. During passing time, when you brush arms with the gorgeous black-haired boy you've loved forever and notice that he's glanced back at you, you almost walk into a door.

So maybe *that's* how you're going to die.

And then you do even stranger things like driving out into the woods, all alone, to see the witch.

I'd never visited her before. I'd only seen her around town, stalking through the hardware store or the supermarket while other shoppers sidled out of her way. Everybody knew that she could see things. Past and future things. Secret things. For a fair price, she'd tell them, too. But I hadn't ever been near her until I was standing on her rickety little porch, staring at her splintering front door.

I couldn't quite get myself to knock. I glanced around instead. At the pile of rabbits' feet in a basket by the doorstep. At the dark stains on the wooden boards. At the windchime made of something's hollowed bones. I'd just made up my mind to run away when the door flew open.

She smiled at me from across the threshold.

She was tall, much taller than me. Big-boned. She wore plaid flannel and dusty denim, heavy boots, and a thick short braid. She could have been a farmer. Maybe someone's sharpshooting grandma. But the eyes in her leathery face—the eyes staring into mine—were like embers, black, and amber, much too bright.

"Knew I heard someone out here," she said. "Come in."

If I hadn't known I was going to die soon anyway, I probably wouldn't have obeyed. But I didn't think I had anything else to lose.

Inside, the little house was cluttered. Mason jars, drying herbs, old quilts, and animal hides. Almost cozy. But the strange smells in the air—rusty, meaty smells—weren't cozy at all.

She took a seat on a stool at a small wooden table and gestured for me to take the other one. She lit the candle on the table between us. I say *candle*, but it was really just a wick in a bowl of fat. The bowl looked like it might have been bone. What bone, and what fat, I didn't know. Didn't want to know.

For a quiet minute, she stared into the flame. Then her eyes seared toward mine.

"So," she said. "You're going to die."

A sick feeling flooded through me. Like my stomach, heart, and lungs had all sunk to the muddy bottom of a stream.

She knew. And if she knew, then there was something to know. Something true.

"I'm guessing you don't *want* to die," she went on.

"I mean ... no." My voice came out sticky and cracked. "Not *yet*."

She watched me with those bright eyes. I felt them on my skin, like sparks.

"Well," she said. "Too bad. You can't cheat death."

The mud started to crawl up from my stomach into my throat. My fingers were freezing. I put them in my lap, where they twitched around like injured birds.

I don't know what I'd expected, coming here. I didn't know what I wanted. I didn't know what to do next.

Before I could decide, before I could even stand up, she grabbed my arm. Her hand was huge. Knobby knuckled. Dirty nailed.

"You can make a trade, though. A fair trade."

"What do you mean?" I rocked forward on my chair's edge, ready to run.

"You don't give someone who wants a meal a couple of crumbs and pretend that's enough," she said, still holding my arm. "You can't give death a mouse or a fly or something and think that's going to work. It needs to be fair."

"You mean—I need to pick somebody?" My thoughts and words came out in broken pieces. "Somebody like me. Or enough like me. For death to take instead?"

Her eyes burned. "Oh, you've already picked someone."

I almost jumped out of my chair.

How did she know? How could she know there was already a face in my mind—someone I'd always wanted to trade places with, someone I'd have loved to trade with at that second, maybe more than ever?

She didn't let go of my arm.

"A fair trade," she said again.

"But—"I took a breath. The oily smell of the candle was making me sicker. "I can't—" I looked over the leaping flame, straight into her eyes. "Would—would I have to kill them? In exchange?"

She didn't answer this. Not aloud. But she smiled in a way that meant yes.

"And you'll need to take a piece of her," she said. "Her flesh for yours." She smiled wider. "Just a little bite."

My stomach lurched. "You're saying I need to—I'd need to eat—"

I broke off, but she just went on smiling. Her teeth were gray. Straight. Too large.

"I can't." I choked out the words. I swear I could already taste blood in my mouth. Blood and fat and gristle, along with that river mud. "No. *No.*"

I pushed back from the table hard enough that her grip broke.

"Never mind. I shouldn't have—just—" I didn't finish.

I scrambled out the door into the daylight. Her bloodstained porch creaked under my shoes. A few skinny hens flapped out of my path as I ran to my car, jumping in and tearing away so fast that I didn't even remember the roll of cash I'd meant to leave her, still wadded in my pocket, until I was out on the county road, and it was much too late.

I didn't tell anyone where I'd gone.

I didn't tell anyone what I was thinking, feeling, dreading. I kept everything inside. Silent.

No one seemed to notice the difference.

I went to school. Drifted through classes. Sat with Alex and Marina and Sasha at lunch. As usual, I dropped Sasha off at her house on my way home.

One of the few things I had that Sasha didn't was a car. It

was a rusty gray three-time hand-me-down that had belonged to both of my brothers first, but it was mine. My hands on the steering wheel. My shoe on the accelerator. My choice to steer off the road at the big bend on County FF and head straight for that huge oak tree, making sure the passenger side hit head-on.

If I chose it, but I didn't.

I just thought about these things every time we whipped past. I thought about how this might have been the witch's real message to me—to make me see that what I thought I wanted wasn't really what I wanted at all. To show me who I really was. And who I wasn't.

Then I tapped the brake and kept my wheels on the road, and I left Sasha safely at the end of her long driveway, at her family's house in the maple woods.

I never made that choice.

As it turned out, I never had to.

One evening, when Sasha was out alone on that same stretch of road through the woods near her house—maybe she was going to the mailbox, maybe she was just out for a walk in the September light—someone came roaring down the road and hit her. They found her body in the ditch the next morning. She'd been dead for hours by then. I heard they had to shoo the crows and vultures away, that they were already picking at her, like any other piece of roadkill. Whoever had hit her probably thought she was a deer, too. Red-brown hair. Delicate limbs. Big eyes.

She died.

And I lived.

We all grieved—her friends, relatives, neighbors, everyone in our little north woods town. But inside my grief, holding me up like a brace, was the certainty that it wasn't my fault.

I'd made the good choice. For whatever reason, death had picked her instead. Maybe death liked Sasha more, just like everybody else. Maybe, I told myself, it had been Sasha's flower wreath that sank all along.

For once, I was the lucky one. For once.

I took that little bit of strength and used it to comfort others. Marina and Alex. And Leo, gorgeous, black-haired Leo, most of all.

Leo, who leaned on me—*me*—all through the funeral. Who called me over and over afterward to talk. Who started to invite me out in such a gradual, natural way that no one ever judged us for it.

We graduated. We got engaged.

We had a small, quiet wedding. Alex and Marina were bridesmaids. I carried a bouquet of violets and columbines in memory of Sasha.

No one needed to know that inside our little rented house, Leo would call me by her name.

"Sasha," he'd whisper. Or, sometimes, just "Sash." It had happened for the first time after a kiss on one of our early dates, and then again. And again. And again. I'd thought it would stop with time—and there was nothing that would have made me let go of someone as beautiful as Leo. But it never stopped at all.

So I started responding to it. Like it was my own name. It was easier than the other choice, another conversation that would hurt us both. Better if it only hurt one of us.

He asked me to change my hair, just for fun. Grow it a little longer. Add some red. He bought me gifts, clothes in styles I'd never worn. Always a little too small.

So I made myself smaller.

I clenched my hands. I ate less and less. Gradually, I learned to talk like her and almost to move like her, though I'll never get her gracefulness down. I made myself fit, sliver by sliver, into the space that had been left for me, like a stepsister cutting off bits of her own foot until she slips into that blood-soaked shoe.

I didn't see the witch again until a year or so after our wedding.

"Hanna," a voice said. My name. My *own* name.

And there she was, smiling at me from the other side of a stack of apples in the supermarket.

I had changed. But she looked no different. Same flannel shirt. Same thick braid. Same eyes, like fire pits full of sparks.

"So," she said, still smiling. "You made the trade."

That cold sickness, that river mud, surged straight up from my stomach into my mouth.

"What?" I whispered.

She didn't repeat herself. She knew I'd heard. She just waited, grinning, until I pushed myself on.

"No," I said. "I didn't. I didn't do it."

Her grin widened. She leaned a little closer. "I know," she said, low but clear. "You chickened out. We took care of it for you."

I jerked backward. My elbow hit the stack of apples, sending several bouncing to the floor.

I might have said something else. *No,* maybe. Or *stay away from me.* Those were the things in my head. Then I ran home and locked myself in the bathroom of my house.

But it wasn't my house.

It smelled like her. I'd started buying her brand of shampoo. Her favorite kind of soap.

The clothes I wore—too tight. The shoes on my feet—too small. The gold ring on my left hand that had never been meant for me. The one who'd put it there.

It was hers. Everything.

I knew it all then as I huddled on the edge of the empty bathtub, making myself as small as I could.

My life had been traded for hers. But that didn't make me *her.*

And the hole left by a dead girl was all the space I'd ever have.

STORK BITES

BY EV KNIGHT

The baby squirming in my arms awakened my nausea. This time, it would not be breathed away. Activated salivary glands worked overtime as jaw muscles quivered in anticipation. I shoved my niece into my brother's arms and took off to the bathroom. Why my mother thought it was a good idea to drag me here to talk to Natalie, I couldn't imagine. Kids freak me out, but babies—I heaved—babies made me sick.

So what if Natalie had been my best friend? She was my brother's wife now. Her postpartum depression was not my problem. He knocked her up. He should be dealing with her refusal to leave her room. All I could do was commiserate with her. The difference, I guessed, was that Natalie wanted to have this baby. I never wanted one. And now, for whatever reason, she didn't want to hold her daughter. She wouldn't care for her, feed her, or even acknowledge her existence. Admittedly, it was strange. I probably would need to try to talk to her before we left.

Once my stomach was sufficiently empty of my breakfast sandwich, and the rest of my guts felt vacuumed sealed, I stood up, wiped the sick-tears from my face, and flushed. Surely somewhere in that bathroom of domestic bliss, where couples woke up in the morning and weren't completely disgusted by each other's breath, I could find an old bottle of mouthwash. My stomach lurched at the idea of gargling anything, but it had to be done.

An opened box of two pregnancy tests glared at me accusingly, beside the bottle of green "alpine mint" flavored breath freshener. Until then, I'd managed to block the idea from my mind. Sure, I had skipped a period or two. I was in college. Life was stressful. Stress screwed up my cycles. As for puking every morning, well, it was September, so allergies and post-nasal drip and all that.

The truth was, I knew. I knew, and I had no idea what to do about it. It's not like I had a choice, not anymore. However, I'd seen the coat hanger drawn on the protest signs, back when there was still a chance, back when the courts had all but dismantled Roe v. Wade. I couldn't bear to think about how to do it. I fiddled with the single test, still in its package, until finally, I decided to face my doom head-on.

The second line showed up immediately, so I didn't have to wait the full two minutes before having a breakdown. I tried to stifle my sobs with a hand towel, but apparently, no one was allowed to be sad in that house because a short knock preceded the door opening.

"Shit, Mom. Privacy?" I shoved the test into the trash.

"It's just me," Natalie said.

I looked up. Her bloodshot eyes almost glowed red within the puffy black circles of skin surrounding them.

"You look like I feel," she said and sat down on the edge of the tub across from me.

"Oh, yeah? That obvious?" I sniffled.

"You're pregnant." She didn't ask, she simply stated a fact.

"How'd you know?" I rubbed my temples. We'd been friends for a long time, but then she started dating Brad, and I went off to college. By the time we'd become sisters, we'd drifted apart as friends. But there, in the bathroom, our bond came back, sobbing over babies, but for different reasons.

"You don't want it." Again, not a question.

"Of course not, I never wanted kids. They creep me out ... no offense. Abby seems super sweet." What an idiot. Here was my friend, who'd always wanted kids, suffering for some unexplained reason, and I was making this about me and my unwanted pregnancy.

I expected tears. Instead, she brightened. "Are you sure?"

At first, I assumed she was asking if I was sure I found my niece to be sweet but then realized she was asking if I was sure I didn't want it.

"I do not want it." It was enough to bring on the tears again. "And I don't know what to do."

"But are you sure? Like, you never ever, ever want kids? If this happened again, in the future, and say you're happily married."

"Stop. I don't want this baby. I don't ever want to have kids. And I don't want a husband ever either, for that matter. Nat, what is this even about—do you know someone?" I'd forgotten about Natalie's depression, and frankly, it seemed she had as well. Her eyes were suddenly clear, and there was no lethargy to her movements.

She hugged me and cried on my shoulder. "If you are sure you don't want it, then I know what to do. It's just, it hurts, I mean, the … um … procedure. It hurts."

"Is it the coat hanger thing?" I asked.

"No. It's quite different. I just need you to be sure you never want a baby after this."

"God, Natalie, stop. I get it. It's wrong, it's illegal. You don't have to have anything to do with this if you don't want, and yes, I've learned a valuable lesson, and no, I will never do this again. Don't you think I feel like shit about it?"

She held a hand up to stop me.

"Jess. It isn't about any of that. I promise. It's your body, I respect that. I want to be there for you through this. Actually, I need to be. If you go through with it, then I really think I will start feeling a lot better."

It made no sense, but I'd heard of women drowning their kids from postpartum depression, so her weird talk wasn't bad in comparison. Plus, if she was willing to help me solve my problem, who was I to question her reasoning?

"How soon do you think I can get an appointment?" I asked.

"Today. Let's go now. The sooner, the better, I'd say."

"Should we call or something ahead of time."

"No. It's not like that, they don't have a phone anyway. We should go now. It's a bit of a drive. Let me go get dressed."

I didn't have to convince Mom or Brad that Natalie and I needed to go for a ride. They were thrilled she wanted to get out of the house and that she and I would talk.

Natalie drove. I asked a few times if she wanted to talk about her depression. I tried to come up with a way to ask if it had anything to do with Abby's dark red birthmark on her forehead. I wondered if Natalie could be so shallow as to be depressed over her daughter not being born blemish-free and "perfect." That didn't seem like her at all, and Mom said most "stork bites" faded away as the child grew.

"Abby's birthmark is so cute. It's like an angel kissed her right between the eyes." It was the dumbest thing I could have said and super cheesy. It made Natalie cry, too, so officially I was the winner of the Foot-in-Mouth of the Year award.

I shut up. My nerves tried to fill the silence with their agitated screams, but I was the only one that could hear them, and it only made things worse. I turned on the radio, and we rode the rest of the way in silence.

Had it been Sunday, and Nat and I an old married couple, the drive would have been pleasant and relaxing. But we were far from that, and the road in the middle of nowhere, Connecticut felt like the opening scene for a horror film. A light autumn rain lacquered the fallen leaves and brightened their colors but pushed the branches down, closing them around our car. The ambiguity of bright seasonal beauty mixed with menacing trees and darkened skies reminded me of Dorothy setting out on the yellow brick road. Was I going to make it home in one piece, or would the wicked witch destroy me? I tapped my toes with nervous anticipation. Looking back, maybe I should have clicked my heels.

Finally, just as I was about to ask her if we were lost, Natalie turned left into a drive that was so well hidden among the overgrown shrubs and naked berry bushes, I had to wonder how many times she'd been there. Many years ago, a small, wooden sign warned us that this drive was for "The Covenant of The Sisters Only. No Trespassing."

"Is this some sick joke?" I snapped. Was this some kind of joke? She brought me to an all-women's church for an illegal abortion? No. She tricked me. That's what this was all about. Bring me to religion, save an unwanted pregnancy, and her good deed would somehow be rewarded by curing her depression. Depression that somehow her god didn't cause but could take away when he is appeased? "Just let me out, Nat. Thanks a lot."

Natalie slowed the car on the drive but did not stop; she didn't even look at me. Her knuckles were white from her grip on the wheel, and I could see how tense her jaw sat. She spoke through clenched teeth. "It's not at all what you think. Do you want rid of it or not?"

"Yes," I said, my mouth just as tight.

"Then shut up and trust me."

The ramshackle wooden cabin of sorts waited at the end of a drive, devoid of majestic color but surrounded by more chickens than I had ever seen in my life. They all milled about happily, clucking and pecking at the ground right beside the house. I wondered if it was the heat that kept them there or what exactly, but they all stayed close. There was no way this place was even still operating as a medical clinic. It looked centuries old—

dirty, chipped stone steps, dusty dark windows, and a mildewed wooden door. If we used the heavy, cast-iron knocker in the shape of a chicken foot, I feared we might put a hole through the wood. But Natalie had clearly been here before because she walked past the front door and around the side of the dilapidated hut to a side entrance with an old pull rope that rang a gong-like bell somewhere inside.

A waft of dried herbs and day-old hamburger assaulted my nose. But the sight of the old crone answering the door was worse. When I say, "old crone," I mean an old woman who looked more like the wicked witch than a nun. She wasn't wearing a habit, but a babushka on her head and an old gray housedress like I'd seen women in pictures from the great depression wearing. Overtop, she wore a probably once-white apron which was now covered in what looked like old rust-water stains. Her teeth were darker than anything else about her when she smiled at us. I shivered and secretly hoped she was just a receptionist.

"You were almost too late," she said. I opened my mouth to tell her we didn't have an appointment when Natalie spoke.

"I know, I know, but I've brought my friend, Jessica. She is my second."

I looked at Natalie. What was she up to? The old woman turned to me; her eyes went straight to my middle. "Have you come of your own free will, child?"

"Yes, I need your help," I said, unsure if I wanted the help.

"And you present yourself as this girl's second?" I didn't know what that meant, I looked to Natalie for help, and she gave a quick short nod. "Yes, I do."

"Come then." The old woman gestured with gnarled fingers, and we followed.

In my memory, the hall was long and lit only by torches angled off the packed dirt floor. The air was dank, and everything was draped in red cloth. But that is the memory of my nightmares and probably not the truth. The walk was short before we turned into the kitchen. Warmed by a large hearth fire, the room was actually cozy. Another old woman was working a mortar and pestle, grinding away at a bundle of dried herbs sitting beside her on the counter. More bouquets hung from the ceiling in various states of desiccation. She wore the same-colored headscarf and dress as what I assumed was her sister. She, unlike our greeter, hunched from an osteoporotic humpback, but when she turned to us, I gasped. She otherwise looked exactly like the first woman.

"So, she returns?" the kitchen crone said to her twin.

"She brings a second in her place."

"It is my turn." The hunchback clapped her hands. "I'll prepare the cuppa."

"Uh, maybe there's been a miscommunication," I interjected. Natalie elbowed me. I shut my mouth.

"Please, sit. Agatha, my sister, will prepare the test, and then we will begin," the entry witch said while she rummaged through drawers, gathering what looked to me to be cookie-making supplies rather than surgical tools. Natalie paid no attention. She stared at the wall beside the kitchen table where a ceramic owl stared at us all accusingly above a large mirror. I hadn't seen her bite her nails since high school final exams, but she had the thumb down to a nub, and her pointer finger was bleeding.

"Aren't there any forms or paperwork I need to fill out?" I asked. The sisters looked at each other.

"No, dear. We never forget a ... face." They broke out in a fit of chuckles before falling strangely silent again. Agatha brought me a teacup filled with a faint yellow herbal tea. "Let me take your hand." She grasped my fingers, and I felt a sharp prick. I pulled my hand back. The tip of my ring finger welled up with a bloom of crimson.

"It is said that you wear your wedding band on your left fourth finger because its vein goes directly to the heart. You wear

no ring, but this is no matter, for it is your heart's blood I need."
She snatched my hand back and squeezed my bleeding digit over
the cup until a single drop fell into the concoction. I expected the
tea to turn from yellow to faint rose, but instead, it darkened into
a deep royal purple.

"Adelaide! 'Tis a boy! It's mine, my turn, dear sister, as I
know you must remember."

"Yes," hissed her sister. "I'm well aware. Perhaps you should
busy yourself preparing the mamaliga."

The hunchbacked Agatha skipped across the kitchen like a
child, clapping her hands and muttering to herself.

"Drink your tea," Adelaide said to me.

"This purple stuff? With my blood in it? No. No way," I said.

"Please, Jess, just drink it. There are pain killers and like
antibiotics and stuff in there. And it's only a drop of your own
blood. Please, you'll wish you had."

I wrinkled my nose but downed the drink. No self-respecting
college girl says no to a shot, no matter how nasty. At least that's
what the old me thought.

"Now, disrobe and climb up onto this table." She pulled off
the worn plaid table cloth and then began covering it with tufts
of moss she pulled from a burlap sack sitting in the corner.

Natalie stood up and turned away from me. I hesitated,
unsure of what I'd just heard.

"Do it, girl. Time is of the essence." I'd come that far. I'd
drank their rotten potion, so at this point, why not? I watched
myself undress in the mirror and waited until Adelaide finished
icing the table with moss before I gingerly climbed up, trying not
to knock any of it off.

I turned my head toward the mirror as I listened to her lay
out her "instruments" and waited for Natalie to turn back around
to face me. I don't think she ever did, not until I was redressed. I
say this because things started to get weird after that. The mirror

rippled like a funhouse mirror, distorting my reflection. But that wasn't all. Agatha hummed a tune far away in the back of the kitchen, but it too was warped like an old record. My inner ears roared as if I was listening to the ocean through a seashell. But the smell in the room was pleasant like corn on the cob on the fourth of July.

Adelaide's dried husks that served as hands touched my thighs, pushing them open. I tried to focus on her in the mirror. I didn't see her put on any gloves before I felt her fingers probing inside of me. First one, then two, then more and more.

"Agatha, is it almost ready? You'll want to have the plate here soon."

That couldn't have been what she said. I squinted; my head was spinning. I could feel myself stretching down below as if I was having a baby in reverse. In the mirror, I watched Adelaide's face inching closer and closer to my nethers. No, that couldn't be right. She couldn't have had her entire arm up to the shoulder inside of me.

"I'm taking the spoon up now," she announced. The pain was immense, as if I was taking the whole world into me. The stretch, the burning, searing pain, was like nothing I could ever have imagined. Impossibly, the scene in the mirror played out to my drugged senses. Adelaide, an old woman of average height and weight, was hip-deep inside me and crawling farther. I kicked and tried to close my legs on her, to smother her, but her strength was beyond reality. Then, as if I hadn't suffered enough, I felt the spoon.

She was inside to her ankles, and I was being drawn and quartered—ripped apart from the inside, split into two pieces, and cored-out like a jack-o'-lantern. Scrape, scrape, scrape. I heaved and screamed and spit and vomited. I cried. I could hear the gritty scratching from inside me. It transmitted from my uterus to my ears, through cell after cell after cell. Nerve endings worked the same way to send panicked signals to my brain to fight for my life or die—because I was dying. I was about to die with another human being inside of me. When they performed my autopsy, I'd look like a turducken—me, the embryo, and Adelaide—layer after layer of different flesh.

My friend Natalie had her back turned to me somewhere in that room. No one would know my story or understand how it happened. I chose death and closed my eyes. As soon as I relaxed and gave in to my fate, I felt her backing out. In the mirror, I saw my body deliver a grown human in breach, feet first position. My womb collapsed behind her like an empty toothpaste tube. Bloodied and wet, she emerged, holding a spoonful of raspberry-colored gelatinous tissue.

"Give it, give it! It's mine, it's mine!" Agatha danced at my side. She held a small plate of yellow mush. "I'm hungry, so very hungry."

Again, I plead that the drugs must have provided me this nightmare because I watched Adelaide plop her spoon filled with my uterine contents onto her sister's plate. That smell of herbs and raw hamburger filled my nose again. Just before I passed out, I swear I watched Agatha bury her face in her plate and gobble up the slop like a barnyard pig.

I was dressed and resting on an old Victorian fainting couch when I woke up. Natalie sat in a chair, hands gripping the arms, bouncing her leg up and down.

"Jess? You okay? It's all done. It's all over." She came over to me and fell on her knees beside the couch. She grabbed my hand and held it against her heart.

"I'm thirsty," I croaked.

"I'll get the sisters," she said. But I held on tighter.

"No!" I tried to raise my voice, but it just got squeakier. "No, they … they're monsters."

"It's just the drugs they gave you. I had some crazy nightmares, too."

"You've been here before? You had an," I couldn't even say the word. What they'd done was not an abortion.

"My ex. When your brother and I started dating, he followed me home one night after work. He knew where the hide a key was, and he came in while I was asleep. And he …"

"No," I said. "You don't have to tell me anymore. I just didn't know you'd had one before. You never told me. I would have been there …"

"It's okay. It's not like something you go around telling all your friends, especially not these days."

I nodded. She was right. "But you came here? Why?"

"First of all, it's not like a girl has a lot of options anymore. Secondly, a co-worker offered to bring me here when she caught me puking at work."

I nodded again, but my thoughts were racing. Adelaide came into the room with two glasses of what looked like iced tea.

"Thirsty?"

I was, exceedingly, but I wasn't sure I wanted to drink anything they had to offer.

"It's just a couple glasses of sweet tea. Nothing more. Your procedure is over. If you drink it, you may go."

Natalie took her glass and sipped. I gulped mine down to empty.

"There now, don't you feel better?" She smiled that brown toothy smile.

"Yes. What do I owe you?"

"You've paid your deposit already. Come, I'll show you out." Adelaide answered.

Natalie stepped ahead of me, and without giving me the opportunity to pay the rest, they headed to the door.

"I'll go start the car, you might be chilled," Nat said and squeezed by us. I stopped and turned to Adelaide, though I had trouble looking her in the eye after what I felt and saw her do. Dream or not.

"So, how much more do I owe?"

"My sister and I have no need of money."

"Oh, so ..."

"We have a roof above our heads, a hearth to keep us warm, but what we require is sustenance. You've fed my sister well." She turned around, and I looked over her shoulder to see what she was looking at. About six feet back stood Agatha. Let me rephrase it, Agatha stood straight in the background. Her hair darkened to salt and pepper and was full of life. She looked twenty years younger and free of thinning bones. "But I'm still hungry." This time her smile revealed a set of blackened, sharp teeth. "Until you've fed us both, you remain in our debt, and we never forget."

"So, I have to go get pregnant and go through this all again? Just to *feed* you?"

Agatha came bounding down the hall. "Or we'll take a baby, a whole, live one. Fleshy and juicy like your friend's."

"Stay away from her baby," I warned.

"Of course. Tell her the debt is paid, the mark of her womb has been lifted." Adelaide said and slammed the door on my face.

Natalie had the radio on when I got in the car. I shut it off and glared at her.

"What exactly did they mean when they asked me if I was willing to be your second?" I thought I knew the answer, but I needed to hear it from her.

"There are two of them, I think, you know, that maybe they've been alive for a really long time doing this ... surgery.

And I think they sort of need each other. So, they both need to be fed somehow. When you go to them, they require a future payment, and it has to come from you, but see, there's a loophole. Someone else can agree to pay your debt and take on the future payment as well. I mean, I guess as long as they're fed."

"This is some fucked up Grimm Brothers shit, Nat," I said, and suddenly what I saw in the mirror seemed more likely.

"I know, I know. I'm so sorry. I never ever wanted to put this on anyone, and for a long time, I tried to avoid getting pregnant. But, you know, it's been five years, and I thought, what were the chances? It seemed like a nightmare, so I took a chance." She sobbed. She would wreck the car if she didn't pull over, and I told her so.

"But do you really think they would come for Abby? Really?" I remembered Adelaide saying the mark of the womb was lifted. And thought of the stork bite between Abby's eyes. Shit.

"You asked me if I was upset about her birthmark. I was. I want to love my daughter. My empty arms are aching for her. But when I saw that mark, I knew what it meant. I knew I better not get too attached. I tried to pretend she was gone, that she was stillborn, so when they came and took her away to pay my debt, maybe it wouldn't hurt so bad."

All of it made sense—*if* we were in some horror movie. But we weren't, and it was all too much for my exhausted and drug-addled brain to consider. I nodded and looked out the window.

"I'm so sorry, Jess. I should have told you. It wasn't fair to pass this curse on to you, but when you said you never ever wanted to have babies, I figured it was the best way out. I could help us both, and then the curse would die with you. I'm really sorry, I should have said something."

"It's fine. I'm ready to go home, though, I'm tired, and honestly, I'm pretty sore."

"Yeah, for sure. You can stay with us tonight. I'll drive you back to school tomorrow night."

Abby's birthmark was gone, just as Adelaide had promised. Her little angel face was without a hint of it. And neither Mom nor Brad seemed to remember it ever being there. I watched Natalie hold her daughter, singing softly to her and rocking her, feeding her, trying to make up for two weeks of absence.

When I got back to school that Monday, I signed up to volunteer at a local pregnancy support clinic. I couldn't imagine ever putting myself in a position where I would need to rely on the Sisters of St. Margaret again or that I might ever need a "second," but I thought, in this day and age, it's best to have a plan B in your pocket.

CHICKEN FOOT

BY OCTAVIA CADE

S ource material: domestic canary, *Serinus canaria domestica*.
Yellow feathers, paling at wing and tail-tip. The cage is strewn
with seeds, and there are sprays of millet woven through the bars,
a cuttlefish bone wedged between. There are swings, greens, oyster
shells—a small red water dish. At the time of purchase, the canary
showed no sign of disease or stress; it was certified to be in perfect
health.

I chose the canary for musical ability and its current research
status as a vertebrate neurogenetic model. Perhaps, if successful,
this experiment will result in a house that learns faster than the
chicken foot did.

The little thing seems so unafraid. I believe it is used to
company—I've found it most inclined to friendliness when
presented with fruit. It appears fondest of apples. If this works,
I shall set up a cider press and let apple juice flow through the
gaps between floorboards and down onto bird legs. It may only
be a canary, but it deserves to be happy.

The canary, I'm told, was previously known as "Sparky."

I can't recall the name of the chicken.

It doesn't matter anyway. The dead can't be called back by
names.

After separation, the canary legs were successfully engorged.
They fixed to the house easily enough. I burnt the rest of the

bird, let its ashes fly up into the sky. There'll be no more cages for it, poor pretty thing.

The hypothesis of transferred musical ability is proved accurate. I can't explain why the characteristics and behavior of the bird re-assert themselves in the legs after attachment. It's as if the house takes the place of the body and brain on a structural level. There must be some transfer of memory, of information, that passes between the biological to the architectural. Strange. I would have thought that if any part of the bird were capable of such defining behavior, it would be the wings. Yet I know of no experiment in which wings have been attached to a house, certainly none where the attachment was successful. I think that the house must, in such circumstances, weigh too much for the wings to lift. The legs at least act as stabilizing pillars.

The pillars have begun to sing.

It did not happen in the instant of transformation, but the house was not staggering an hour before the songs began. I can only guess it took time for the sedative to wear off. The singing started slowly, and at low levels—wavering—but within minutes had reached a volume such that it was all that I could hear.

The canary's legs have taken on the tones of woodwind instruments; however, the pitch is higher than expected from the length and breadth of available leg.

It does not sound like screaming.

Wind whistles through the canary legs, and they sing—a high, sweet honeycomb sound. Resonance sets the house to shaking. Kitchen cupboards snap open, spatulas and saucepans fall off their hooks, and knives are gleaming on the floor, tin plates, spoons, salt cellars, broken jam jars. The kitchen smells of fruit and sugar.

The rest of the house smells of small animals and uncleaned cages. I don't know why. The cage was never unclean, and the animal—what remains of it—is no longer small.

Perhaps the canary legs miss their home. Perhaps that home smelled less clean to the bird than it ever did to me. I hope not; I tried to give it a comfortable habitat. Yet the bird is part of a new home now. I can only hope it will adjust.

The song does not ring well with adjustment.

A tuning fork brought to the same pitch shatters glass. It's a good thing all the windows are absent—since I lost the chicken, they have gone unreplaced. It was cheaper that way. Less messy when the transplants failed. Instead, shutters bang against frames and leave changing light patterns on the walls. This is distracting in heavy winds, so I am contriving latches to keep them still in storms.

Note: if this experiment is successful, I must reinforce my precautions for quakes. There's no telling what will happen if the house sings as it walks.

It appears the tensile strength of the canary legs is less than calculated. The house buckles first on one side, then another. It stumbles, crouches, and the ground is suddenly closer than it was. The canary legs are crushed beneath the weight of the house, and the music squealed and ceased. Shuddering continued for approximately four and a half minutes, after which there was no further sign of life.

As long as the shuddering continued, I sang to it, to the canary feet, so that the part of the house that is canary knew it wasn't alone. Afterward, the legs take such a long time to burn. They're wide and heavy as tree trunks, but in the end, they too go flying into ashes. These are the only comforts I can give.

There is no longer any intact crockery in the house, and the slop bucket has overturned.

There was never this trouble with the chicken.

Emotional attachment to a chicken is irrelevant.

If the legs of a single canary are too frail for houses, I wonder whether two of them might be support enough. Perhaps the singing might be kinder, too, if they had a friend other than myself to sing with.

Source material as before. Their names, I am told, were "Screech" and "Squeak." They share a cage, they sing and preen. They treat each other beautifully.

It hurts to watch them, to remember the time when I had a friend as well, when I fed her from my own hands, felt the beak and scratch of claws.

Friends die, I tell the canaries. *I hope that you will not, but if you do, it will be together.*

The tensile strength of four legs is adequate, the suspension resulting from four legs is superior than that of two, but the rhythm of the house is ... different. It does not feel like home.

The legs have begun to fight. They kick and scratch, and there is bleeding where they join with the foundations of the house. The blood is thick; it has the taste and consistency of tar. It is possible that the trauma of transplantation has induced psychosis in the subject species.

The legs sing to each other as they fight, but the result is not harmonic. It cracks shutters clean across, and even the bathtub has begun to leak. Milk curdles in saucers, and the potatoes in the cupboard sprout white roots and wither. The mirror turns cloudy, and the fireplace ash levitates and sinks again, covering the carpets in dust.

The songs do not, *do not,* sound like screaming.

The chicken never screamed.

Not until the end, when there was nothing more to be done to defend it.

It is no use thinking about the chicken. That is the price of a home that is a living thing—the living parts of it die, and the rest of us go on.

I tried to replace it with canaries, which are light and delicate and nothing like a chicken, but their singing is a terrible screaming thing, and when the canary legs are removed from the house to still the fighting, they curl and wither. I send the ashes to the sky, as I always do, but it's clear they are not a good replacement.

The house, legless, has sunk on itself next to a lake. The lake has pelicans in it. They look so unafraid.

Their legs are strong and beautiful.

WHERE THE HORIZON MEETS THE SKY

BY R. J. JOSEPH

T he normally sure-footed and nimble, voted "Most Likely to Join a Professional Track Team" in high school, Naomi faceplanted over the tree roots she didn't see on her regular morning run.

She stood up and dusted off her hands, glad she didn't feel any injuries. "Where did those come from?"

The roots hadn't been there the previous day. Naomi had run or walked that isolated route in the East Texan piney woods at the outskirts of town pretty much every day since she'd been in high school thirty years prior. She knew the paths the same way she knew the wrinkles that appeared weekly in her face. Every time there was a change in her forest, however gradual, she noticed it.

This change hadn't been gradual.

She poked at the huge roots with her sneakered foot, gently brushing the freakishly long grass that had already grown up around them. *What was that?* Naomi gazed up along the trunk attached to the weird roots and gasped. The trunks were covered in scales, very unlike the patches of bark that covered the other evergreens. A hint of yellow beneath the gray made the large stems look almost like chicken legs. Naomi looked up, puzzled, directly into the eyes of an older woman standing in a doorway at the top of the legs.

"Well, stop being rude and get on up here, gal. May as well get all in my business up inside my house since you are investigating all outside."

Mortified to have been caught staring, Naomi took one step back—right into a wooden lift made of intertwined tree branches that closed as soon as she was inside. The lift flew up toward the woman and deposited Naomi inside what was supposed to be the belly of the chicken, but was instead an almost regular-looking cabin. *Almost.*

Naomi gawked at the abode despite herself and forgoing all her impeccable Southern manners. The cabin was made of windows all around, visible from the outside and below as three solid walls. She shivered as she gazed out the side that featured a frozen wasteland, wind whipping everywhere, blowing snow and ice throughout. She tried to focus on the small structure in the far distance but was distracted by the rays of heat coming through the second glass wall.

Naomi walked over to the display and pressed her hand to glass that was extremely warm to the touch. Beyond were expanses of sand, a molten desert with ripples where the wind took pity and blew for a long, slow moment as she watched. Again, she squinted and looked toward a tiny speck amid the grains, unable to quite make out what it was that called to her through that window, just at the edge of the scene, where the horizon kissed the sky.

"You done? Wanna tell me about this man you're pining over, so you're tripping over your own feet?"

Naomi turned around, grasping for pearls she wasn't wearing. "Wh-what do you mean?"

How did the woman know her thoughts?

"Oh, I know a lot. About a whole lot. Ain't no secrets from me around here. No, siree." The woman was older than Naomi had first thought. She couldn't place her exact age, though. Surely, she was too wizened to stretch her arms as far as she did across the cabin—several feet—to grab a chair and pull it close to where Naomi stood. *Surely*.

"Sit. Can't help you if you don't tell me what you want. You gotta say it."

Naomi supposed she should be frightened by the strange woman and her even stranger ways. She would've thought she was drunk. But she didn't drink. And though she might need reading glasses soon, her eyesight wasn't afflicted, either. She was seeing the woman, clear as day. She saw the woman's every move just as clearly.

And something made her sit in that strangely offered chair. She wasn't drawn to it in the same way she was drawn to the scenes outside the woman's windows but drawn to sit, nonetheless.

"I ... I'm not sure what you want me to say." Honesty seemed the best way to go. Things definitely couldn't get any more weird—or so she thought.

The elder woman cackled, and even though Naomi heard her raspy delight in her ears and all around her, the woman's neck stretched to the far corner of the room, now twice as large as it had been when Naomi first arrived moments before. The gnarled hand that had moved the chair Naomi sat in crossed the slender, berobed torso, and picked up a mortar and pestle. She began to work with the single appendage.

"You gotta say it," she repeated.

Naomi felt tears sting behind her eyes. She twisted her hands in her lap, intertwining her fingers in a mimicry of how the other woman twisted the fingers of her other hand—*her third hand?*—around various ingredients she added to her concoction.

"I don't think my husband loves me anymore, and I don't know what to do about that. I keep myself looking nice. I stay busy with my job. I thought all I wanted was to be his wife and be happy with him." She swallowed. "I'm not even sure if that's what I want anymore. Or ever wanted."

The woman sucked at her teeth in a loud, rude sound. "He

stepping out on you?"

"I really don't know. We don't … I mean—"

"Ain't much heat between you no more?"

A heated blush burned Naomi's neck and chest. She'd never spoken of such things so openly with a stranger. She shook her head.

"Oh, ain't no shame in wanting to screw your own husband. You got a lot of passion in you waitin' to come out."

Naomi stammered again. "I don't really want, um, relations with him all the time. I just want him to, maybe, pay more attention to me. The way he used to when we were younger. He's hardly ever home nowadays." The tears that threatened spilled over onto her cheeks. "I don't want to feel so lonely anymore, especially when he's physically right there. Maybe then we can rekindle the love that isn't so strong between us anymore."

The witch stood in front of Naomi, just an older woman again. "That all you askin' me for?"

Naomi met her gaze, swiping at her eyes. Her voice was strong when she spoke again. "Yes. I want my husband to spend more time with me."

As soon as the words left her mouth, her eyes began to burn from the substance the conjure woman blew into her face. Naomi coughed, and nausea churned in her belly. Then, the yearning she'd felt earlier came rushing back, more intense than before. Although her face also stung, she rose and returned to the window closest to her. Movement caught her eye, and she stood, transfixed, wanting to vocalize the longing she felt. She could find no words.

"You best go home to your husband, girl. Go on, now."

When Naomi could turn away from the window, she found the other woman staring at her with slitted eyes.

"Go on, now."

Naomi found herself bundled back into the lift and on the ground below the cabin before she fully comprehended what had happened. Then, the chicken legs unrooted themselves and sprinted through the forest, the house disappearing deep into the foliage.

She didn't have much time to think about the strange happenings in the forest that day because of what manifested at her home.

When she'd walked back toward the house, the first thing Naomi saw was Devon's sports car sitting in their driveway. As she approached, she reached out to feel the hood. Cool to the touch. That meant he hadn't just gotten there in a hurry to beat her home and had likely been there for a while.

But when she went inside, the house was dead quiet. "Devon …?" She squatted to take off her running shoes, and he appeared in front of her bent-over form.

"Where have you been?" His typically ebullient, full voice fell flat across the short distance between them.

"I always take my runs at this time during the summer. Keeps me busy." Part of her relished in the thought of her husband looking for her and him being the one all alone for a change. The feeling quickly abated when Naomi realized she didn't like being questioned by a virtual stranger.

"I've been waiting for you."

Naomi stood up and tried to walk around him into the kitchen. He shifted to allow her to pass and followed her into the brightly lit room.

She spent the rest of the day trying to walk around him.

While she cooked their lunch, he was right there, standing at her side. When she went to the backyard to water the plants, he joined her. When she tried to go use the bathroom, he went too and only stayed outside the door when she looked at him pointedly, pressed her hand to his chest, and closed the door in his face. He waited there until she came out and resumed dogging her every step.

The next morning, he hadn't gone in to work. It was sweet to think he had taken the day off to spend time with her. He never did that. In fact, she had a difficult time getting him to stay home from work for any reason, a multitude of accrued personal and sick time and special occasions be damned.

"What are we going to do today?" She had already decided she'd skip her run that morning since Devon wasn't much into outdoor activities.

"Whatever you want to do." The monotone hadn't left his voice.

"Are you feeling okay? You sound like you might be coming down with something." She stretched out her arm to feel his forehead, and he lay there, allowing her investigation. Not swatting her hand away like he usually did when she doted on him.

"I'm fine." And he continued to lay there in the bed next to her until she got up and began to get dressed. He did the same and followed her out of their bedroom. They spent that first full day in relative silence, him only responding when she asked him something. He never looked at her or started an interaction. And when they went to bed that night, he lay motionless, on his side of the bed, staring at the ceiling until she fell asleep watching him.

By the fourth day, Naomi was unbearably uncomfortable with Devon's presence. His movements grew slower, and she often caught a grimace on his face, as if he was in pain.

"I made you a doctor's appointment for today. I don't think you're feeling well."

"Okay."

He followed her to her car and allowed her to drive him into town. She didn't know what to do when the doctor didn't find anything wrong with her husband. Something was way, way off.

"I guess you should go on into work this afternoon," she said, "since the doctor gave you a clean bill of health."

He didn't turn to face her. "Okay. But where will you be?"

"I'll be waiting at home for you like always." She patted his stiff hand with an enthusiasm she didn't feel. When they returned home, she got his briefcase and his car keys and led him to his own car. He got in and drove away.

She headed back into the forest.

There was no sign of the old woman's house where she last encountered it. She wandered deeper into the trees, listening and watching for any sign of the chicken legs and the wooden lift.

"You looking for me, girlie?"

Naomi gasped at the voice speaking right in her ear.

"Guessin' that's a yes." The crone stepped out from beneath a distant tree, beckoning Naomi to come to her. Before she could close the distance between them, the wooden lift appeared and tipped her, face front, into it.

"What did you do to him?" She wasn't sure if she was angry or just curious. Then she decided she was a bit of both, curiosity winning out as stronger.

"What did I do to who?" The older woman smirked and pushed her curtains apart to reveal the same desert and ice landscapes Naomi had seen on her first visit.

Instead of answering, she went toward the cold emanating from the glass. Much more detail showed through the pane—Naomi could now make out a little house on the horizon, with smoke coming from the chimney. A tiny figure walked in the snowdrift outside the house, deep tracks appearing in its wake as it slowly made its way out into the expanse.

A yearning Naomi only recognized as deep want started low in her belly. She hadn't felt that magnetism since the last time she'd talked to Devon about having a baby. She'd thought they would have as much time as they wanted to start a family, so when he evaded her talking about it, she took it in stride, determined to bring it up again later.

But soon, later was too late. She was already in her late

forties when Devon finally told her he'd never wanted children. The pain of that stabbed through her, and she flinched.

She'd told herself that if it had been meant to be, it would have. Maybe she had been barren. Maybe he had been. Now that she'd started perimenopause and they rarely had sex, she'd probably never find out.

"I always wanted kids." Naomi spoke the words aloud. She placed her hand on the cool glass in front of her.

"Sometimes what we want ain't necessarily what we need."

"I suppose. That's why I pour my all into my little charges at school." She smiled. "No one stays in the first-grade classroom for more than a couple of years while they establish themselves as teachers. I never wanted to be anywhere else." She thought she had never wanted to be anywhere else until right then, looking out that window.

The glass grew hot underneath her fingers, and she drew her hand back. The scape changed to the desert, and the light from the sun's reflection heated the glass until it appeared molten. A lone figure trudged through the sand toward a house built into a dune in the far corner of the picture. Despite the heat, Naomi pressed her face against the window, leaning into the pulling sensation.

"What you need?"

Naomi sighed and turned to face the other woman. "I need my husband to want me. To desire me. To not just go through motions you're making him go through. It has to get better if we do it right."

"I knew you wanted something more. That heat is burning off your ass." She cackled loudly and snorted. "And I ain't making him do nothin'. I did what you said. Just like I'll do what you said now."

Naomi felt the woman's breath on the back of her neck, and her skin began to burn.

She was tired but couldn't quite place the source of her exhaustion. She headed back home to take a nap before Devon arrived home from work.

Naomi woke from her nap to Devon fervently pressing his body onto hers. His intensity startled her, his heat unlike that of the yearning she'd experienced earlier. She tried to lose herself in what was obviously pleasurable for her husband. She missed making love with him.

She just wasn't sure that love was what they were making at that moment. Gone was the ever-patient and gentle Devon she'd known. Even when they were in the throes of youthful passion, he had always been courteous and took his time with her. The man on top of her was anything but courteous.

He rained kisses all over her face and stuck his tongue down her throat. Naomi didn't resist because she wanted to be with him. Just not like that.

"Devon. Baby. Please. Slow down."

He seemed to hear her but didn't heed her request.

She soon told herself there was no need for him to slow down because her passion had finally caught up to his, and she joined him in their wanton abandonment of propriety, in steamy, satisfying daytime sex.

Devon fell asleep as soon as they finished, leaving Naomi awake. Sated, but unsettled. She'd wanted her husband to desire her, and he had. Surely, at their age, there could only be so much of that—it wasn't like he could physically get on-demand erections all the time, nor could she want to match his desire, even if he could.

Naomi was wrong on all counts. She endured the next three days of non-stop sex until she had a perpetual ache between her legs and bruises on her breasts where Devon grabbed at them.

She woke up the fourth day, determined to tell him she was tired and needed a break. She rolled over to where he lay on their bed and shook his shoulder. A gurgling sound came from his throat, but he didn't move. Naomi raised up to see what was happening. Devon's eyes were bulged open, brown eyes turned cloudy. A heavy trickle of dried blood crusted his jaw. The gurgles turned to a rasp, and Naomi grabbed her cell phone to call 911.

"Devon. Devon! Hang on. They're coming."

She started CPR and tried to distract her mind from the feeling of his cold, hard lips beneath hers, the unyielding flesh beneath her hands preventing her from pressing his chest inadequately.

When the EMS arrived, they pulled Naomi away from him and continued her ministrations for a short time before telling her he was gone and had been for hours.

Gone? "What do you mean? We just woke up," she said. "He was trying to tell me something just before you got here."

Naomi tried to focus on what the woman was saying, but she could still hear Devon gurgling, trying to say something. The others didn't seem to hear it.

Then she ran. Out of the house. Into her beloved forest. Straight into the wooden lift.

"What did you do? What did you do to him?" She screamed, anguish ripping across her vocal cords as she twisted her hands together to ground herself in the moment.

"I ain't do nothing but what you asked for." The crone seemed sad but not repentant.

"I don't ... I don't understand. What happened to my husband? What did you do?"

"It was his time to go. I ain't do nothing to speed that along."

Naomi wailed and dropped to the floor. "Did I kill him? Was his heart too weak to have all that sex? Did I do this?"

The other woman wrapped her arms around her and rocked. "No. Was just his time. He was gonna go then anyway, no matter what you had been asking for."

"Why didn't you tell me that? You knew. I could've asked for different things. I could've asked for him to—to stay alive, or to be healed, or … something." She left her biggest thought unspoken—*I could have asked for something I really wanted and needed.*

The witch let go with a melancholy chuckle. She seemed to have heard the thought as clearly as if Naomi had spoken it. "Yep, you shoulda done that. Oh, but you done more than that. You wanted him to spend more time with you and to desire you. That don't stop with death. He gonna keep wantin' you. Always."

Naomi stopped rocking and drew away from the witch. "What do you mean?"

"He gonna keep coming for you, wanting to love on you. That's the power you held and used."

"I don't want him to come for me like that. I want him to rest in peace." Her eyes widened. "You did this. You knew, and you let this happen." She pushed the woman away and clawed at her face.

"Calm down, girlie. Your problem is you don't know what you want or need. I just did what you said." She slapped Naomi. "Now. Think. For real, this time. What you want? What you need?"

Naomi cried, gut-wrenching sobs filling the space in the enormous cabin. "I don't know what I want. I wanted my husband. I thought I needed him."

"Maybe you did. But he gone now, only to return to fill the need you said you had before." She sucked her teeth. "But it ain't gotta be that way."

Icy heat prickled through Naomi, and she crawled across the floor to the expanse of windows pulling her in.

"You could join me and my sisters. It's only three of us, and we mighty tired. Wanna take a rest. We can't, 'less we find somebody to join us."

Naomi continued toward the far wall of windows. "You did all this to trick me?"

"No tricks. You always got a choice."

When she reached the window, one pane revealed the forest below, where she saw Devon's reanimated corpse shambling through the brush. He sniffed the air, and she knew he could smell her. He would never rest. She would never rest.

That wasn't what she wanted or needed.

She pressed her face fully into the icy section of the window and relished in the blast of cold jolting through her when her body followed. She turned around in the snow and looked at the deep footsteps behind her.

Naomi raised one leg and placed it in the hole in front of her. She repeated the same with the other. Step by step, she marked the progress of the figure before her, back to the cabin, where the horizon kissed the sky.

MAW MAW YAGA AND THE HUNTER

BY ALEXANDREA WEIS

Angry black ribbons wove through the last traces of white in the sky, creating a gnawing urgency in Camille. A storm approached the swamps, and her small metal skiff couldn't ride out the high winds and waves. Her hand on the outboard's throttle, Camille glanced at her empty crab traps, disappointed in her haul. She'd hoped to add a hearty contribution to the *Boucherie*. With the storm closing in, Camille wondered if searching the shores for a fat possum or raccoon might appease the other families taking part in the food festival for the coming winter.

Camille looked up at the sky again, and a jolt of trepidation shot through her. The blackness was everywhere. Soon the heavens would open. She needed to find shelter. She searched the shore for an alcove to secure her boat, but the shoreline was nothing but twisted branches of cypress trees, and their unforgiving knees were sure to damage the bottom of her skiff.

She turned up the throttle on the motor, wanting to cut through the dark, briny swamp water faster, but the way ahead remained murky. The last traces of light snatched away by the eerie sky made it dangerous for her to continue. Camille cursed her luck, wishing she'd stuck to her favorite hunting routes, but the desire for an impressive haul sent her to the farthest reaches of the swamps.

She reached for her back pocket, eager to call her mother. Something broke through the blackness—a glowing yellow light.

It didn't move or bob, which meant only one thing—a structure. But who would live way out here? Even the most diehard Cajun had moved to the small towns along Barataria Bay, wanting to enjoy more of the amenities modern life offered.

A crash ripped across the sky, briefly lighting up the swamps. In that instant, Camille saw the building sending out its ray of sanctuary. A house made of rough cypress timbers and sitting on stilts resembling chicken legs rose out of the water ahead. The rickety abode lay nestled next to a high ridge of land covered with brush and knotted pines.

Relief coursed through Camille. She'd found refuge. She might be a stranger, but the first rule of the swamps was always to care for those who land on your doorstep. It was what her mother called the Cajun way.

Camille sped the boat toward the building, searching the porch with her flashlight. A chill went through her as the beam landed on a few skulls set along the porch's eaves. Possum, coon, and an alligator added a macabre ambiance. Camille remembered what her grandmother told her about such oddities. *Gris-gris,* she called it. The bones of the dead kept evil away.

Another crack from the ominous sky put aside Camille's reservations about the shack. She needed shelter, not superstition. That was the old ways of the swamp, and she considered herself a modern woman.

A pier of planks spread over uneven posts jutted from the water. Camille pulled her boat alongside while surveying the home with her flashlight.

The moment she cut the engine, she called, "Anyone in there?"

She held her breath, running her hand through her short black hair. Perhaps this was an old camp used by gator hunters who'd left the light on to find their way back.

A flood of light washed over the dock as the front door of the home swung open, and a thick shadow stood in the doorway.

"Whatchya doin' out in this, girl? You gonna catch ya death."

The voice was gravelly and peppered with the Cajun hints she'd grown up listening to. Camille relaxed, relieved to be among her kind.

She climbed from her boat. "I was collectin' for our *Boucherie* festival. But the crabs, they ain't bittin', and I don't see no coon or possum 'round to bring back for the feast." She pointed at the skulls hanging on the porch. "But I see you got plenty of them 'round here."

The occupant stepped onto the porch, and Camille cringed. An old crone, hunchbacked with silvery wisps of hair, a wizened face, and long, crooked nose, stared at her. Rags fashioned into a dress and made from a hodgepodge of colored fabrics clung to her round figure.

Camille moved closer to the porch steps and spied the woman's cane and how she leaned on it for support. Carved with the faces of raccoons, squirrels, possums, foxes, birds, and with a handle shaped like an alligator head, the beauty of the piece took her breath away.

The old-timer held up the cane. "My children," she said in her throaty voice. "I keep them with me."

Camille ignored her yearning to ask more questions and wiped her hands on her jeans. "Can I tie up to your pier until the storm passes? I won't be no bother."

The hunched matron peered down from her porch with a cool gleam in her eyes. Even though she struck Camille as weak, a nudge of warning told the experienced huntress to watch her back.

The frail woman waved her inside. "Better get in here, girl. Can't leave ya for the rain to swallow."

Camille never ventured from the dock, continuing to weigh her options.

"What's wrong with ya?" she asked. "You slow or somethin'."

A rolling rumble overtook the sky. The dock shook, and a

frigid wind blew past. Camille suppressed her reservations and moved toward the porch. Better to take her chances inside than die in the swamps.

The closer she got, the uglier her hostess became. Her face was a roadmap of wrinkles, and her knotted hands reminded Camille of her grandmother's before she passed. She chastised herself for fearing the old woman. She shouldn't have let a few animal skulls scare her off.

The interior comprised one room with dull hardwood floors, roughhewn walls, cobweb-riddled ceiling beams, a black potbellied stove, and a deep sink with a hand pump. The furniture consisted of a chair and table made of unfinished pine. A black stone mortar and pestle waited on the tabletop with green sprigs sticking out. The lamps gave off the black smoke and acrid stench of kerosine. There were no photos. No radio, phone, or any other modern amenities. The threadbare red rug under the table awakened a pang of guilt. The poor spinster had nothing.

"Hope ya hungry," the stranger said while closing the door. "I got soup on the stove. It ain't got no meat, but it will fill ya belly and warm ya bones."

Camille reached into her back pocket for her phone, eager to call her kin.

"Don't bother tryin' to call nobody," the old woman told her. "Ain't got no signal. Nothing works here." She arched a black eyebrow. "You're pretty even if your hair's too short. Whatchya name, girl?"

"Camille." She smoothed her unruly bangs. "My family lives on the edge of Barataria Bay."

Her gnarled finger tapped the head of the cane as she appraised her guest. "You're far from home. Don't get nothin' but *cocodree* … what you say, gator hunters here."

Camille kept her gaze on the piercing eyes of the alligator carved into the cane's handle. "What do I call you, *sha*?"

The old gal let out a deep, scary cackle, shaking the house and sounding more unworldly than wise.

She shuffled across the room, leaning heavily on her cane. "No one's called me *sha* in a long time. Not even the hunters who come out this way." She set her walking stick aside and checked a cast-iron pot atop the stove. "They're all lookin' to make a bounty off the land. Don't seem right to take what ain't theirs."

Camille's shoulders tensed. "What's wrong with it? People gotta eat."

A smile lifted her craggy features. "What about the innocent animals murdered? I saw them traps in ya boat. You're no better than the rest."

Camille wiped her face, confused. Hunting was a way of life among the Cajuns. She'd never met anyone who didn't accept what they did unless they were city folk. She'd heard about their weird vegan and gluten-free diets from a cousin who lived in New Orleans. It seemed unnatural and unhealthy.

"You got animal skulls on your porch," she argued. "I bet you trapped them. You ain't no different from me. How else are you gonna survive in the swamp?"

The elderly woman lifted a wooden spoon from the side of the stove. "Those skulls belong to the ones I protect. My children suffered because of people like you."

Camille glanced at the door, her skin prickling with unease. The discomfort she felt since entering the cabin intensified. "You never told me your name?"

She set the spoon down and walked toward the table. "You can call me Maw Maw Yaga, just like the rest of my family."

Camille eased closer to the table. "What family would leave their Maw Maw alone in the swamps? Don't seem right."

Yaga eased her bulk into a chair. "I'm not alone. My family's here. All around me." She flashed a gap-toothed grin.

The cold permeating the home seeped into her bones. Camille

wasn't sure if the coming storm or the crone bothered her more.

The drum of a thousand fingers erupted on the roof. Whatever fears Camille harbored about the strange woman, she had to remain until the tempest passed.

"Sit yourself." Yaga motioned to the chair across from her. "We got a while till this blows over."

Camille approached the chair. "How can you tell?"

Yaga glanced at the ceiling. "Those angry drops comin' down. It means nature wants to cleanse the land of all its sin."

"Sin?" Camille frowned. "What ya talkin' about?"

She leaned into the table, her eyes glinting in the faint lamplight. "The stain on the land. The one left by man. Ya think all that killin' and blood don't leave a mark? Nature remembers all crimes."

The din of the rain grew louder, blotting out the crackle of the fire in the stove. Thunder, deeper than the loudest motor, shook the home. Camille grabbed the table, certain the flimsy shack would tumble into the swamps.

Yaga picked up a knife on the side of the mortar and pestle. "This house has stood up to worse. Ya got nothin' to fear, honeychile."

She sharpened her knife on the side of the motor, using it as a whetstone. Camille remembered her grandmother doing the same thing. The grinding noise sent a tingling along her spine then, just like it did now.

A window by the door flew open, letting a barrage of damp cold inside. Camille stood and was about to rush to close the window when a small bird flew into the room.

It was unlike any other bird she'd seen, with golden feathers and a beak of bright blue. It flitted and hovered around Camille, chirping and flapping its wings.

Camille stared in dismay. "What's with this bird?" She studied the tiny creature, questioning why it stuck so close.

The bird landed on her right shoulder. Camille froze.

She swore she detected its rapid breathing and frantic heartbeat. Then a high-pitched voice rose around her.

"Run," came from the bird. "She means to kill you."

A rush of air swept past her right cheek.

Something thudded on the floor, and before she could sense what was happening, Camille saw the golden bird fly out the window. When she peered down, the pestle settled next to her rubber boot.

"They call them *cho chos* and are believed to be messengers sent by the swamps to protect people." Yaga's deep voice saturated the room. "The birds like to tell me all the going's on, but this one told ya about me, didn't she?"

A frigid rush of air embraced Camille. Her mouth went dry, and her heart pounded in her ears.

"I should go," she muttered. "My family might be searchin' for me."

Yaga straightened her back, her slight hunch disappearing. "Ain't no one gonna head out in this mess. You're mine now."

Camille eased closer to the door, a thousand scenarios of escape formulating in her head. She was just an old woman, after all. She'd wrestled alligators, and gar—Yaga was no match for her.

But the suddenly agile old woman moved faster than any critter Camille had seen. Yaga wielded the mortar, appearing ready to bludgeon her with a single blow. She wasn't the same person plodding around the shack. This was a nimble creature with hungry black eyes, and her lips pulled back in a fiery sneer. She bared her razor-sharp teeth at Camille.

She barely got out of the way before Yaga landed on top of her. Camille skirted to the side of the door, hoping to reach for the knob and get away. But Yaga blocked her escape, taking a stance in front of the only exit. Camille rocked from side to side, anticipating her next move.

"What are ya doin'?" she demanded. "You're mad."

The woman's cackle iced the blood in Camille's veins.

Yaga juggled the mortar in her hands. "You never paid attention when the old ones talked about me, did ya? I protect the land and all those livin' on it. I summon the storms, just like the one that brought ya here. I own these waters, and soon I'm gonna own your soul."

Camille curled her hands into fists. She would not take such talk from a crazy woman. No wonder they left her in the swamps to die.

She charged, anxious to be on her way, but Yaga remained swift-footed and quickly ducked. She seemed to float around the room, almost like the bird that flew in through the window. Camille chased after her, swinging as she went, mindful of the mortar. But every time she got close to her, Yaga dashed out of reach. Her ire swelled, and her determination to end the foolish game of cat and mouse fueled her hurried steps.

She swung again, and Yaga quickly slipped out of range. Sweat beaded her brow, and a swell of worry rose in her gut. What if this hag was a witch, a demon, or worse?

Fear slowed her chase, and soon Camille no longer wished to silence Yaga but to flee. She worked her way toward the door, and she was within feet of gaining his freedom when Yaga barreled in front of her, holding the mortar above her head.

"It ends here, girl."

An intense pain sent shooting lights across her eyes. She wavered, dizzy and confused. The ground came up, and she heard the thud of her body on the old floorboards, but there was no pain. Camille summoned her strength, attempting to crawl toward the door. A pair of soft leather shoes with small birds painted along the toe appeared before her. She marveled at how the birds looked like the one that flew in the window. Another agonizing bolt shot through her head. Then everything went black.

The sting of cold drops on her face stirred Camille, rousing her from dreams of chasing an old woman around a rundown shack. A flash made her wince at the headache brewing behind her eyes. Something tugged along her wrists and ankles. She tried to move and discovered she couldn't budge. Camille glanced down at her legs before panic closed her throat.

Tethered to an X-shaped frame, she was outside in the rain, the lights from Yaga's shack just ahead. Trees, their branches weighed down with droplets, dipped around her, brushing against her legs and arms. She struggled, glimpsing the old rope securing her to the wooden structure. Her dread morphed into sheer terror as the events before she blacked out returned.

"Whatchya fightin' for?" the gravelly voice asked from the shadows. "You can't get free."

Yaga emerged from a thicket of brush carrying her cane and no longer leaning on it for support. The rain fell, but Yaga remained dry, and as she moved, the pelting drops magically parted.

"Let me go," Camille shouted. "My family will come for me."

"Out here?" Yaga laughed. "Not likely. This part of the swamp is haunted, or didn't ya know that? Only the foolish come out this far."

Camille looked around for a means to escape, but all she could see were trees and the gentle waves of the rain dancing on the pools of black water nestled in the swamp. She tried to work one of her hands free, testing the ropes.

Yaga tapped the cane's tip against a jutting cypress knee. "By the time ya get out of those ropes, it'll be too late. My children will have taken what they needed."

Camille stopped and glowered at the crone. "What are ya gonna do? Kill me?"

Yaga chuckled. "Oh, it will be much worse than death."

She lifted her cane and pounded it into the ground three times until it became wedged deep into the soil.

A slow rumble grew beneath the swamp's surface, like the sound of a wave crashing on the shore.

Yaga stepped back from the cane and held up her hands. "Come, my babies. Time to eat."

Camille rocked back and forth as she attempted to work her way off the stand. The cacophony of rain, crickets, the buzz of mosquitoes and gnats became deafening. Her eyes bulged, and her heart rose in her throat as anticipation's grip tightened. Then the surrounding swamp stilled.

The rain stopped, the crickets went silent, and even the constant buzzing of insects vanished. The disconcerting quiet was worse than the pull of her restraints.

A funny hum surrounded her. The cane still stuck in the ground seemed to swell and contract in time with the strange noise. Camille blinked several times, believing her eyes played tricks in the dim light. One face carved into the walking stick, the alligator in the handle, opened its enormous jaws as if yawning after a long nap.

Panic laced with disbelief zoomed through her. Camille flinched when a squirrel in the shaft's side flicked its tail and chattered its teeth. A raccoon rubbed its whiskers and leveled its dark eyes on her. More animals materialized, emerging like hatchlings rising from the nest. A pair of snakes slithered toward her while a possum set its pink feet on the ground. What bothered Camille the most was how the creatures looked at her—as if she was their prey.

She rocked back against the stand. "What's happening?"

Yaga folded her hands. "They're wakin', and they're real hungry."

Camille grappled with her ties. "Stop this!" Her voice cracked with fear. "I will do anythin' you want."

Yaga stood, a loving smile on her lips as the creatures made their way toward the X-frame. "Retribution's a painful process. But necessary."

Splinters cut through the back of Camille's T-shirt. "I haven't done anythin' wrong."

The first snakes appeared at her feet, their pink tongues popping in and out.

"It's not for me to decide," Yaga told her. "They're the ones who hold ya fate."

The last of the creatures to leave the cane was the alligator. It started as a baby when it climbed down the wooden shaft, but the dangerous predator grew as it lumbered toward Camille. Its snout and tail lengthened until it became a magnificent beast, opening its wide mouth, showing off its craggy teeth as it got closer.

Camille became so terrified of the alligator she didn't notice the black snake slithering up her leg. The bite on her thigh made her cry out. She shook her leg to get the critter off, but to no avail. It only incensed the animal, and it bit again. A searing sensation burned like a blowtorch crept along her flesh.

Then the sharp stab of teeth attacking her ankle sparked an unbearable rush of hysteria. The raccoon worked the edge of her boot down with its nimble hands, exposing her flesh. It took a chunk from her ankle, and a metallic essence permeated the air.

Camille screamed as the bites overwhelmed her. But when she saw the alligator open its wide jaws, aiming for her lower leg, her shrill cry echoed across the swamp.

The wretched torture of her leg bone snapping in two bought a wave of black spots, and Camille teetered in and out of consciousness. Tears filled her eyes as she thought of her family, her home, and the people she would never see again.

"There, there," Yaga said in a motherly tone. "It'll be over soon, and then your work can begin."

The agony vanished. Peace filtered through every fiber of Camille. She was free. She flexed her hands, but the usual crackles and pops her joints made when moving didn't resonate.

She glanced at the wooden planks beneath her and saw the flow of the swamp through the slats. There was no briny aroma and no trickle of running water. She felt nothing—no chill in the night air, no rub of the rough boards against her skin. She touched her jeans, thankful to find her clothes intact. The nightmare of being eaten faded. It was just a dream. But when Camille ran her hand along the fabric of her pants, no soft texture, no brush of the denim greeted her.

She glanced around and then sat up, alarmed to find she was still on the old witch's porch. Camille scrambled to her feet, about to bolt for her boat sitting in the water. The moment she reached the edge of the porch, an ungodly iciness cut through her. She could not move or breathe.

She took a step back and then spotted the skulls perched above the porch. The animal bones were no longer there. Human skulls replaced the shiny white heads of possums, raccoons, and alligators. The black holes where eyes once stared out, and the shiny white teeth caught in freakish grimaces didn't belong to the creatures of the swamp but humans.

She ran her hand through her hair, disturbed by the sensation of nothingness. "What the hell?"

"You're one of us now," a deep male voice said at the side of the porch.

Camille spun around. In the corner, crowded against the railing, three men wearing the camouflage of hunters cowered. Deathly white faces stared back, sending a shiver through her. Their shimmering images contrasted against the flat, stained, cypress boards.

"Who are you?" Camille demanded.

One in a green hat pointed at the clearing next to the ramshackle structure. "What we are makes no difference."

Camille eased closer to the men. "What happened to me?"

The hunter in the cap continued to motion to the clearing. "Take a look."

Camille reached the edge of the porch and peered into the darkness. She squinted at first, but then the flash of something white showed behind the green of a few low-lying branches. Bones, some secured to an X-frame made of bleached wood and a few scattered on the boggy ground, stood out. Strips of clothing, tattered legs to jeans, discarded rubber boots, and a shredded black T-shirt appeared.

Camille ran her hand across her chest, desperate to feel the fabric of her black T-shirt.

"That's what remains," another man added. "After she lets her creatures rip you apart."

The crunch of bones as the alligator ripped off her leg, the venom of the snakes coursing through her veins like fire, returned.

She crumpled to her knees. "It was real?"

The hunter in the red cap nodded at the end of the porch. "You're like us—souls to do her bidding."

Camille followed the man's eyes to the array of skulls set along the eaves. At the very end, a shriveled head caked in mud and dried blood boasted a familiar mop of thick black hair.

Camille covered her mouth, holding back her scream. She stared in terror at her eyeless face. Her lips peeled away, and her cheekbones jutted through bits of the dead, black skin.

The last of the men curled his arms around his legs. "Once Maw Maw Yaga got ya," he said with a shudder. "She ain't never gonna let you go."

BABA YAGA IN REPOSE

BY HEATHER MILLER

The forest stretches for miles. Trees older than memory spread their branches both tall and wide, leaves still flush with summer's green, only a few spots of color to indicate the coming autumn. Within the branches, birds flit and hop, the bright red of cardinals and the subdued brown of sparrows mixing with a hundred other colors and shapes and sizes. Great black crows and enormous owls sit half-hidden, watching the frolics of the smaller birds with disdain. Squirrels, a thousand times a thousand in number, leap from branch to branch, chittering their excitement. Lower down, beneath the trees, the forest floor is a mosaic of fallen leaves, centuries' worth, rotting away slowly to the deep, dark, fragrant loam that sustains the forest's life. If one were to sit, very still and very quiet, eventually one would see the other creatures that dwell in the twilight world of the undergrowth—sleek red-brown foxes, rabbits with quivering whiskers, great fat raccoons making their ponderous way between the trees, snakes and spiders and insects that creep and crawl and slither beneath the leaf litter.

Late afternoon sun filters down through the treetops, making dappled shadows that dance along the forest floor. A person could walk for days among these trees and never leave the forest, never see another human soul. There is an air of magic about the place, of unseen things that linger just beyond mortal sight, a whisper of wonder, a prickling of power along the spine. This forest speaks, its voice a long, low hum that reverberates through the ground and vibrates the very air.

The forest seems endless, the trees march onward north,

south, east, and west, and yet the forest holds a secret at its center that few ever discover.

If one were to walk far enough, if one were to walk long enough, if one were to wander with despair in one's heart, with longing, or yearning, or heartbreak strong enough … one would see up ahead an unexpected sight. Through a thinning of trees—a mist, a fog, a haze turned golden with September sunlight—and if one were brave enough to push through that haze, to wander just a little farther, one would leave the forest behind and discover the meadow.

A clearing so large the trees on the other side are nothing more than a dark shadow on the horizon, the meadow is a rippling ocean of knee-high grasses, wildflowers blue and red and yellow, a thousand times a thousand of them, waving and nodding among the grass. Pale golden light shines upon the clearing like heavenly rays, tiny nameless insects flying through the drifting dust motes.

A path appears, a path which is barely a path at all, a faint line through the grasses, a track just wide enough for a single person. Quail scurry away through the grass as one passes, butterflies lift lazily into the air, flutter their wings, a dozen tiny air currents, before settling back onto the flowers that sustain them. Grass with seed heads soft as feathers brush against one's hands and whisper lullabies that flow upward, swirling around one's fingers and arms and settling comfortably and warm upon one's shoulders.

A person could pass an hour or a day along that path, lost in reverie, but eventually, finally, one would come to realize that the grasses are thinning, and the light is dimming, that the sun no longer sits high in the sky but has made its way closer to the horizon and now long shadows stretch across the golden meadow.

The prairie grasses fade to hard-packed dirt, and a sight greets one's eyes that seems like something from a dream, half solid and half illusion. A fence surrounds a small round hut thatched with yellow hay. The fence looks like a white picket, but as one approaches, one realizes that the fence shifts as one walks, one moment simple white wooden stakes, and with a step forward, the stakes turn to something unnervingly like bones, leaning against each other at raucous angles, the fence caps changed to skulls, bleached white in the sun. Another step forward, and the fence is just a fence again, straight and true, clean and white pickets all in a row.

There is no gate, but the path leads to an opening in the fence. As one steps through this opening, a surge of something, some deep primal emotion, washes over one, a mixture of fear, curiosity, danger, longing, and strong, strong magic. Turning back, one sees that the fog which hovered at the edge of the forest has crept forward across the meadow, tendrils twisting along the ground toward the little cottage at the heart of it all. There's no going back now.

The fence makes a complete circle around the house, shutting out the fog and field and forest beyond. Around the back sits an ancient well, a worn wooden bucket hanging on frayed rope, moss deep and green growing along the pale stones. Deep into the earth the well goes to cool, clear water that no self-respecting fairytale heroine would ever trust.

Beyond the well, a smaller building, also round and thatch-roofed, a replica of the hut in miniature. A spider sits amid a sparkling web across the corner of the doorway. Within, the light comes dimly through cracks between the wooden boards that form the walls, and by this light, a curious sight is revealed.

This building is a barn of some sort. Along one wall, three stalls, full of golden hay, hold three animals. In the first, a horse, old and gray and bony, with black spots along its hindquarters and an ancient saddle hung on the wall. In the second stall, an old brown cow, its flank soft as velvet and its udder full and pendulous. In the third, a bristly black pig, big enough for a full-grown woman to ride on.

Along the opposite wall, a series of large roosting boxes hold not chickens but a dozen geese, black as night and big as dogs.

However, the curious thing is that every single one of these animals is asleep. The geese are nestled together in their roosts, the pig and the cow curled up on their hay-strewn floors, the horse standing, unmoving, barely breathing, eyes closed.

Curious as the animals are, something perhaps even stranger sits at the very back of the barn. A structure which resembles nothing so much as a large stone bowl sits, hay packed around it. The bowl is at least four feet high and wide, big enough for a woman to climb inside. Against the wall next to it leans a huge stone, long and bulbous at one end. If one were to reach a hand toward it, it would shiver slightly, a vibrational warning that some things are best left alone.

Outside the stable, a small garden is laid out. Cabbages and carrots, turnips and onions grow in neat rows, surrounded by masses of ferny foliage topped with great blood-red blossoms. A long, thin worm, at least a foot from tip to tip, and black as the earth from which he emerges, pops his head up next to a cabbage and slithers across to the turnips, where he burrows once more beneath the soil.

The sun is sinking lower now, a pumpkin-orange glow in the western sky. Its light reflects back from the hut's diamond-paned windows, a mirage of fire within.

The hut, like all things within this circle, this meadow, this never-ending woodland, has a strangeness about it. No door marks the front or back, but rather two identical doors sit opposite each other on the sides of the house. Thick drifts of hay line the structure's perimeter, as if the house itself has settled down to roost like the great black geese in the stable.

Each door enters the same room, which forms one-half of

the circular hut. Two windows, like eyes, look out onto the front of the fenced circle, the gap which the path leads through just visible through the encroaching fog. A wall stretches across the back of the room, cutting the circle in half. In the middle of this wall, an enormous stone fireplace sits, nothing but cold ash

piled up beneath the chimney. An enormous armchair, covered in threadbare upholstery, sits before the fireplace. On either side of the fireplace, a door.

The rounded walls of the room are covered with cabinets and shelving, intricately carved with flowers and vining branches, but if one steps nearer and looks closer, faces appear, impish and grinning, half-hidden behind the vines. Crockery sits stacked neatly, wooden spoons and disturbingly sharp knives lay arranged in straight lines across the wooden countertops. Dozens of glass jars line the shelves, full of herbs and spices and other, darker things, things which strongly resemble claws and beaks and feathers, uncanny eyes floating in cloudy liquid. From the rafters hang bunches of dried flowers, their papery scent filling the space. A simple wooden table and two chairs sit to one side, a dark stain covering the tabletop.

Like the two outer doors, both of the inner doors, to either side of the fireplace, lead to the same place. Pick one, it matters not which. Through these doors lies a darker room, thick hangings over the two windows. The fireplace, double-sided, takes up the center of the straight wall here in a mirror image of the front room. A few shelves are mounted to the walls, and on these rest a dozen books, thick and old, with yellowing pages and bound in something that would cause most people to draw away in horror.

But softly, quietly, carefully, one must explore this room. For in the center, a bed sits. Its head abuts the center of the circular wall, its foot extends outward to the center of the room. The bed is old wood, scarred, but heavy, sturdy, built to withstand a thousand times a thousand years. Upon the bed, a pile of quilts, colors faded, pieces stitched with dark thread.

But, beneath the quilts. Oh! Beneath the quilts!

Beneath the quilts lies a woman. The bulk of her body makes a hill of the quilts in the center of the bed. One gnarled hand rests atop the quilt, clutching arthritically at the blanket, the skin as brown and furrowed as the rough-hewn wood of the bed, the nails long and yellow. Shoulders clothed in a faded nightgown protrude from the blankets, curls of coarse gray hair lay spread around the woman's head. The face! Ancient, wizened, lined with wrinkles (a thousand times a thousand, at least). Bloodless lips curl inward over toothless gums, the eyelids droop but do not quite cover the spheres beneath them, leaving thin lines of jaundiced white showing beneath. And the nose—the nose is hardly to be believed. Somehow both squashed and hooked, it extends down past the lips, curving till it almost touches the chin, a large hairy mole perched on one side.

The woman's chest rises and falls so slightly, so slowly it might almost not be moving at all. Her breath escapes her gummy mouth in the faintest of whistles, odorous and foul.

The woman is Baba Yaga, Grandmother Witch, keeper of the forest, punisher of those she deems unworthy, patron saint of those who please her, and she has slept here, unmoving, in this enchanted repose for years upon years. Her house sleeps, her animals sleep, her garden sleeps. Once she was feared and revered, spoken of in whispers in towns and villages.

But that was long ago. The world changed, you know, changed around her, and the number of people who cared about her, whose stories and beliefs and fears and dreams kept her alive, became less and less with each passing year until no one spoke her name in reverence any longer until her story became simply that, and her power waned.

She put it off as long as she could, but she felt the life flowing out from her little by little, day by day, felt the loneliness eating away at her, felt the world as she'd known it coming to a sad end, and finally one day she'd done it. She'd saved up her strength for weeks, and that final day, as the sun set, she'd cast her last bit of magic, covering her forest, her fields, her garden, her pets, her house, and finally herself in the spell of a long slumber.

But, wait.

The sun has disappeared from the sky. The moon, half-full, shines down, haloed in cloud, and something is coming from the woodland beyond the little round hut. Out from the mist, shapes emerge, hazy and nebulous at first, taking form as they draw nearer to the house, shapes and shades of women, dressed in fashions the world has not seen for centuries, hair long and loose, woven with pale flowers.

Once these spirits were mortal flesh, once they had lost themselves in the great unending forest beyond, once they had come to Baba's house, some searching it out, some stumbling upon it by chance, all filled with despair and pain and longing and yearning and heartbreak and need. All had found Baba, with her demands and her temper and her magic which could kill or heal, and all had learned from Baba the power that dwelt inside themselves, all had grown strong of body and heart and mind in her keeping, all knew the truth that lay beneath Baba Yaga's ugly exterior. All knew that the worthy found help within her walls.

And, when Baba began to fade, all, in whatever realm they drifted once their mortal lives had ended, mourned her and wept.

That first night, as Baba lay fading into enchanted slumber, as the forest pulled into itself and away from the world beyond, as the fireflies lit up the night and the nocturnal creatures began to scurry in woods and field, they had come. The ghosts of the women Baba had gifted with her help, wisdom, and love came back to care for her.

Now, on this night, as the air fills with fireflies and the wind moans through the trees, and the starlight falls soft upon the little hut in the midst of the wood, they come as they have come every night, for countless nights. They sweep the floors and light the fire which will burn itself out by the time the sun rises. They wipe the counters and dust the books and tuck the quilts in warmly around the old woman in the bed. They go silently about their duties, each with her assigned task. One brushes the cow and the horse and the pig, one rakes the leaves that have gathered against the back wall. One whispers words in a long-forgotten tongue, caressing the side of the house, until the house itself raises on scaly, spindly legs and turns half a circle, settling back down in its hay-strewn pit so that the doors now face opposite ways.

At last, as the first pale glow of sunrise begins to shimmer above the forest to the east, the shades gather in the old woman's bedroom. In turn, they lay a hand on her slumped shoulders, in turn, they each lay a gentle kiss upon her sleeping brow. Then wordlessly, they drift from the house, through the field, and into the forest, dispersing into the fog as the bright sunlight burns it away.

They will return each night, every night, to care for old Baba as she slumbers, until the day comes when the people of the world remember her and come searching for her once more.

SHADOW AND BRANCH, GHOST FRUIT AMONG THE LULLABIES

BY SABA SYED RAZVI

At the edges of the threshold, they tell stories about leaving. They say a girl cannot ever really return once she leaves home. They speak of monstrous wolves. The wisest know to seek the shadows at the edge of every road.

Guard your steps on this or any path beyond the busy rush of light.

The crush of autumn leaves echoes louder in the forest, a song in pieces, a symphony swirling along the bark of trees. Those who live among the birds and foxes find their meals in berries and hares, in moss and bones. In the cadence of stories slipping from huts standing on chicken legs or crow's talons.

There is a reason the girls do not venture through the border of night, falling fiercely between the branches, at least not without a doll to eat the offerings that keep them safe. And, there is a reason the mothers and maidens keep their distance from the wisdom of those hearths shimmering like comfort in the thrum of the woods.

Baba Yaga lives in the woods, in a hut they say—or is it a cave? She appears as an old woman to maidens, and as a young girl to mothers, and maybe a little of both to the little ones who haven't yet decided what it is that revolts them about themselves. Her voice is like apples, a scent that calls you to curiosity and longing. In the space around the simple boundaries of the self, all senses come together and twist into others. The roots speak of nesting in love, while the moss invites the thrill of a sudden gust of wind. The light falls in flecks like glittering snow.

Every girl carries in her hands a shadow that seeks the thrill of the forbidden, like the crush of leaves as they crumble, like the earth shifting into the softness beneath beckoning feet.

Every home has a hearth, and its ashes serve as a reminder of the ends of all things—of changelings from the wilds, offerings to gods that do not wish to hear, of beauty evaporating like morning dew. What mother is not a blossom ripening too soon, while the bud grows again before her? What maiden doesn't think her bloom will linger eternal?

Guard your hearts from wishes lost in the darkness of what has failed to find a place in your home. What lines the darkness is also called light.

The story of the crone is the story of the fruit, formed and fallen, bitten and bruised, sticky with the rot of neglect. The story of the crone is the story of every wisdom, hard-won through the rewards of pain. The story of the crone lies in the spaces just beyond looking, in the reflections and shadows, in the echoes and the sweet silences, in the suffocating softness of something spun of yarn.

Guard your voices from the forest, from the harvest, from the garden. Find your goblins in the market and your faeries in the lullabies. Find your sugar in the warmth of the cauldron, weaving breath from blood and leaf and bone.

Every reason has a rebellion, born of a spark of something haughty and high. They say the hag will find you in your dreams to lure you to the woods. They say to hang bells on the window, to wear bells on the ankles, so you may wake before your heart song steals your stones. But the maidens love to tempt their fate, to prove their beauty by the sneer carved of the bounty of time. Her wrinkled gray is the wrong kind of mushroom, the wrong kind of fable, and the wrong kind of reminder that all possibilities end. And the mothers sometimes lose themselves in the fantasy beyond the drudgery of day, loving and hating the twisted inverse of their faces in the young, their admiration just a wish to hold fast another day against the burden of milk or oats, of flower crowns and stitching. A yarn is a tale and also a trap.

And, so, she appears as the fears you do not own.

For every story about Baba Yaga is a forgotten memory. No one remembers meeting her, and no one knows her face. The legends tell of houses spun with sugar and sweets, baked under a moon that illuminates bread and pebbles. The legends tell of caverns filled with drying blossoms and grasses, pelts and skins, and things pickled in jars, with fires from which to find potion or spice. But if you look for her, you will not find her.

Every goddess-shaped traveler will come back with an invisible glimmer. Every gleam will creep into the windowsill to light the way. Though none remember the shapeshifter in the woods, all come back to make a rendering. They sing of their loves while weaving. They chatter about their hopes while brewing. They reach for what is forbidden, snatching a secret treat. We know who has seen her, not by what they have said but what they have made. No painting, weaving, or drawing is ever the same, but every one bears eyes. And through the eyes is a passage from the woods to the heart, from the darkness to the dusk.

She finds her way through the tapestries and paintings, weaving herself into the shadows of hearth-fire and candle-flame. She finds her way into the bed, through the dreaming. She finds her way through the haughty edge of cruelty of those who trespass on her land and who refuse to see her truth. She favors the cruel. She favors the arrogance of youth. She favors the resentment of the aging. In this edge is an opening, and in the darkness, she breaks a space big enough to suck the life from the marrow, night by night. The girls wither slowly and either find their hearts becoming caverns of stone or sinking into beds of moss. The mothers wizen slowly, finding their arms as hasty as branches or as welcoming as nests.

Baba Yaga feeds on their beauty, on their demanding and reckless tongues, on their shrewd and intolerant eyes. Living endlessly to cast the dirge of the promise of death. If they soften, she leaves them to ripen and bloom and rot. Most never understand their transgressions at all, the penalty of failing to see her, themselves in her reflection, their paths in her footfalls. In the shadows, she creeps through them, haunting their hearts. In the mirrors, she hovers around them, a phantom dimming their lights. There is nothing to guard, no path to discern. The forest claims the fire for its own.

When stories are woven with howls, the echoes beckon beyond the light. They call us from homes into the night-blooming song of crickets, of insect and stream, of bats and screeching, slithering things. The shadows still creep inside. The wilderness carries the cavernous, the crones, the lost little girls. The crush of leaves under footfalls says every girl and every reason knows the way through the shadows. They say to guard the hearts of your own. They say their steps beat in time. They say that every leaf carries the cost of leaving.

AFTERWORD

by Laura West

Women and horror stories go hand in hand. We know fear. We know pain. And as the expression of the female voice grows louder over time, so does our appreciation for Baba Yaga—the wild witch of Slavic folklore.

The roots of Baba Yaga stem from a place that is dark and sinister—a nightmare. In the old-school Russian tales that I was raised with, Baba Yaga was a conniving, wicked, dangerous old hag who murdered and ate little children. She represented a manipulative woman who lured children for her own vicious benefit, keeping herself hidden from societal punishment by lurking in the shadows of the woods. An evil murderer, she was not what anyone strived to be. However, like so many folktales, Baba Yaga's have evolved over time, and the stories in this anthology capture the essence of an ever-changing tale that has been altered with every translation, every decade, and within a constantly changing society.

Many stories in this anthology capture an exalted image of Baba Yaga as a symbol of femininity, a wild rebellious soul in a positive sense, and almost a yearning to be like her, or with her. This modern take on Baba Yaga's folklore makes it easier and more palatable for our human conscience—a constant strive for a "happy ending" if you will, or for things to not be so terrible as they may seem. The lightening of dark fairy and folktales, or the attachment of a heroic element to somebody so heinous, is not uncommon. Many tales have been sanitized over the years before being exposed to a wider audience. For example, "Sleeping Beauty" is kissed awake by true love rather than raped and impregnated while in a coma, "Snow White" doesn't dance on coal and die on her wedding day, and "The Little Mermaid" gets her legs instead of having her tongue cut out.

Despite her evildoings, Baba Yaga still attracts new readership. Both heroes and villains represent the conflicting and complex human experience, and we flock to Baba Yaga's malevolence because her tale brings with it the possibility of hope. She is the one who controls the elements in the woods, who embraces the most fundamental inner-conflict of human nature—that we are all flawed, with good and evil coursing in tandem through our veins. The lure that Baba Yaga creates, hidden in the wild, is a place of danger, mystery, and challenge.

Stories evolve and change with culture. This anthology is a beautiful reminder and commentary of Baba Yaga's modern alterations and older tributes alongside new innovations that have left a mark all over the world. But, standing the test of time, Baba Yaga will always be a phantasm of horror and a symbol of fear for readers in generations to come.

Thank you for joining us *Into the Forest*. Be joyous you've found a way out—so many of us have not, and perhaps never will.

ABOUT LAURA WEST

Laura West studied screenwriting as a full scholarship recipient at NYU Tisch School of the Arts and began her career working at companies including Martin Scorsese's *Sikelia Productions*, *Scott Rudin Productions*, and as head of development for *Sterling Films*. She grew up in a Russian/Armenian home where her father, Vlad West, was a legendary jazz musician who played with Duke Ellington, Gerry Mulligan, Thad Jones, and Tony Scott. The film *Moscow on the Hudson,* starring Robin Williams, was based on his life.

ABOUT CHRISTINA HENRY

Christina Henry is a horror and dark fantasy author whose works include *Horseman, Near the Bone, The Ghost Tree, Looking Glass, The Girl in Red, The Mermaid, Lost Boy, Alice, Red Queen,* and the seven-book urban fantasy Black Wings series. She enjoys running long distances, reading anything she can get her hands on, and watching movies with samurai, zombies, and/or subtitles in her spare time. She lives in Chicago with her husband and son.

ABOUT THE EDITOR

Lindy Miller Ryan is an award-winning author/editor, short film director, and professor at Rutgers University. Prior to her career in academia, Ryan was the co-founder of Radiant Advisors, where she led the company's research and data enablement practice for clients that included 21st Century Fox Films, Warner Bros., and Disney. She is the founder of Black Spot Books, a small press with a mission to amplify voices of women-in-horror, serves on the Board of Directors for IBPA, and is co-chair of the Horror Writers Association Publishers Council. Ryan was named one of *Publishers Weekly*'s Star Watch Honorees 2020. She has published numerous academic texts and writes clean romance novels under the name Lindy Miller, which are being adapted for the screen. Lindy's horror-thriller debut novel, BLESS YOUR HEART, is forthcoming from Minotaur Books. LindyMillerRyan.com

ABOUT THE AUTHORS

Jill Baguchinsky is the award-winning author of young adult novels *Spookygirl: Paranormal Investigator* and *Mammoth*. Jill is known for quoting Ghostbusters at inappropriate moments and being that person at a party who spends the whole evening befriending the host's cat.

Carina Bissett is a writer and poet working primarily in the fields of dark fiction and fabulism. Her work has been published in multiple journals and anthologies, including *Upon a Twice Time*, *Bitter Distillations: An Anthology of Poisonous Tales*, and *Arterial Bloom*. She is also the co-editor of *Shadow Atlas: Dark Landscapes of the Americas*. Links to her work can be found at carinabissett.com.

Octavia Cade is a New Zealand writer. She's sold over sixty stories to markets, including *Clarkesworld*, *Strange Horizons*, and *Fantasy & Science Fiction*. Her most recent book, the climate fiction novella "The Impossible Resurrection of Grief," was published by Stelliform Press. She attended Clarion West 2016 and was the 2020 writer in residence at Massey University.

Jess Hagemann's recent work has appeared in *Southwest Review*, *Castle of Horror: Femme Fatales*, and on the HorrorGirl podcast. She holds an MFA from the Jack Kerouac School. Her debut novel Headcheese won an IPPY Award in Horror.

R. J. Joseph is a Stoker Award®-nominated, Texas-based academic and creative writer/professor whose writing regularly focuses on the intersections of gender and race in the horror and romance genres and popular culture. She has had works published in various applauded venues, including the 2020 Halloween issue of *Southwest Review* and *The Streaming of Hill House: Essays on* *the Haunting Netflix Series*. Rhonda is also an instructor at the Speculative Fiction academy. She occasionally peeks out on Twitter @rjacksonjoseph or at www.rhondajacksonjoseph.com

Jo Kaplan is the author of *It Will Just Be Us* and *When the Night Bells Ring*. Her work has appeared in *Fireside Quarterly*, *Black Static*, *Nightmare Magazine*, *Nightscript*, *Vastarien*, *Horror Library*, and numerous anthologies. She teaches English and creative writing at Glendale Community College.

EV Knight is the author of the Bram Stoker Award®-winning debut novel *The Fourth Whore*. She released her sophomore novel, *Children of Demeter*, and a novella, *Partum*, in 2021. EV lives in one of America's most haunted cities—Savannah, Ga. She is a huge fan of the Savannah Bananas and the beauty of Bonaventure Cemetery. When not out and about searching for the ghosts of the past, EV can be found at home with her husband Matt, her beloved Chinese Crested Gozer Augustus, and their three naughty sphynx cats.

Gwendolyn Kiste is the Bram Stoker Award®-winning author of *The Rust Maidens, Reluctant Immortals, Boneset & Feathers*, and *The Invention of Ghosts*. Originally from Ohio, she lives on an abandoned horse farm outside of Pittsburgh with her husband, two cats, and not nearly enough ghosts. Find her online at gwendolynkiste.com.

Donna Lynch is a horror and dark fiction author, singer, lyricist, spoken word artist, and two-time Bram Stoker Award®-nominated poet. She has published eight poetry collections, as well as two novels and a novella, and several short stories. She and her husband, artist and musician Steven Archer, are the founding members of the dark rock band Ego Likeness (Metropolis Records). They live in Maryland.

Catherine McCarthy Catherine McCarthy is a spinner of stories with macabre melodies. Her published work includes the collection *Mists and Megaliths* and the novella *Immortelle*. Her Gothic novel *A Moonlit Path of Madness* will be published by Nosetouch Press as well as her cosmic horror novella *Mosaic* published by Dark Hart, both forthcoming in 2023.

Lindz McLeod is a queer, working-class, Scottish writer who dabbles in the surreal. Her prose has been published by Catapult, Flash Fiction Online, Pseudopod, and many more. Her short story collection *Turducken* is forthcoming with Bear Creek Press in 2022 and her debut novel *Beast* is forthcoming with Brigids Gate Press in 2023. She is a full member of the SFWA and is represented by Laura Zats at Headwater Literary Management. www.lindzmcleod.co.uk.

Heather Miller reads and writes horror in a century-old house (surely haunted) in a small town in Oklahoma. She released her first novella, *Knock Knock*, a modern Gothic ghost story, in 2021. You can see what she's up to at www.heathermillerhorror.com.

Lisa Quigley is a Bram Stoker Award®-nominated horror author and a pagan witch. She holds an MFA in Creative Writing from the University of California, Riverside's low-residency MFA program in Palm Desert. Her work has appeared in such places as *Unnerving Magazine*, *The Lineup*, *Journal of Alta California*, and *Automata Review*. She is the co-host and co-creator of the TIH award-winning horror fiction podcast Ladies of the Fright and Senior Editor of *The Lineup*. *Hell's Bells* (2020) and *Camp Neverland* (2021) from Unnerving are her novellas. The Forest (PMMP 2021) is her debut novel. Lisa lives in New Jersey with one handsome devil and two wild monsters. Find her at www.lisaquigley.net.

Saba Syed Razvi, PhD is the author of: "In the Crocodile

Gardens" (Elgin Award-nominee), "heliophobia," "Limerence & Lux," "Of the Divining and the Dead," and "Beside the Muezzin's Call & Beyond the Harem's Veil." She's an Associate Professor of English & Creative Writing at the University of Houston in Victoria.

Christina Sng is the three-time Bram Stoker Award®-winning author of *A Collection of Nightmares*, *A Collection of Dreamscapes*, and *Tortured Willows*. Her poetry, fiction, essays, and art appear in numerous venues worldwide, including *Interstellar Flight Magazine*, *Penumbric*, *Southwest Review*, *Weird Tales*, and *The Washington Post*.

Monique Snyman lives in Pretoria, South Africa, with her husband, daughter, and an adorable Chihuahua. She's the author of the Bram Stoker Award®-nominated novels, *The Night Weaver* and *The Bone Carver*, and the upcoming South African horror series, *Dark Country*.

Sara Tantlinger is the author of the Bram Stoker Award®-winning *The Devil's Dreamland: Poetry Inspired by H.H. Holmes*, and the Stoker®-nominated works *To Be Devoured*, *Cradleland of Parasites*, and *Not All Monsters*. She is a co-organizer for the HWA Pittsburgh Chapter. Find her on Twitter @SaraTantlinger and at saratantlinger.com.

Alexandrea Weis RN-CS, PhD, is an IPPY Award-winning author, registered nurse, and wildlife rehabber who was born in the French Quarter. She has taught at major universities and worked in New Orleans area hospitals for thirty years. Weis grew up in the motion picture industry as the daughter of a director. She is a member of the HWA and ITW Association. www. AlexandreaWeis.com

Jacqueline West's work includes the *New York Times*-bestselling middle-grade dark fantasy series The Books of Elsewhere, the YA horror novel *Last Things*, and the middle-grade ghost story *Long Lost*. An award-winning poet and active HWA member, Jacqueline lives with her family in Red Wing, Minnesota.

Stephanie M. Wytovich is an award-winning American poet, novelist, and essayist. Follow her at http://stephaniewytovich. blogspot.com/ and on Twitter and Instagram @SWytovich and @thehauntedbookshelf. You can also find her essays, nonfiction, and class offerings on LitReactor.

Mercedes M. Yardley is a dark fantasist who wears red lipstick and poisonous flowers in her hair. She is the author of *Beautiful Sorrows*, the Stabby Award-winning *Apocalyptic Montessa, and Nuclear Lulu: A Tale of Atomic Love*, *Pretty Little Dead Girls*, and *Nameless*. She won the Bram Stoker Award for her story *Little Dead Red* and was a Bram Stoker Award® nominee for her short story "Loving You Darkly" and the *Arterial Bloom* anthology. Mercedes lives and works in Las Vegas with her family and strange menagerie. You can find her at mercedesmyardley.com.

In 2011, **Yi Izzy Yu** left Northern China for the US. Since then, she has taught Chinese and English in high schools and colleges, given birth to the now eight-year-old visual artist Frankie Lu Branscum, and published work in magazines ranging from *New England Review* to *Samovar* and in the collections of translated Chinese weird fiction, *The Shadow Book of Ji Yun* and *Zhiguai*. Currently, she lives outside of Pittsburgh, where she teaches, translates Chinese, and investigates shadows.

OTHER ANTHOLOGIES FROM BLACK SPOT BOOKS

A Midnight Clear
Dead of Winter
Under Her Skin